CAN YOU SOLVE

. . . the bizarre murder by a blind man?

. . . the mystery of the missing manuscript?

. . . the riddle of a dying soldier's last words?

. . . the "barest" baffler that could mean a fortune?

. . . the time of day the loan shark died?

. . . the cryptic call to arms that could crack a big-city burglary ring?

Can you outguess the Black Widowers— and Isaac Asimov? Join the feast and find out. The cuisine is sublime, the vintage rare, and the Widowers await you. . . .

CASEBOOK OF THE BLACK WIDOWERS

Isaac Asimov

FAWCETT CREST • NEW YORK

Acknowledgments

"The Cross of Lorraine" originally published in *EQMM*.
   Copyright © 1976 by Isaac Asimov

"The Family Man" originally published in *EQMM* under the
   title "A Case of Income-tax Fraud." Copyright © 1976 by
   Isaac Asimov

"The Sports Page" originally published in *EQMM*. Copyright © 1977 by Isaac Asimov

"The Missing Item" originally published in *IASFM*. Copyright © 1977 by Davis Publications, Inc.

"The Next Day" originally published in *EQMM*. Copyright ©
   1978 by Isaac Asimov

"Irrelevance!" originally published in *EQMM*, under the
   title of "A Matter of Irrelevance." Copyright © 1979 by
   Isaac Asimov

"None So Blind" originally published in *EQMM*. Copyright ©
   1979 by Isaac Asimov

"The Backward Look" originally published in *IASFM*. Copyright © 1979 by Davis Publications, Inc.

"To the Barest" originally published in *EQMM*. Copyright ©
   1979 by Isaac Asimov

CASEBOOK OF THE BLACK WIDOWERS

to Alex Zupnick, Don Laventhal, and Bob Zicklin, who labor to keep me out of trouble.

Contents

Introduction

For some reason, possibly because of the sweet and lovable modesty with which I am imbued, I live in constant dread that someone will try to stop me from pouring out my endless stream of published material.

For instance, back in March 1971, I wrote a short mystery for *Ellery Queen's Mystery Magazine* (*EQMM*) about an organization I called "the Black Widowers." I meant it as a one-shot, but Frederic Dannay ("Ellery Queen") introduced it as "the first of a new series." So I wrote a second—then a third—

And with each one, I trembled lest Fred, or somebody, would say, "Okay, that's enough."

Fortunately for me, no one did.

Eventually, when I had written twelve stories of the series I decided I had enough for a book I called *Tales of the Black Widowers* (Doubleday, 1974). When I had written twelve more, there was *More Tales of the Black Widowers* (Doubleday, 1976).

You're ahead of me, I know, but now I have completed a third set of a dozen stories, so here is *Casebook of the Black Widowers*.

And *still* no one has told me to stop. On occasion, I wonder about that. After all, there is no denying that my Black Widowers stories run against the current of contemporary fashions in mysteries. In fact, these stories are virtually nineteenth-century.

The notion of having a group of men from the upper strata of society sitting around a leisurely and sumptuous meal, while discussing and solving some mystery, is a thoroughly Victorian convention. Nor does it help that there is no violence or sex to speak of; in fact, there often isn't even very much of a crime. Yet the mail I receive is very gratifying.

The results of my thinking about the matter are these:

1. The mysteries are as fair as I can make them. I try to have everything out in the open and I arrange it so that at the crucial moment the reader can come up with Henry's reasoning and beat him to the punch. And, if I may trust the letters I get, readers occasionally do.

2. The mysteries, as mysteries, can be described, discussed, and solved in about a quarter of the space I devote to each. The other three quarters are given over to the leisurely dinner conversation of the Black Widowers, and apparently this, too, pleases the readers.

This makes me happier than I can say, because I myself enjoy the game of constructing fair mysteries and I enjoy, just as much, the construction of intelligent conversations.

So, Gentle Readers, here I am with the third volume in the series. And you all have my assurance that while I live I will not stop!

1.

The Cross of Lorraine

Emmanuel Rubin did not, as a general rule, ever allow a look of relief to cross his face. Had one done so, it would have argued a prior feeling of uncertainty or apprehension, sensations he might feel but would certainly never admit to.

This time, however, the relief was unmistakable. It was monthly banquet time for the Black Widowers; Rubin was the host, and it was he who was supplying the guest; and here it was about twenty minutes after seven and only now—with but ten minutes left before the banquet was to start—only now did his guest arrive.

Rubin bounded toward him, careful, however, not to spill a drop of his second drink.

"Gentlemen," he said, clutching the arm of the newcomer, "my guest, the Amazing Larri—spelled L-A-R-R-I." And in a lowered voice, over the hum of pleased-to-meet-yous, "Where the hell were you?"

Larri muttered, "The subway train stalled." Then returned smiles and greetings.

"Pardon me," said Henry, the perennial—and nonpareil—waiter at the Black Widower banquets, "but there is not much time for the guest to have his drink before dinner begins. Would you state your preference, sir?"

"A good notion, that," said Larri, gratefully. "Thank you, waiter, and let me have a dry martini, but not too darned dry—a little damp, so to speak."

"Certainly, sir," said Henry.

Rubin said, "I've told you, Larri, that we members all have our *ex officio* doctorates, so now let me introduce them in nauseating detail. This tall gentleman with the neat mustache, black eyebrows, and straight back is Dr. Geoffrey Avalon. He's a lawyer and he never smiles. The last time he tried, he was fined for contempt of court."

Avalon smiled as broadly as he could and said, "You undoubtedly know Manny well enough, sir, not to take him seriously."

"Undoubtedly," said Larri. As he and Rubin stood together, they looked remarkably alike. Both were of a height—about five feet, five—both had active, inquisitive faces, both had straggly beards, though Larri's was longer and was accompanied by a fringe of hair down either side of his face as well.

Rubin said, "And here, dressed fit to kill anyone with a *real* taste for clothing, is our scribble expert, Dr. Mario Gonzalo, who will insist on producing a caricature of you in which he will claim to see a resemblance. Dr. Roger Halsted inflicts pain on junior-high students under the guise of teaching them what little he knows of mathematics. Dr. James Drake is a superannuated chemist who once conned someone into granting him a Ph.D. And finally, Dr. Thomas Trumbull, who works for the government in an unnamed job as code expert and who spends most of his time hoping Congress doesn't find out."

"Manny," said Trumbull wearily, "if it were possible to cast a retroactive blackball, I think you could count on five."

And Henry said, "Gentlemen, dinner is served."

It was one of those rare Black Widower occasions when the entrée was lobster, rarer now than ever because of the increase in prices.

Rubin, who as host bore the cost, shrugged it off. "I made a good paperback sale last month and we can call this a celebration."

"We can celebrate," said Avalon, "but lobster tends to kill conversation. The cracking of claws and shells, the extraction of meat, the dipping in melted butter, takes one's full concentration." And he grimaced with the effort he was putting into the compression of the nutcracker.

"In that case," said the Amazing Larri, "I shall have a monopoly on the conversation," and he grinned with satisfaction as a large platter of prime-rib roast was dexterously placed before him by Henry.

"Larri is allergic to seafood," said Rubin.

Conversation was indeed subdued as Avalon had predicted until the various lobsters had been clearly worsted in culinary battle, and then, finally, Halsted asked, "What makes you Amazing, Larri?"

"Stage name," said Larri. "I am a prestidigitator, an escapist *extraordinaire*, and the greatest living *exposeur*."

Trumbull, who was sitting to Larri's right, formed ridges on his bronzed forehead. "What the devil do you mean by *exposeur*?"

Rubin beat a tattoo on his water glass at this point and said, "No grilling till we've had our coffee."

"For God's sake," said Trumbull, "I'm just asking the definition of a word."

"Host's decision is final," said Rubin.

Trumbull scowled blackly in Rubin's direction. "Then I'll *guess* the answer. An *exposeur* is one who exposes fakes; people who, using trickery of one sort or another, pretend to produce effects they attribute to supernatural or paranatural forces."

Larri thrust out his lower lip, raised his eyebrows, and nodded his head. "Pretty good for a guess. I couldn't have put it better."

Gonzalo said, "You mean that whatever someone did by what he claimed was real magic, you could do by stage magic."

"Exactly," said Larri. "For instance, suppose that some mystic claimed he had the capacity to bend spoons by means of unknown forces. I can do the same by using natural force, this way." He lifted his spoon and, holding it by its two ends, he bent it half an inch out of true.

Trumbull said, "That scarcely counts. Anyone can do it that way."

"Ah," said Larri, "but this spoon you saw me bend is not the amazing effect at all. That spoon you were watching merely served to trap and focus the ethereal rays that did the real work. Those rays acted to bend *your* spoon, Dr. Trumbull."

Trumbull looked down and picked up his spoon, which was bent nearly at right angles. "How did you do this?"

Larri shrugged. "Would you believe ethereal forces?"

Drake laughed and, pushing his dismantled lobster toward the center of the table, lit a cigarette. He said, "Larri did it a few minutes ago, with his hands, when you weren't looking."

Larri seemed unperturbed by exposure. "When Manny banged his glass, Dr. Trumbull, you looked away. I had rather hoped you all would."

Drake said, "I know better than to pay attention to Manny."

"But," said Larri, "if no one had seen me do it, would you have accepted the ethereal forces?"

"Not a chance," said Trumbull.

"Even if there had been no way in which you could explain the effect? Here, let me show you something. Suppose you wanted to flip a coin . . ."

He fell silent for a moment while Henry passed out the strawberry shortcake, pushed his own out of the way, and said, "Suppose you wanted to flip a coin, without actually lifting it and turning it—this penny, for instance. There are a number of ways it could be done. The simplest would be simply to touch it quickly, because, as you all know, a finger is always slightly sticky, especially so at mealtime, so that the coin lifts up slightly as the finger is removed and can be made to flip over. It is tails now, you see. Touch it again and it is heads."

Gonzalo said, "No prestidigitation there, though. We see it flip."

"Exactly," said Larri, "and that's why I won't do it that way. Let's put something over it so that it can't be touched or flipped. Suppose we use a . . ." He looked about the table for a moment and seized a salt shaker. "Suppose we use this."

He placed the salt shaker over the coin and said, "Now it is showing heads? . . ."

"Hold on," said Gonzalo. "How do we know it's showing heads? It could be tails and then, when you reveal it later, you'll say it flipped, when it was tails all along."

"You're perfectly right," said Larri, "and I'm glad you raised the point. Dr. Drake, you've got eyes that caught me before. Would you check this on behalf of the assembled company? I'll lift the salt shaker and you tell me what the coin shows."

Drake looked and said, "Heads!" in his softly hoarse voice.

"You'll all take Dr. Drake's word, I hope, gentlemen? Please, watch me place the salt shaker back on the coin and make sure it doesn't flip in the process. . . ."

"It didn't," said Drake.

"Now to keep my fingers from slipping while performing this trick, I will put this paper napkin over the salt shaker."

Larri molded the paper napkin neatly and carefully over the salt shaker, then said, "But, in manipulating this napkin, I caused you all to divert your attention from the penny and you may think I have flipped it in the process." He lifted the salt shaker with the paper about it and said, "Dr. Drake, will you check the coin again?"

Drake leaned toward it. "Still heads," he said.

Very carefully and gently, Larri put back the salt shaker, the paper napkin still molded about it, and said, "The coin remained as is?"

"Still heads," said Drake.

"In that case, I now perform the magic." Larri pushed down on the salt shaker, and the paper collapsed. There was nothing inside.

There was a moment of shock, and then Gonzalo said, "Where's the salt shaker?"

"In another plane of existence," said Larri airily.

"But you said you were going to flip the coin."

"I lied."

Avalon said, "There's no mystery. He had us all concentrating on the coin as a diversion tactic. When he picked up the salt shaker with the napkin around it to let Jim look at the coin, he just dropped the salt shaker into his hand and placed the empty, molded napkin over the coin."

"Did you see me do that, Dr. Avalon?" asked Larri.

"No. I was looking at the coin, too."

"Then you're just guessing," said Larri.

Rubin, who had not participated in the demonstration at all, but who had eaten his strawberry shortcake instead and now waited for the others to catch up, said, "The tendency is to argue these things out logically and that's impossible. Scientists and other rationalists are used to dealing with the universe, which fights fair. Faced with a mystic who does not, they find themselves maneuvered into believing nonsense and, in the end, making fools of themselves.

"Magicians, on the other hand," Rubin went on, "know what to watch for, are experienced enough not to be misdirected, and are not impressed by the apparently supernatural. That's why mystics generally won't perform if they know magicians are in the audience."

Coffee had been served and was being sipped at, and Henry was quietly preparing the brandy, when Rubin sounded the water glass and said, "Gentlemen, it is time for the official grilling, assuming you idiots have left anything to grill. Geoff, will you do the honors today?"

Avalon cleared his throat portentously and frowned down upon the Amazing Larri from under his dark and luxuriant eyebrows. Using his voice in the deepest of its naturally deep register, Avalon said, "It is customary to ask our guests to justify their existences, but if today's guest exposes phony mystics even now and then, I, for one, consider his existence justified and will pass on.

"The temptation is to ask you how you performed your little disappearing trick of a moment ago, but I quite understand that the ethics of your profession preclude your telling us. Even though everything said here is considered under the rose, and though nothing has ever leaked, I will refrain from such questions.

"Let me instead, then, ask after your failures. Sir, you describe yourself as an *exposeur*. Have there been any supposedly mystical demonstrations you have not been able to duplicate in prestidigitous manner and have not been able to account for by natural means?"

Larri said, "I have not attempted to explain all the effects I have ever encountered or heard of, but where I have studied an effect and made an attempt to duplicate it, I have succeeded in every case."

"No failures?"

"None!"

Avalon considered that, but as he prepared for the next question, Gonzalo broke in. His head was leaning on one palm, but the fingers of that hand were carefully disposed in such a way as not to disarray his hair. He said, "Now, wait, Larri, would it be right to suggest that you tackled only easy cases? The really puzzling cases you might have made no attempts on."

"You mean," said Larri, "that I shied away from anything that might spoil my perfect record or that might upset my belief in the rational order of the universe? If so, you're quite wrong, Dr. Gonzalo. Most reports of apparent mystical powers are dull and unimportant, are crude and patently false. I ignore those. The cases I do take on are precisely the puzzling ones that have attracted attention because of their unusual nature and their apparent divorce from the rational. So you see, the ones I take on are precisely those you suspect I avoid."

Gonzalo subsided and Avalon said, "Larri, the mere fact that you can duplicate a trick by prestidigitation doesn't mean that it couldn't have been performed by the mystic through supernatural means. The fact that human beings can build machines that fly doesn't mean that birds are man-made machines."

"Quite right," said Larri, "but mystics lay their claims to supernatural powers on the notion, either expressed or implicit, that there is no other way of producing the effect. If I show that the same effect *can* be produced by natural means, the burden of proof then shifts to them to show that the effect can be produced after the natural means I have used are made impossible. I don't know of any mystic who has accepted the conditions set by professional magicians to guard against trickery and who then succeeded."

"And nothing has ever puzzled you? Not even the tricks other magicians have developed?"

"Oh yes, there are effects produced by some magicians that puzzle me in the sense that I don't know quite how they do it. I might duplicate it but perhaps using a different method. In any case, that's not the point. As long as an effect is produced by natural means, it doesn't matter whether I can reproduce it or not. I am not the best magician in the world. I am just a better magician than any mystic is."

Halsted, his high forehead flushed with anxiety, and stuttering slightly in his eagerness to speak, said, "But then nothing would startle you? No disappearance like that you carried through on the salt shaker? . . ."

"You mean that one?" asked Larri, pointing. There was a

salt shaker in the middle of the table, but no one had seen it placed there.

Halsted, thrown off a moment, recovered and said, "Have you ever been *startled* by any disappearance? I heard once that magicians have made elephants disappear."

"Actually, making elephants disappear is childishly simple. I assure you there's nothing puzzling about disappearances in a magic act." And then a peculiar look crossed Larri's face, a flash of sadness and frustration. "Not in a magic act. Just . . ."

"Yes?" said Halsted. "Just what?"

"Just in real life," said Larri, smiling and attempting to toss off the remark lightheartedly.

"Just a minute," said Trumbull, "but we don't let that pass. If there has been a disappearance in real life you can't explain, we want to hear about it."

Larri shook his head, "No, no, Dr. Trumbull. It is not a mysterious disappearance or an inexplicable one. Nothing like that at all. I just lost—something, and can't find it and it—saddens me."

"The details," said Trumbull.

"It wouldn't be worth it," said Larri. "It's a—silly story and somewhat . . ." He fell into silence.

"Goddamn it," thundered Trumbull, "we all sit here and voluntarily refrain from asking anything that might result in your being tempted to violate your ethics. Would it violate the ethics of the magician's art for you to tell this story?"

"It's not that at all. . . ."

"Well, then, sir, I repeat what Geoff has told you. Everything said here is in confidence and the agreement surrounding these monthly dinners is that all questions must be answered. Manny?"

Rubin shrugged. "That's the way it is, Larri. If you don't want to answer the question, we'll have to declare the meeting at an end."

Larri sat back in his chair and looked depressed. "I can't very well allow that to happen, considering the fine hospitality I've been shown. I will tell you the story and you'll find there's nothing to it. I met a woman quite accidentally; I lost touch with her; I can't locate her. That's all there is."

"No," said Trumbull, "that's not all there is. Where and how did you meet her? Where and how did you lose touch with her? Why can't you find her again? We want to know the details."

Gonzalo said, "In fact, if you tell us the details, we may be able to help you."

Larri laughed sardonically, "I think not."

"You'd be surprised," said Gonzalo. "In the past . . ."

Avalon said, "Quiet, Mario. Don't make promises we might not be able to keep. Would you give us the details, sir? I assure you we'll do our best to help."

Larri smiled wearily. "I appreciate your offer, but you will see that there is nothing you can do sitting here."

He adjusted himself in his seat and said, "I was done with my performance in an upstate town—I'll give you the details when and if you insist, but for the moment they don't matter, except that this happened about a month ago. I had to get to another small town some hundred fifty miles away for a morning show and that meant a little transportation problem.

"My magic, unfortunately, is not the kind that can transport me a hundred fifty miles in a twinkling, or even conjure up a pair of seven-league boots. I did not have my car with me—just as well, for I don't like to travel the lesser roads at night when I am sleepy—and the net result was that I would have to take a bus that would make more stops than a telegram and would take nearly four hours to make the journey. I planned to catch some sleep while on wheels and make it serve a purpose anyway.

"But when things go wrong, they go wrong in battalions, so you can guess that I missed my bus and that the next one would not come along for two more hours. There was an enclosed station in which I could wait, one that was as dreary as you could imagine—with no reading matter except for some fly-blown posters on the wall—no place to buy a paper or a cup of coffee. I thought grimly that it was fortunate it wasn't raining, and settled down to drowse, when my luck changed.

"A woman walked in. I've never been married, gentlemen, and I've never even had what young people today call a 'meaningful relationship.' Some casual attachments, perhaps, but on the whole, though it seems trite to say so, I am married to my art and find it much more satisfying than women, generally.

"I had no reason to think that this woman was an improvement on others, but she had a pleasant appearance. She was something over thirty, and was just plump enough to have a warm, comfortable look about her, and she wasn't too tall.

"She looked about and said, smiling, 'Well, I've missed my bus, I see.'

"I smiled with her. I liked the way she said it. She didn't fret or whine or act annoyed at the universe. It was a flat, good-humored statement of fact, and just hearing it cheered me up tremendously because actually I myself was in the mood to fret and whine and act annoyed. Now I could be as good-natured as she and say, 'Two of us, madam, so you don't even have the satisfaction of being unique.'

" 'So much the better,' she said. 'We can talk and pass the time that much faster.'

"I was astonished. She did not treat me as a potential rapist or as a possible thief. God knows I am not handsome or even particularly respectable in appearance, but it was as though she had casually penetrated to my inmost character and found it satisfactory. You have no idea how flattered I was. If I were ten times as sleepy as I was, I would have stayed up to talk to her.

"And we did talk. Inside of fifteen minutes, I knew I was having the pleasantest conversation in my life—in a crummy bus station at not much before midnight. I can't tell you all we talked about, but I can tell you what we *didn't* talk about. We didn't talk about magic.

"I can interest anyone by doing tricks, but then it isn't me they're interested in; it's the flying fingers and the patter they like. And while I'm willing to buy attention in that way, you don't know how pleasant it is to get the attention without purchase. She apparently just liked to listen to me, and I know I just liked to listen to her.

"Fortunately, my trip was not an all-out effort, so I didn't have my large trunk with the show-business advertising all over it, just two rather large valises. I told her nothing personal about myself, and asked nothing about her. I gathered briefly that she was heading for her brother's place; that he was right on the road; that she would have to wake him up because she had carelessly let herself be late—but she only told me that in order to say that she was glad it had happened. She would buy my company at the price of inconveniencing her brother. I liked that.

"We didn't talk politics or world affairs or religion or theater. We talked people—all the funny and odd and peculiar things we had observed about people. We laughed for two hours, during which not one other person came to join us. I had never had anything like that happen to me, had never felt so alive and happy, and when the bus finally came at 1:50 A.M., it was amazing how sorry I was. I didn't want the bus to come; I didn't want the night to end.

"When we got onto the bus, of course, it was no longer quite the same thing, even though it was sufficiently nonfull for us to find a double seat we could share. After all, we had been alone in the station and there we could talk loudly and laugh. On the bus we had to whisper; people were sleeping.

"Of course, it wasn't all bad. It was a nice feeling to have her so close to me; to be making contact. Despite the fact that I'm rather an old horse, I felt like a teen-ager. Enough like a teen-ager, in fact, to be embarrassed at being watched.

"Immediately across the way were a woman and her young son. He was about eight years old, I should judge, and *he* was awake. He kept watching me with his sharp little eyes. I could see those eyes fixed on us every time a street light shone into the bus and it was very inhibiting. I wished he were asleep but, of course, the excitement of being on a bus, perhaps, was keeping him awake.

"The motion of the bus, the occasional whisper, the feeling of being quite out of reality, the pressure of her body against mine—it was like confusing dream and fact, and the boundary between sleep and wakefulness just vanished. I didn't intend to sleep, and I started awake once or twice, but then finally, when I started awake one more time, it was clear that there had been a considerable period of sleep, and the seat next to me was empty."

Halsted said, "I take it she had gotten off."

"I didn't think she had disappeared into thin air," said Larri. "Naturally, I looked about. I couldn't call her name, because I didn't know her name. She wasn't in the rest room, because its door was swinging open.

"The little boy across the aisle spoke in a rapid high

treble—in French. I can understand French reasonably well, but I didn't have to make any effort, because his mother was now awake and she translated. She spoke English quite well.

"She said, 'Pardon me, sir, but is it that you are looking for the woman that was with you?'

" 'Yes,' I said. 'Did you see where she got off?'

" 'Not I, sir. I was sleeping. But my son says that she descended at the place of the Cross of Lorraine.'

" 'At the what?'

"She repeated it, and so did the child, in French.

"She said, 'You must excuse my son, sir. He is a great hero-worshiper of President Charles de Gaulle, and though he is young he knows the tale of the Free French forces in the war very well. He would not miss a sight like a Cross of Lorraine. If he said he saw it, he did.'

"I thanked them and then went forward to the bus driver and asked him, but at that time of night, the bus stops wherever a passenger would like to get off, or get on. He had made numerous stops and let numerous people on and off, and he didn't know for sure where he had stopped and whom he had left off. He was rather churlish, in fact."

Avalon cleared his throat. "He may have thought you were up to no good and was deliberately withholding information to protect the passenger."

"Maybe," said Larri despondently, "but what it amounted to was that I had lost her. When I came back to my seat, I found a little note tucked into the pocket of the jacket I had placed in the rack above. I managed to read it by a street light at the next stop, where the French mother and son got off. It said, 'Thank you so much for a delightful time. Gwendolyn.' "

Gonzalo said, "You have her first name, anyway."

Larri said, "I would appreciate having had her last name, her address, her telephone number. A first name is useless."

"You know," said Rubin, "she may deliberately have withheld information because she wasn't interested in continuing the acquaintanceship. A romantic little interlude is one thing; a continuing danger is another. She may be a married woman."

"Or she may have been offended at your falling asleep," said Gonzalo.

"Maybe," said Larri. "But if I found her, I could apologize if she were offended, or I could reassure her if she feared me; or I might cultivate her friendship if she were neither offended nor afraid. Rather that than spend the rest of my life wondering."

"Have you done anything about it?" asked Gonzalo.

"Certainly," said Larri, sardonically. "If a magician is faced with a disappearing woman he must understand what has happened. I have gone over the bus route twice by car, looking for a Cross of Lorraine. If I had found it, I would have gone in and asked if anyone there knew a woman by the name of Gwendolyn. I'd have described her. I'd have gone to the local post office or the local police station, if necessary."

"But you have not found a Cross of Lorraine, I take it," said Trumbull.

"I have not."

Halsted said, "Mathematically speaking, it's a finite problem. You could try every post office along the whole route."

Larri sighed. "If I get desperate enough, I'll try. But, mathematically speaking, that would be so inelegant. Why can't I find the Cross of Lorraine?"

"The youngster might have made a mistake," said Trumbull.

"Not a chance," said Larri. "An adult, yes, but a child, riding a hobby? Never. Adults have accumulated enough irrationality to be very unreliable eyewitnesses. A bright eight-year-old is different. Don't try to pull any trick on a bright kid; he'll see through it.

"Just the same," he went on, "nowhere on the route is there a restaurant, a department store, or anything else with the name Cross of Lorraine. I think I've checked every set of yellow pages along the entire route."

"Now wait a while," said Avalon, "that's wrong. The child wouldn't have seen the words because they would have meant nothing to him. If he spoke and read only French, as I suppose he did, he would know the phrase as *Croix de Lorraine*. The English would have never caught his eyes. He must have seen the symbol, the cross with the two horizontal bars, like this." He reached out and Henry obligingly handed him a menu.

Avalon turned it over and on the blank back drew the following:

☨

"Actually," he said, "it is more properly called the Patriarchal Cross or the Archiepiscopal Cross, since it symbolized the high office of patriarchs and archbishops by doubling the bars. You will not be surprised to hear that the Papal Cross has three bars. The Patriarchal Cross was used as a symbol by Godfrey of Bouillon, who was one of the leaders of the First Crusade, and since he was Duke of Lorraine, it came to be called the Cross of Lorraine. As we all know, it was adopted as the emblem of the Free French during the Hitlerian War." He coughed slightly and tried to look modest.

Larri said, a little impatiently, "I understand about the symbol, Dr. Avalon, and I didn't expect the youngster to note words. I think you'll agree, though, that any establishment calling itself the Cross of Lorraine would surely display the symbol along with the name. I looked for the name in the yellow pages, but for the symbol on the road."

"And you didn't find it?" said Gonzalo.

"As I've already said, I didn't. I was desperate enough to consider things I didn't think the kid could possibly have seen at night. I thought, who knows how sharp young eyes are and how readily they may see something that represents an overriding interest. So I looked at signs in windows, at street signs—even at graffiti, damn it."

"If it were a graffito," said Trumbull, "then, of course, it could have been erased between the time the child saw it, and the time you came to look for it."

"I'm not sure of that," said Rubin. "It's my experience that graffiti are never erased. We've got some on the outside of our apartment house. . . ."

"That's New York," said Trumbull. "In smaller towns, there's less tolerance for these evidences of anarchy."

"Hold on," said Gonzalo. "What makes you think graffiti are necessarily signs of anarchy? As a matter of fact . . ."

"Gentlemen! Gentlemen!" And as always, when Avalon's voice was raised to its full baritone splendor, a silence fell. "We are not here to argue the merits and demerits of graffiti. The question is: How can we find this woman who disappeared? Larri has found no restaurant or other establishment with the name of Cross of Lorraine; he has found no evidence of the symbol along the route taken. Can we help?"

Drake held up his hand and squinted through the curling smoke of his cigarette. "Hold on, there's no problem. Have

you ever seen a Russian Orthodox Church? Do you know
what its cross is like?" He made quick marks on the back of
the menu and shoved it toward the center of the table.
"Here. . . ."

He said, "The kid, being hipped on the Free French, would
take a quick look at that and see it as the Cross of Lorraine.
So what you have to do, Larri, is look for some Russian
Orthodox Church en route. I doubt that there would be more
than one."

Larri thought about it, but did not seem overjoyed. "The
cross with that second bar set at an angle would be on the top
of the spire, wouldn't it?"

"I imagine so."

"And it wouldn't be floodlighted, would it? How would the
child be able to see it at four o'clock in the morning?"

Drake stubbed out his cigarette. "Well, now, churches
usually have bulletin board affairs near the entrance. I don't
know, there could have been a Russian Orthodox cross on
the . . ."

"I would have seen it," said Larri firmly.

"Could it have been a Red Cross?" asked Gonzalo feebly.
"You know, there might be a Red Cross headquarters along
the route."

"The Red Cross," said Rubin, "is a Greek Cross with all
four arms equal. I don't see how that could possibly be
mistaken for a Cross of Lorraine by a Free French enthusi-
ast. Look at it. . . ."

Halsted said, "The logical thing, I suppose, is that you
simply missed it, Larri. If you insist that, as a magician,
you're such a trained observer that you *couldn't* have missed
it, which sounds impossible to me, then maybe it was a
symbol on something movable—on a truck in a driveway, for
instance—and it moved on after sunrise."

"The boy made it quite clear that it was at the *place* of the

Cross of Lorraine," said Larri. "I suppose even an eight-year-old can tell the difference between a place and a movable object."

"He spoke French. Maybe you mistranslated."

"I'm not that bad at the language," said Larri, "and his mother translated and French is her native tongue."

"But English isn't. *She* might have gotten it wrong. The kid might have said something else. He might not even have said the Cross of Lorraine."

Avalon raised his hand for silence and said, "One moment, gentlemen, I see Henry, our esteemed waiter, smiling. What is it, Henry?"

Henry, from his place at the sideboard said, "I'm afraid that I am amused at your doubting the child's evidence. It is quite certain, in my opinion, that he did see the Cross of Lorraine."

There was a moment's silence and Larri said, "How can you tell that, Henry?"

"By not being oversubtle, sir."

Avalon's voice boomed out. "I knew it. We're being too complicated. Henry, how is it possible to gain greater simplicity?"

"Why, Mr. Avalon, the incident took place at night. Instead of looking at all signs, all places, all varieties of cross, why not begin by asking ourselves what very few things *can* be easily seen on a highway at night?"

"A Cross of Lorraine?" asked Gonzalo incredulously.

"Certainly," said Henry, "among other things. Especially if we don't call it a Cross of Lorraine. What the youngster saw as a Cross of Lorraine, out of his special interest, we would see as something else so clearly that its relationship to the Cross of Lorraine would be invisible. What has been happening just now has been precisely what happened earlier with Mr. Larri's trick with the coin and salt shaker. We concentrated on the coin and didn't watch the salt shaker, and now we concentrate on the Cross of Lorraine and don't look for the alternative."

Trumbull said, "Henry, if you don't stop talking in riddles, you're fired. What the hell is the Cross of Lorraine, if it isn't the Cross of Lorraine?"

Henry said gravely, "What is this?" and carefully he drew on the back of the menu . . .

Trumbull said, "A Cross of Lorraine—tilted."

"No, sir, you would never have thought so, if we hadn't been talking about the Cross. Those are English letters and a very common symbol on highways if you add something to it. . . . He wrote quickly and the tilted Cross became:

EXXON

"The one thing," said Henry, "that is designed to be seen, without trouble, day or night, on any highway is a gas-station sign. The child saw the Cross of Lorraine in this one, but Mr. Larri, retracing the route, sees only a double X, since he reads the entire word as Exxon. All signs showing this name, whether on the highway, in advertisements, or on credit cards, show the name in this fashion."

Now Larri caught fire. "You mean, Henry, that if I go into the Exxon stations en route and ask for Gwendolyn . . ."

"The proprietor of one of them is likely to be her brother, and there would not be more than five or six at most to inquire at."

"Good God, Henry," said Larri, "you're a magician."

"Merely simpleminded," said Henry, "though perhaps in the nonpejorative sense."

"The Cross of Lorraine"—Afterword

Eleanor Sullivan, the delightful managing editor of *Ellery Queen's Mystery Magazine*, who was the first to see the story after I had written it, was struck by the fact that although she had seen the sign "Exxon" any number of times, she had never noticed the Cross of Lorraine it incorporated.

She decided to try an experiment. Not long after she had read the story, she was driving her car with a friend as passenger.

She said, "There's a prominent Cross of Lorraine on some of the signs of the highway. Can you point it out to me?"

The passenger knew what a Cross of Lorraine was and began to look. (It must have acted as a damper on conversation, I suspect, though Eleanor did not say so.)

Eleanor even made it easier by deliberately driving into an Exxon gasoline station in order to tank up, but the passenger never saw it. In the end Eleanor had to explain.

It's not surprising, really. You don't necessarily see what there is to see; you see what you *expect* to see. You know there are two x's in Exxon and that's all you expect to see and all you do see.

"The Cross of Lorraine" appeared in the May 1976 *EQMM*.

2.

The Family Man

Mario Gonzalo, the artist member of the Black Widowers, seemed oddly disheveled as he said vehemently, "I *cannot* teach what I do because I don't *know* what I do, but that doesn't mean I can't *do* it."

And Emmanuel Rubin, his straggly beard seeming to shoot sparks out of each gray bristle, bent his eyes, magnified through the thick lenses before them, at Gonzalo and said, "If you don't know what you're doing, you're a paint dauber and not an artist."

"You're a madman, Manny. If knowing were everything, Michelangelo could teach you to be Michelangelo, but the fact is that Michelangelo couldn't teach anyone to be Michelangelo. For that matter, no one could have taught Michelangelo to be Michelangelo either. He was *born* Michelangelo."

"You miss the entire point. Teaching doesn't necessarily imply the making of an equal. Michelangelo could give the kind of instruction from which others might profit. If he couldn't create equals, he could create somewhat less miserable marble tappers. You bet he knew what he was doing even if he could only pound a limited amount into the heads of mere mortals."

"Ah," said Gonzalo gleefully. "Mere mortals! And what made them mere mortals? The lack of genius. And what were the components of that genius? Could Michelangelo himself know?"

Thomas Trumbull, staring over his scotch and soda, and apparently irritated at being excluded from a conversation that the loud voices of Gonzalo and Rubin had made into a private dialog, scowled and said, "Since Michelangelo is dead and can't be consulted on the subject, why don't we drop this foolish argument?"

"No," said Gonzalo passionately, "I appeal from the sublime to the ridiculous and ask Manny. You're a writer, Manny—after a fashion. Can you teach what you do?"

"I not only can," said Rubin, "I have. I've written articles for *The Writer* and I've lectured at writers' conferences."

"And you've told them about query letters, and the necessity of rewriting, I suppose. Do you tell them how you know where you start your story, just which incident you put after which, how you break up your dialog, how you make the denouement inevitable without giving it away?"

"I could do that."

"Then do it right now. Explain it to me!"

Roger Halsted, flushing to the roots of his receding line of hair, said, in his soft voice, "Don't do it, Manny. We'll be sitting here all night and none of us is interested. Not even Mario."

"I won't—but I can."

"You *can't*," said Gonzalo, "because you can't describe the intuition involved. Enough intuition is talent, and a hell of a lot of it is genius, and intuition can't be taught."

Geoffrey Avalon, standing tall, said in his solemn baritone, "You stand with the Greeks, Mario. They were quite certain that any outstanding ability was the result of divine inspiration, the working of a god who possessed the person. The word 'enthusiasm,' expressing this process, means 'the god within' in Greek. Naturally, one can't explain the workings of a god to a mere mortal, and that, I take it, is your position, Mario."

"Bull!" said Rubin. "Bull to you, Geoff, and to Mario and to the Greeks. There is nothing mysterious about intuition at all."

"If you can understand it," said Mario, "explain it."

"I will," said Rubin. "All a man knows is what he observes and learns. There is nothing innate except a few biological instincts—certainly nothing cultural. It may be that with experience—with *experience*, damn you, Mario—a person learns to interpret, very rapidly, what he observes, or to draw inferences, or to do something based on deduction or induction from those observations and his past experience. He does it so rapidly that he generally doesn't bother to isolate the steps in the procedure or even to be aware they exist, so he calls it intuition. Yes, Henry?"

Henry, the perennial waiter at the Black Widowers' monthly dinner meetings, his bland and uncreased sixtyish face displaying no emotion, said, gently, "Dinner is served, Mr. Rubin. If you will sit down, I am sure the rest will follow."

Rubin said, "I suppose I *am* the natural leader."

"No," said James Drake, stubbing out his cigarette, "as host today, I'm the leader. However, the rest of us are naturally afraid you'll eat everything in sight if we don't all sit down to protect our rights."

"That depends," said Rubin, "on what we are having today. Henry?"

Henry said, "The chef is in an Old English mood today and it will be rib roast and Yorkshire pudding, preceded by a seafood quiche."

"*That's* not Old English," said Rubin.

"The chef is rarely entirely consistent," said Henry, "and I'm afraid his judgment of what will constitute a success for dinner is largely intuitive."

"And largely right, too," said Gonzalo, approving. "Whatever you say intuition is, Manny, some people have more of it than others, and why is that?"

"Some people have more talent than . . ."

"*Aha!*" said Gonzalo.

Rubin looked haughty and said with stiff politeness. "*If* I am to be allowed to finish my sentence, I will go on to explain that talent is the capacity for such fast thought, plus, perhaps, muscular deftness, and undoubtedly depends on the physiology of the brain and on nothing more mysterious than that."

"That's mysterious enough," said Drake.

"Mysterious now, but not necessarily forever," said Rubin,

"and when we learn enough about the brain, talent and genius will be as nonmysterious as eye color."

"That's just your intuitive guess," shot back Gonzalo.

Rubin's reply was lost in quiche, and the dinner conversation grew more general.

Through all the argument, the guest of the evening had maintained a steady and clearly amused silence. Quietly, he listened and as quietly, he sipped at his martini.

His name was Simon Alexander. His black hair and black mustache, each thick and luxuriant enough to give him a Satanic appearance, or, failing that, a Levantine one, were his most prominent features. The small and persistent smile on his face seemed to accentuate the Satanism.

When the coffee was served, however, and Drake tapped his spoon against the water glass, Alexander, as though in anticipation, grew serious.

Drake said, "Gentlemen, it is time to grill our esteemed guest, and Manny, since you've been clattering away more insupportably even than usual, suppose you supervise the grilling."

Rubin said, "I'm sorry you find mental stimulation insupportable, Jim, but I'm not surprised." He took a quick sip at his coffee, signaled Henry for a bit of a freshener, then said,

"Well, Mr. Alexander, or, if you prefer, Simon, how do you justify your existence?"

Alexander's smile returned. "By seeing to it that the American people pay their legal taxes in full and on time."

There was a stir about the table, and even Henry was betrayed into pausing in the precise performance of his duties long enough to cast a penetrating glance at the guest.

Trumbull said, with a distinct suggestion of outrage, "Are you in the employ of the IRS?"

"I am," said Alexander. "I'm in the Division of Fraud."

"Good God," said Trumbull, "and you offer that as justification for your existence? Horse-whipping with barbed wire is what it justifies." He cast a lowering glance at Drake.

Drake said, "Give him a chance, Tom. It takes all kinds to make a world and, aside from his profession, Simon is one of Nature's noblemen."

Alexander waved his hand. "It's all right, Jim. Tax collectors have always been the favorite villains of humanity from the moment they first appeared on scene in ancient Sumeria five thousand years ago and invented writing in order to keep score. Besides, I think Mr. Trumbull was merely expressing himself colorfully and didn't really mean it."

"The hell I didn't," muttered Trumbull.

Rubin, who had held his peace in a markedly aggrieved manner, now raised his voice, "Since I'm grilling today, may I continue? Do you mind keeping quiet, Tom?"

Trumbull said, "Circumstances moved me."

Rubin waited for silence and said, "Mr. Alexander—I withdraw the Simon, since through the common law of humanity, you can have no friends here, or possibly anywhere—how can your role in tax collection be taken as justifying your existence?"

Alexander said, "I think it is not difficult to see that the IRS represents the single essential arm of the government. Presidents can die and be replaced at once, with but a slight and perfunctory hiccup of emotion. Congress can bumble, the Supreme Court can drag, and we can lose ground diplomatically, economically, even militarily, yet perhaps make it all up afterward. Natural disasters are local, temporary, and pass by.

"However, let the tax structure of the nation falter and the government can no longer function. That would mean a spreading paralysis far wider and longer and deeper than anything that can possibly occur short of a thermonuclear war."

Rubin said, "But the tax structure is not likely to falter, is it?"

"Not in the sense that the physical machinery is likely to break apart or that the computers will stop working. No, the weak link is the taxpayer himself. The American budget now approaches half a trillion dollars annually, and the largest part of this is collected out of the unwilling wallets of Americans everywhere."

"Sorry, Manny," said Trumbull angrily, "but I've got to interrupt. What the hell has 'unwilling' got to do with it? You enforce your own interpretation of the rules, act as prosecuting attorney and judge, hound us relentlessly, treat us as guilty till we prove ourselves innocent, and are perfectly ready to jail us if you can. What do you care if we're unwilling?"

"In the first place," said Alexander, "our judgments can be appealed to the courts. We are not the last word. Second, it would be much more harmful if we were not relentless. Despite everything we do, we cannot audit everyone, we cannot check into everything. If we tried, the cost would far outweigh what additional money we could collect. No, we are forced to depend on the average American filling out a reasonably honest return and we can count on this only as long as that average American is convinced of the essential honesty of the system. Within the bounds of the law—and the law is not completely equitable, but that's not our fault—we must show neither favor nor mercy or the structure will break down.

"Thus, although Al Capone could commit theft on a grand scale and could murder with impunity, he could be grabbed on income-tax evasion. There is nothing ironical in this. Income-tax evasion is the greatest of these. Similarly, nothing that Nixon and Agnew did prior to their forced resignations was as mischievous as their tampering with the IRS and their making out of dubious income-tax returns. That they were willing to shake the faith of the American people in the honesty of the tax structure was of all their misdeeds the most unforgivable."

Rubin said, "You're serious about this now? You're not pulling our legs?"

"Dead serious."

"Good God, Jim," Rubin said, "we ought to ask for your resignation. You've brought in a guy who's going to make it difficult for me to indulge in a little bit of honest expense-padding next time around."

Avalon cleared his throat. "I don't consciously pad, but I must admit that the IRS and I might not agree on just what constitutes a deductible expense in the first place."

"Then you deduct it till we tell you otherwise," said Alexander, agreeably. "That's the tax man's version of keeping you innocent till proven guilty—but none of this is what I came here prepared to talk about."

"Oh," said Rubin, "what are you prepared for?"

"Jim told me," said Alexander, "that the Black Widowers like to hear some tale that involves a bit of a puzzle, and I happen to have one."

"Jim was wrong to tell you that," said Avalon, austerely.

"We meet for the purpose of participating in stimulating conversation, and a puzzle is not necessary; however—"

Alexander smiled. "In that connection, I was amused by the preprandial quarrel over the nature of intuition, since it is with a matter of intuition that my story is concerned."

"Telepathy!" said Gonzalo at once.

"No, I think not," said Alexander. "The whole conversation illustrated Mr. Rubin's thesis, actually. I agree with him that intuition is undetected observation and deduction, and I would like to point out that what is often considered telepathy is the same. Thus, when Jim introduced me, he said—and I think these are his exact words—'This is Simon Alexander, an investigator of sorts and a very good one. He can actually sense criminality by some kind of inner magic, I think.' Isn't that what you said, Jim?"

"I think so," said Drake.

"I notice you said, 'an investigator of sorts,' " growled Trumbull. "You didn't say he was from the IRS."

Alexander said, "I am trying to make the point that the introduction took place when the drinks were being passed around—as the brandy is now, I see. Henry, do we have any curaçao?"

"I believe so, sir."

"I'll have some then. With everyone concentrating on alcohol, I don't think anyone heard the introduction. Does anyone recall having heard it?"

There were no bites on that one, and Alexander smoothed his mustache wtih one forefinger and accepted the small glass with its orange-colored content from Henry.

"But if Rubin and Gonzalo did not *consciously* hear it," he said, "they nevertheless heard it, I'm convinced, and that bit about sensing criminality by some kind of inner magic sparked the argument on intuition. Of course, I *don't* use some kind of inner magic. I use reason, and I am always quite conscious of the details of the reasoning. Except once . . ." He looked thoughtful.

Drake lit a cigarette from the dying stub of his old one and said, "Tell us, Simon."

"I intend to," said Alexander, "but it has a certain personal confidentiality about it. I have been given to understand that everything that goes on here is confidential."

"Everything!" said Trumbull pointedly, "and that includes

everything *we* say. We take it for granted that nothing *you* hear here can be used against us as far as our taxes are concerned."

"Agreed," said Alexander, "but please be careful what you say, as I would rather not be asked to place too great a load on my integrity."

Alexander sipped at his curaçao, looked pensive, and, for some reason, particularly Satanic.

"You know, of course," he said, "that computers are now the lifeblood of the IRS. We couldn't operate without them. Because they never hesitate, never tire, never grow bored, they are our great strength. Because they never think, they are our great weakness.

"To exploit a computer, however, and take advantage of its weakness, one must know every detail of a computer's working, and this eliminates almost all the human race. And it puts us off our guard.

"Some years ago, the IRS was royally diddled by someone who knew his computers, by a mathematician who was tired of the type of remuneration that mathematicians receive."

Halsted, who taught mathematics at a junior high school, sighed and said, "I know the type."

"The long details of his operation don't concern you, but he managed to get a job that would involve the servicing of certain of our computers. For the purpose, he built himself a new statistical background, a new name, a new appearance, all the way down to a new Social Security number. How he managed that I won't tell you since, confidentiality or not, there is no point in spreading knowledge of the techniques of successful knavery."

"I agree," said Avalon, nodding.

"Nor," said Alexander, "will I tell you exactly how he managed to reprogram one key computer—for in that case, I don't understand it myself. I am no mathematician. Still it was done. For a period of five years, our mathematician—let us call him Johnson, to save syllables—received large tax refunds while paying no taxes. He received more money in that interval than he could have earned in a lifetime of honest endeavor.

"He might still be receiving the money but for the accidental uncovering of an inconsistency in the program. The detection was the result of a most unusual coincidence, and I assure you the IRS could not have been more dismayed, or embarrassed, at the event. Naturally, two things were at once essential. Tha money leak must be stopped and the computer programs so modified as to make the Johnson type of knavery impossible in the future. That was carried through at once in the greatest secrecy. The secrecy was needed not so much to keep individual officials from looking personally ridiculous, though that was a factor, but to keep the Service itself from losing the confidence of the American people."

"They will never learn the truth from any of us," said Gonzalo, with suspiciously intense gravity, "I assure you."

"The second thing," Alexander went on, "was to catch Johnson, make him disgorge what money was left, and clap him in jail for as long as ever the law would allow. It was the Al Capone reasoning, you see. Johnson might get away with murder without shaking the foundation of American civilization, but he could not be allowed to get away with income-tax fraud. And that was where I came in. I was placed on the case.

"My reputation in the Service is, perhaps, an exaggerated one. More than one person there suspects, as Jim told you, that I solve my cases with some inner magic, with some mysterious intuitive faculty that defies analysis. It has been said among us, for instance, that I can look at a tax return that seems clean enough to have been etched in snowflakes and yet tell that somewhere money was clinging to fingers that smelled of garbage. Or that I could interview a person and know for certain that there was a thief hidden behind the saint.

"Actually, there was no magic in it at all. I have a certain cleverness at observation and reasoning and a great deal of experience. My memory is excellent and I have encountered all varieties of behavior patterns—and all the ways of laundering returns, too. What seems like magic or intuition boils down to noting small things that others don't and attaching the proper importance to those things.

"It works the other way around, too. I can often detect the saint beneath the thief. I am quite certain, for instance, that you, Mr. Trumbull, are not short on your returns by even as much as fifty dollars. I suspect that you are ashamed of your relative honesty, and take it out by vilifying the office you dare not defraud. And that's not a guess; I've met others like you."

It was hard for Trumbull to flush through his tan, but his expression made the flush unnecessary.

Avalon said, "I'm afraid your reputation is ruined, Tom. Please go on, Mr. Alexander."

"To put in figures, in nearly a quarter of a century at my job, I have almost never pointed a finger in the direction of either guilt or innocence and been proven entirely wrong."

"A quarter of a century?" said Avalon. "How old are you, Mr. Alexander?"

"Fifty-two."

"You don't look it," and Avalon's finger went unconsciously to his own graying mustache.

Alexander said, "There's gray in my hair, too, but I touch it up a little. Not so much out of vanity, you understand, as because the darkness seems to give me a forbidding appearance that is useful to me in my line of work. However . . .

"Johnson was not an easy quarry. He could tell, somehow, that the game was up, and when the next refund came—this time under the eyes of the Service—it remained uncollected. It's not impossible he had an ally within the Service, but never mind that. Tracing him wasn't easy. He had quit his job long before and all records we had concerning him were false, down to his Social Security number, which, we suddenly discovered, was attached to no human being.

"I was forced to follow the most evanescent clues and to build up the picture of the human being who had done the deed. We left absolutely nothing unturned that might lead us to the identity of the thief and we finally had several possibilities, all dim and uncertain. Different operatives were assigned to each one. The task was somehow to locate enough evidence to warrant a concentration of forces, a full-scale investigation of one particular man—an arrest, of course, if possible.

"My own target was a rather mousey man of average weight and height and of undistinguished appearance. That, in itself, was a good sign, because the job had had to be carried through by someone who could be unnoticeable at crucial moments. He had a vague background that could not easily be traced without tipping our hand too soon—again a hopeful circumstance. At crucial periods, he seemed to be particularly untraceable.

"Unfortunately, all this was negative and such things could never be made to stick. We needed some *positive* correspondence. We had to locate him at the site of action each time, prove computer expertise, and so on. For that, I haunted him like a ghost of a vulture.

"In fact, I managed to collect a circle of mild acquaintances that I held in common with him, and I labored to be present at social gatherings along with him.

"Then, at one gathering in early November, where both of us were present, he quiet and watchful, nursing a single drink for an hour; and I almost as quiet, certainly as watchful, and as abstemious, the host spoke of Halloween. He had a seven-year-old daughter who had gone out trick-or-treating, along with several older friends, and who had come back in ecstasies.

"That rang true for me, for I remembered very well my own daughter's first experience of the sort and I said, 'Yes, I have always thought that, were it not for the enormous commercial overweighting of the Yuletide, a child's spontaneous reaction would be to treat Halloween with the full excitement of Christmas.'

"And, surprisingly, my quarry spoke up. As though overwhelmed by an emotion that forced his naturally quiet personality into the limelight; he said, with a warm smile that lightened and almost transfigured his face, 'You are quite right. In a way, Halloween may be considered precisely equal to Christmas.' Those were his exact words, gentlemen, for I noted them at the time with particular care."

Rubin asked, "Why?"

"Because, as a result of that comment, I instantly and completely eliminated him as a suspect. So certain was I that I remember having the distinct impulse to clap him on the shoulder and invite him out for a drink to celebrate his innocence. I couldn't, though, for I suppose his own unexpected warmth had scared him. As soon as he made the remark, he flushed, looked frightened, and melted away. My own attention was distracted for a moment, and when I turned to find him, he was gone."

Alexander paused and finished his last bit of curaçao. He said, "At the time, my sudden conviction of innocence might have seemed pure intuition—even to myself—but it wasn't, of course. I cling to Rubin's hypothesis the intuition is unde- tected reasoning. Here is the reasoning as I worked it out later.

"Working laboriously from the tiniest beginnings, we had drawn a picture of our criminal, this Johnson. He was a mathematician and had no family. The chances were that he was not only unmarried and childless, but also that he had no siblings and that his parents may have died while he was young. He was cold, utterly cold—and I don't mean by that that he was ruthless and sadistic—merely that he lacked any occasion or desire for love and affection. Let me put it in a way that has great significance for me. He was not, in any way, a family man."

Halsted pleated the tablecloth absently and said, "You, I take it, *are* a family man."

"Completely. My parents, two brothers, and a sister all live, and we are all close. I married a childhood sweetheart, have three children, and a grandson newly born, plus nieces and nephews. I know the emotions of a family man and no one, *no one*, could have spoken with such genuine warmth of children's holidays unless he had experienced the kind of love and affection that accompanies those days. My quarry spoke that way; Johnson could not have; conclusion, my quarry was not Johnson and was innocent. What seemed like intuition was, after all, reason.

"Intuition or reason, I reported my belief in his innocence to my superiors, and the tracking of the remaining possibili- ties grew correspondingly more intense. Five months later we caught the criminal, and he is now in prison and likely to remain there a long time. Some of the money has been recovered; not all, of course."

He paused and Avalon broke the short silence that fol- lowed, saying, "I am delighted to have a happy ending for the department, but you spoke of a puzzle and I see none."

Simon Alexander sighed. "The happy ending is a qualified one. Having dismissed my suspect, we nevertheless found the other suspects fading as well. One after another, they proved to be incompatible with the conditions of the fraud. One day, out of nothing but desperation, I returned to my own dis- missed suspect and, in the interval, something unexpected that had arisen cast a new light on affairs. Astounded, I followed it up and had him—my own suspect whose innocence I had previously maintained and, virtually, guaranteed. He was the criminal after all.

"What puzzles me and, even now, keeps me awake occasionally, is the incongruity of it. He did indeed turn out to be what we had suspected he was—a man without family, love, or affection. Yet his remark about Christmas and Halloween, and the tone in which it was uttered, indicated the reverse. How is this contradiction possible and how could he have used it to throw me off the scent?"

There was a silence around the table as Alexander waited for an answer.

Avalon finally spoke, staring at his empty brandy glass, "Mr. Alexander, despite easy theorization, the fact remains that human beings are complicated and inconsistent creatures. There are undoubtedly contradictory aspects in the character of your suspect or of any man. You'll have to chalk it up to a bad break."

"I'd like to," said Alexander, "and I've tried to do so, but it is my experience that in fundamentals human beings are *not* inconsistent. A man who always puts on his left shoe first, may switch party allegiance and swap wives, but he will always put on his left shoe first."

"Nothing will stop him from putting on his right shoe first, however uncomfortable that might be," said Halsted, "if it is necessary to do so to fool someone. He stepped purposely out of character to mislead you."

Alexander didn't answer at once. Then he said, "I doubt that. Even if he knew I was at his heels, and that's a possibility, he couldn't possibly have known me so well as to be sure that one short, apparently irrelevant sentence would deflect me."

Rubin said, "The remark might have been misanthropically in character, and you interpreted it wrongly because of your own happy associations with the holidays. What the suspect might have meant was that Christmas was just as superstitious and nonsensical as Halloween."

Alexander said, "An interesting thought, but the expression on his face and the tone of his voice did not fit. They were happy, delighted. I am *still* sure he meant it sincerely as a loving remark."

Gonzalo said, "He could be a 'Peanuts' fan and was think-ing of Linus's 'Great Pumpkin,' which is a kind of satire on Santa Claus. That would set up a strong association between Halloween and Christmas."

There was a general hoot from the audience, but Alexander held up his hand. "Actually, that's the first suggestion I hadn't thought of myself. It doesn't sound in the least likely to me, but I will check whether the thief was a 'Peanuts' fan."

Trumbull said, "We don't have enough to go on. I don't think anything can be deduced from what he said to set your mind at ease. Sorry!"

Drake said, "I agree, but we haven't heard from Henry yet."

"Henry?" said Alexander in surprise, swiveling in his seat.

Henry cleared his throat. "I admit, gentlemen, that a thought had entered my mind at the moment Mr. Alexander gave us the suspect's remark."

"Oh?" said Alexander, "and just what thought was that?"

"The suspect, sir, did not say, as you or I might have said, that Halloween was just like Christmas or just as good as Christmas, or even equivalent to Christmas. If you quoted him correctly he said Halloween was 'precisely equal' to Christmas. Surely that sounds like a mathematician speaking and would be in character."

Alexander snorted. "Feeble. Feeble. A nonmathematician might have happened to put it that way if he were a prissy and meticulous person."

Henry said softly, "Perhaps. Yet we might find more in the statement if we treat it mathematically than anyone has yet pointed out. After all, if your suspect were indeed the guilty man he would be not only a mathematician, but also a computer specialist."

Alexander looked annoyed. "What has that to do with it?"

Henry said, "Mr. Alexander, listening to the gentlemen of the Black Widowers month after month is an education in itself and there have been times when I have directed my readings in the directions they have opened up for me. Mr. Halsted, for instance, once discussed the rationale behind positional notation, the manner in which our Arabic numer-als are constructed, and I went on to read further concerning the matter. If you'd care to have me explain it, I'm sure Mr.

Halsted will be glad to correct me if I've made a mistake."

Halsted said, "I'll be glad to, Henry, but I don't see what you're driving at."

"You will in a moment, sir. Our ordinary numbers are written to the base ten. The first column at the right are the ones. The next to the left are the tens, the next are the hundreds or ten times tens, the next are the thousands or ten times ten times ten, and so on. Thus the number 1231 is one times a thousand plus two times a hundred plus three times ten plus one and that comes to one thousand, two hundred thirty-one."

"Right so far," said Halsted.

"But there's no need to consider ten the only possible base for a number system," said Henry. "You could use nine, for instance. The right-hand column in a nine-based system would be ones, the next to the left would be nines, the next would be eighty-ones or nine times nine, the next would be—uh—seven hundred twenty-nines or nine times nine times nine, and so on. The number 1231 would, in the nine-based system, be one times seven hundred twenty-nine plus two times eighty-one, plus three times nine, plus one. That would be, if you would allow me a moment to work it out—the equivalent of nine hundred nineteen in our ordinary ten-based system."

He scribbled hastily on a napkin and held it up. "You could write the result this way: 1231 (nine-based) = 919 (ten-based)."

Halsted, Drake, and Rubin nodded. Avalon and Trumbull looked thoughtful, and Alexander shook his head impatiently.

Gonzalo said, "That's ridiculous. Why would anyone use that nine-based system and multiply nines?"

Halsted said, "The other number bases look complicated, Mario, only because our number system is designed to fit ten as a base. Mathematically, all are equivalently rational, though some are more convenient than others. For instance, in computers, it is particularly useful at times to use—uh, oh . . ."

He looked at Henry with a grin and said, "I may be getting it, Henry, but you keep on and finish."

"Thank you, sir," said Henry. "As Mr. Halsted was about to say, the eight-base system is, I understand, useful to computers. The number 31, for instance, in the ten-base system is, of course, three times ten plus one, or thirty-one. In the eight-base system, however, it is three times eight plus one, or twenty-five.

"We can therefore write"—he used the napkin again—" this: 31 (eight-base) = 25 (ten-base).

He went on, "The different number bases are sometimes given names derived from the Latin names of the numbers. The Latin for ten is *decem*, so a ten-based number belongs to the decimal system. The Latin for eight is *octo*, so eight-based numbers are octal. We can therefore write this: 31 (octal) = 25 (decimal).

"By coincidence, we have the months October and December. . . ."

Rubin roared out in sudden delight, "No coincidence at all. The ancient Romans started their year in March before Julius Caesar's time. By that system, October was the eighth month and December the tenth month and they were named accordingly."

Henry nodded his head and said, "Thank you, sir. If, then, we abbreviate the terms 'octal' and 'decimal' in a natural way and omit the parentheses, we have 31 October = 25 December. How can this be described better than by saying that Halloween, which falls on 31 October, is precisely equal to Christmas, which falls on 25 December."

Alexander's mouth had tended to slacken through this but now he tightened his jaw muscle and said, "Are you trying to tell me that the thief, blurting out his remark without thinking, gave away the fact that he was a computer expert?"

"Yes, sir," said Henry. "It was not out of shyness that a look of alarm crossed his face and that he left as soon as he could. It must have been out of fright at the thought of having slipped into his real character. At that moment, if the significance of his remark had been seen by you, it would have been wise to begin arrangements for having him arrested."

Alexander looked chagrined. "Well, I didn't see it. I interpreted it just wrong. But wait, all this is clever and may even be right considering that the man in question proved to be indeed the criminal, but how would you account for that look of love on his face? *That* was what threw me."

Henry said softly, "You are a family man, sir, and that is

your weakness. You naturally interpret love in human terms
alone. I, myself, am not a family man, and I know that love is
broader than that. Even a misanthrope who hates the human
race could love, and deeply, too."

"Love what?" said Alexander impatiently.

"The beauty and surprises of mathematics, for one thing,"
said Henry.

"The Family Man"—Afterword

Those of you who have read the first two volumes of the
Black Widowers tales know that there is a real organization
called "the Trap Door Spiders" to which I belong, and which
serves as an inspiration for everything about the Black
Widowers, but the mysteries. Occasionally, I even make use
of a real-life guest—at least for appearance and general
background.

For instance, there was indeed a meeting of the Trap Door
Spiders at which a magician, very much like the Amazing
Larri of the first story in this volume, did dine with us as our
guest. (There was no mystery introduced, of course, in the
real-life occasion.)

And at another meeting, which I hosted, I brought my
accountant as my guest. He is a very amiable gentleman
with whom I share a million laughs as he strips me to the
bone for the sake of good old Uncle Sam and then gnaws at
the bones for his fee.

I used him as an inspiration for Simon Alexander in "The
Family Man," changing him from an accountant to a tax
auditor (the enemy) and carrying on from there.

As to the point about numbers to different bases, this was
presented to me by a fellow member of another organization I
belong to, the Baker Street Irregulars. It was presented to me
with the urgent suggestion that I base a Black Widowers
mystery on it, and I was delighted to oblige.

"The Family Man" appeared in the November 1976 *EQMM*
under the title "A Case of Income-tax Fraud." All things
being equal, I prefer a short title, however, so I here restore
my own.

3.

The Sports Page

"Is 'blain' an English word?" asked Mario Gonzalo, as the company of the Black Widowers sat down to their monthly banquet.

"Brain?" asked James Drake, scraping his chair toward the table and looking over the selection of bread and rolls.

"Blain," said Gonzalo sharply.

"How do you spell it?" asked Roger Halsted, who had no difficulty in deciding to take two slices of pumpernickel. He was buttering them.

"What's the difference how it's spelled?" said Gonzalo in annoyance. He placed his napkin carefully over his lightly striped and definitely pink trousers. "Spell it any way you want. Is it an English word?"

Thomas Trumbull, host for the evening, furrowed his bronzed forehead, and said, "Damn it, Mario, we've had a pretty sensible session so far. What's all this about 'blain'?"

"I'm aking you a question. Why don't you answer it?"

"All right. It's not an English word."

Gonzalo looked about the table, "Everyone agree 'blain' isn't English?"

There was a hesitant chorus of agreement. Even Emmanuel Rubin, his eyes magnified by his glasses and his straggly beard a bit shorter than usual, as though it had recently been absent-mindedly trimmed, finally muttered, "No such word."

Lawrence Pentili, who had arrived as Trumbull's guest, and who was an elderly man with sparse white hair, and with muttonchop side-whiskers grown long, as though they were announcing that hair could still be produced, smiled and said, "Never heard that word."

Only Geoffrey Avalon held his peace. Sitting bolt upright as always, he frowned and with his middle finger stirred the ice in the unfinished half of his second drink.

"All right," said Gonzalo, "we all agree it's not an English word. You can see that in a second. But *how* do you see it? Do you go through a list of all the English words you know and see that 'blain' isn't on it? Do you check the sound for familiarity? Do you . . ."

Halsted's soft voice interrupted, "No one knows how human recall works, so why ask? Even people who have theories about how the mechanism of memory works don't understand how information can be fished out once it has been inserted. Every word I use has to be recalled from my vocabulary, and each is there when I need it."

Trumbull said, "There are lots of times when you can't think of the word you want."

Halsted had just turned with satisfaction to the turtle soup that Henry, the incomparable waiter of the Black Widowers, had placed before him. He said, stuttering slightly as he often did under stress, "Yes, and that upsets you. Most people take it hard when they can't think of a word, get very upset, as though something has gone wrong that shouldn't have gone wrong. Me, I tend to stutter when I can't think of a word."

Now at last Avalon's deep baritone sounded, and dominated the table. "Well, wait now. As a matter of fact, there *is* such a word as 'blain.' It's archaic, but it's English. It's some sort of animal ailment, or blister."

"Right," said Gonzalo with satisfaction. "The word is used in the Bible in connection with the plagues of Egypt in the Book of Exodus. I knew someone here would get it. I thought it would be Manny."

Rubin said indignantly, "I thought you meant *current* English."

"I didn't say so," said Gonzalo. "Besides, it's part of the word 'chilblains,' and that's current English.

"No, it's *not*," said Rubin, heating up further, "and besides . . ."

Trumbull said, loudly, "Don't get defensive, Manny. What I want to know is how Mario knows all this. And, incidentally, we're having finnan haddie today at my request, and if anyone here doesn't like it, he can negotiate with Henry for substitutes. Well, Mario?"

Gonzalo said, "I read it in a psychology book. There's nothing that says I have to be born knowing everything, the way Manny claims he's been. I pick up knowledge by keeping my eyes and ears open. And what I want to do now is make a point. Remembering too well is dangerous."

"It's a danger you'll never face," muttered Rubin.

"I don't care," said Gonzalo. "Look, I asked a question and I got a quick and certain response from everyone here but Jeff. He was uncertain and hesitated because he remembered too much. He remembered the use of 'blain' in the Bible. Well, human beings are faced with choices every minute. There has to be a decision and the decision has to be based on what he knows. And if he knows too much, he'll hesitate."

"And so," asked Drake who, having speared some of the finnan haddie on his fork and placed it in his mouth, looked first thoughtful and then satisfied.

"So that's bad," said Gonzalo. "In the long run, what counts is a quick response and action. Even a less than good decision is better than indecision, most times. That's why human beings have evolved an imperfect memory. Forgetting has survival value."

Avalon smiled and nodded. "That's not a bad notion, Mario," he said, with, perhaps, a trace of condescension. "Have I ever told you my theory of the evolutionary value of contentiousness? In a hunting society . . ."

But Gonzalo held up both arms. "I'm not finished, Jeff. Don't you all see that's why Henry here does so much better than we do in solving the puzzles that arise from time to time? Every one of us here at the table practices being deep . . ."

"Not everybody, Mario," said Rubin, "unless you're about to start."

Gonzalo ignored him. "Henry doesn't. He doesn't gunk his

mind up with irrelevant information, so he can see clearly."

Henry, who was clearing some of the excess dishes, said gently, "If I may interpose, Mr. Gonzalo, I'm afraid that whatever I do could not be done, were it not that you gentlemen usually eliminate all that would otherwise confuse me." His unlined, sixtyish face showed only imperturbable efficiency, as he next poured several refills of the white wine.

Trumbull said, "Mario, your theory is junk and, Henry, that false modesty is unbecoming to you. You have more brains than any of us do, Henry, and you know it."

"No, sir," said Henry. "With respect, the most I'll admit is that I have a faculty for seeing the obvious."

"*Because*," said Gonzalo, "you don't have the difficulty of trying to look at the obvious through layers of crud, as Manny does."

Henry bowed his head slightly and seemed almost relieved when the infuriated Rubin launched into an analysis of the value of miscellaneous knowledge to the writer, and of the fact—which he announced as such with fervor—of the equation of general intelligence with the ability to remember, recall, analyze, and synthesize.

But Pentili, the guest, seemed to have lost interest in the conversation. His eyes followed Henry thoughtfully.

Waiting for the precise moment when the desserts had been eaten and when several of the coffees were about ready for the refill, Trumbull tapped his water glass with his spoon and announced it was time for the grilling.

"Since I am host," he growled, "I am delighted to be disqualified as griller. Mario, you did all that preaching over the soup. Why don't you grill out guest?"

Gonzalo said, "Dee-lighted," and cleared his throat ostentatiously. "Mr. Pentili, how do you justify your existence?"

Pentili smiled broadly so that a round little ball of flesh bunched up over each cheekbone, giving him the look of a beardless Santa Claus in mufti. "Thank heaven, I no longer have to. I am retired and I have either already justified my existence or have already failed."

"And in the days when you might have been justifying it, what were you doing to make your existence possible?"

"Breathing. But if you mean, how did I make my living, I

served Uncle Sam in the same fashion, more or less, that Tom does."

"You were a cipher expert?"

"No, but I was involved in intelligence."

"And *that* justifies your existence?" put in Rubin.

"Shall we argue the point?" said Pentili agreeably.

"No," said Trumbull. "It's been argued fifty times. Go ahead, Mario."

Gonzalo looked eager. "The last time Tom had a guest here, he had a problem. Do you have one?"

"At the present time, certainly not. I leave problems to Tom and the others these days. I'm a more or less happy observer. But I have a question, if I may ask one."?

"Go ahead."

Pentili said, "You had said that Henry—who, I take it, is our waiter . . ."

Trumbull said, "Henry is a valued member of the Black Widowers and the best of us all."

"I see. But I take it that Henry solves puzzles. What kind?"

A shade of uneasiness crossed Henry's face but disappeared almost at once. He said, "Some questions arise at one time or another on the occasion of these banquets, sir, and the members have been able to propose answers."

"*You* have proposed them," said Gonzalo energetically.

Avalon raised his hand. "I protest. This is not a fit subject for discussion. Everything said here is entirely confidential, and we ought not to talk about previous sessions in front of our guest."

"No, no," said Pentili, shaking his head. "I ask for no confidences. It just occurred to me that, if it were appropriate to do so, I could pose a problem for Henry."

Gonzalo said, "I thought you said you didn't have a problem."

"I don't," said Pentili, twinkling, "but I once had a problem, many years ago, and it was never solved to my satisfaction. It is of no importance any longer, you understand, except as an irritating grain of sand inside the tissues of my curiosity."

"What was that, Larry?" asked Trumbull with sudden interest.

"You had just entered the department, Tom. It didn't involve you—or almost anyone, but me."

"May we hear it?" said Gonzalo.

"As I said," said Pentili, "it's entirely unimportant and I

assure you I had not meant to bring it up. It was just that when mention was made specifically of Henry's facility with . . ."

Henry said softly, "If I may be allowed a word, sir. I am not the expert at solving puzzles that Mr. Gonzalo is kind enough to think me. There have been occasions when, indeed, I have been helpful in that direction but that has only been when the membership has considered the problem and eliminated much of what is not essential. If, in that case, some simple thread is left exposed, I can pick it up as well as another, but I can do no more than that."

"Oh." Pentili looked abashed. "Well, I'm perfectly willing to present the problem to the membership generally."

"In that case, sir," said Avalon, "we are all ears."

Pentili, having finished his brandy and having declined a refill, said, "I will ask you, gentlemen, to cast your mind back to 1961. John F. Kennedy was in the first months of his tragically abbreviated Administration, and an invasion of Cuba by Cuban exiles was being planned. Kennedy had inherited those plans and had refused to chance the repercussions of having the invaders granted American air support. He was assured by intelligence reports that it was quite certain the Cuban populace would rise in support of the invaders. A free Cuban Government would quickly be formed, and at *its* request the United States might move.

"It is easy, in hindsight, to realize how wretchedly we had underestimated Castro's hold on his army and his people, but at the time we saw everything through a pinkly optimistic haze. You all know what happened. The invaders landed at the Bay of Pigs and were met at once by well-organized Castroites. The Cuban people did *not* rise, and in the absence of effective air support, the invaders were all either killed or taken. It was a tragic affair for them and an embarrassing fiasco for the United States. Kennedy accepted the responsibility since he was President and had given the final kickoff signal. Although others were clearly more to blame, no one stepped forward to take his medicine. As Kennedy said, 'Victory has a thousand fathers, but defeat is an orphan.' "

Rubin, who had been staring at his coffee cup, said suddenly, "I remember that. At the time, Kennedy said it was an old saying, but no one, to my knowledge, has ever discovered the source. It will have to go into the quotation books with Kennedy's name under it."

Avalon cleared his throat. "A defeat or even a humiliation does not stand alone in time. Smarting from the Bay of Pigs, Kennedy was determined not to submit again, so the next year he faced down the Soviets on the Cuban missiles affair and won for us our greatest victory of the Cold War."

Rubin said, with vehemence, "And victories don't stand alone, either. President Johnson, determined not to appear less *macho* than his predecessor, led us step by step into the quagmire of Vietnam, and this led to our . . ."

"Come on, you idiots," shouted Trumbull. "This isn't a contemporary history class. We're listening to Larry Pentili."

In the sudden silence that followed, Pentili said, with a bit of gloominess flitting over his face, "Actually, it is all pertinent. You see, the real villain of the Bay of Pigs affair was faulty intelligence. Had we known quite accurately what the situation was in Cuba, Kennedy would have canceled the invasion or given it effective air support. In that case, there would have been no fiasco to give either Castro or Khrushchev the false notion that they could get away with establishing missile sites ninety miles off Florida and then, if we accept Rubin's psychohistorical interpretation, there would have been no Vietnam.

"And in my opinion, information need *not* have been faulty. We had one operative who had been planted in Cuba and who was back in Washington some half a year before the Bay of Pigs with reports he had been unable to radio out. . . ."

"Why not?" said Gonzalo, at once.

"Because he was playing a difficult role that he dared not risk. He was a Soviet agent, you see, and his whole value to us was that the Soviets allowed him to travel to the United States freely and to circulate in Washington freely because they thought he was spying on us for them."

"Maybe he was," said Drake, peering through his cigarette smoke. "How can you tell which side a double agent is fooling?"

"Maybe both sides," said Halsted.

"Maybe," conceded Pentili, "but the Soviets never discovered anything more than we deliberately had this Russian of ours reveal. On the other hand, through him we learned a

great many useful things that the Soviets could not con-
ceivably have wanted us to know."

"I wonder," said Rubin, with something more than a trace
of sarcasm in his voice, "if the Soviets might not have
reasoned in precisely the same way."

"I don't think so," said Pentili, "for in the end it was the
Soviets who eliminated him and not we. How they caught on
to him, how he had given himself away, we never discovered,
but it was clear that the Soviets finally came around to
agreeing with us that he was essentially our Russian and not
theirs. Too bad, but, of course, from their standpoint he was a
traitor. In reverse, we'd have done the same thing."

Avalon said, "Frankly, I would hesitate to trust a traitor. A
man who betrays once can betray again."

"Yes," said Pentili, "and for that reason he never knew
anything more than it was considered safe for him to know.
Yet I, for one, *did* trust him. It was always my opinion that
he chose us because he came to believe in the American ideal.
During the three years he worked with us, he never gave us
any ground for concern.

"His name was Stepan and he was an earnest man, rather
humorless, who went about his task with a conscious dedication. He was determined to learn idiomatic English and to
speak it with a general American accent. He was therefore a
faithful listener to news programs not for their contents but
for the sanitized pronunciations of men like Walter Cronkite.
To develp his vocabulary, Stepan worked at crossword puzzles, with indifferent success, and was very fond of the word
game Scrabble, at which he usually lost."

Avalon said, "Scrabble is that game that involves small
wooden tiles with letters on them out of which you form words
on a board?"

"It has its complications. . . ." began Rubin.

Pentili overrode him. "You have the essentials, Mr. Avalon. I mention the game because it has something to do with
the problem. Stepan never achieved his aim fully. He re-
tained his Russian accent, and his vocabulary was never as
unlimited as he would have liked it to be, but we encouraged
him because we felt it to be a sign of increasing dedication to
us. The Soviets probably supported it because they felt it
would make him a more efficient spy on us and for them."

"They may have been right," said Rubin dryly.

"*They* killed him, remember," said Pentili. "In September 1960, Stepan arrived from Cuba. We had only the most indirect notion of his activities in that country, but his initial guarded contact with us gave us every reason to think he had information of the most vital importance. It remained only to get that information in such a way as not to blow his cover.

"In very indirect fashion, we arranged to make contact with him in a hotel room. The trouble was that, although neither he nor we knew it at the time, his cover was already blown. Someone got to him before we did, and when our man finally arrived, Stepan was dead; knifed. What it was he meant to tell us, we never learned."

Avalon ran his finger thoughtfully around the rim of his long-empty coffee cup. "Are you certain, sir, that he was killed by the Soviets? We live in a violent society and people are killed every day for a variety of reasons."

Pentili sighed. "To have an agent killed just at the point of delivery of a vital message, and to have that killing come about through some unrelated cause, is asking too much of coincidence. Besides, the Washington police were bound to treat it as an ordinary killing, and we helped them since the man was a Soviet national. Nothing was turned up, no theft, no plausible motive arising out of his private life. There were no traces left behind of any kind; an ordinary culprit would have left some.

"Second, there was some interest in the murder on the part of the Soviet embassy, but not enough. They were just a shade too easily satisfied. Third, certain avenues of information, which would have remained open had Stepan been in the clear and had he died for reasons not connected with his work, were closed. No, Mr. Avalon, there was no doubt in my mind that he died the death of an agent."

Gonzalo, suddenly aware of crumbs defacing the fine cut of his lapel, brushed at himself delicately and said, "Where's the puzzle, though, Mr. Pentili? You mean who killed him? Now? After all these years?"

"No, it doesn't matter a hippie's curse who killed him. Even after he was knifed, though, Stepan must have tried to get across *something*, perhaps enough to give us the essential core of what we needed, but if so, he failed. I have been wondering frequently, and painfully, in the years since my retirement whether a greater shrewdness or persistence on

our part might not have saved our country some of its losses
in the years since that murder."

Halsted said, "I'm sorry if this question is embarrassing,
Mr. Pentili, but was your retirement forced on you because of
Stepan's death?"

"You mean that I might have been fired as punishment for
not having kept him alive? No. The episode did not reflect
any discredit on me and I retired only a few years ago, in the
ordinary course of events, with a generous pension, the
expressed esteem of my confreres, and an award handed me
by President Nixon. In fact, danger came to me not through
Stepan's death but through my insistence that he was trying
to tell us something significant. The department dismissed
the matter; erroneously, in my opinion; and I was more or
less forced to dismiss it, too. But I have wondered about it
since; all the more so, since my retirement."

Gonzalo said, "What was Stepan's way of getting across the
information?"

Pentili said, "We are quite certain that Stepan had no
documents on him, no letters, no written message. He didn't
work that way. He had what any traveler might be expected
to have in a hotel room. He had clothes, toiletries, and so on,
in a single suitcase, and an extra suit in a garment bag.
There were signs of a search, but it was a skillful one that left
a minimum of disarray. Something may have been taken
away, of course, but if so, we cannot tell what it was, and that
has nothing to do with the problem.

"The only items that might not be considered perfectly
routine were a crossword puzzle book, with approximately
half the puzzles worked out completely or nearly completely
in Stepan's own handwriting, the Scrabble set he always
carried with him . . ."

Rubin interrupted, "So he could strike up games with
occasional strangers?"

Pentili said, "No. He had the habit of playing four-handed
games with himself when he had nothing to do and using a
pocket dictionary to help. He said there was nothing better
for developing a vocabulary. The dictionary was there, in his
jacket pocket, with the jacket hanging in the closet.

"He was knifed while standing, apparently, and that was
the one flaw in an otherwise flawless performance, for he was
not killed outright. The killer or killers had to leave rapidly,

and they left a spark of life behind. Stepan had collapsed just next to the desk and, when they were gone, he managed to pull himself upright. On the desk was a newspaper—the Washington *Post*, by the way—and the Scrabble set.

"He opened the top desk drawer and pawed about for the pen. He found it and tried to write with it but it was dry—a common situation in hotel rooms—so he dropped it to the floor. His own pen was in his inner jacket pocket at the other end of the room, and he knew he couldn't make it there. He had a couple of minutes to live and he had to make use of whatever objects were on the desk.

"The newspaper, at the time of the knifing, was folded as it had been when he had bought it a hour earlier, but he . . ."

Halsted said, "How did you find out all this?"

"Circumstantial. I assure you we are expert at this. The desk drawer was open; the pen, quite dry, was on the floor. Most of all, Stepan was bleeding, partly from his right hand, which he had instinctively used to try to ward off the weapon, and his own blood marked his every movement and everything he had touched.

"As I say, he unfolded the newspaper to the sports page. He then lifted the top of the box of the Scrabble set, removed the board, and managed to take out five letters, which he put in the wooden holder used for the purpose. Then he died. The letters were 'e,' 'p,' 'o,' 'c,' and 'k.' "

"In that order?" asked Drake.

"In that order, left to right."

"Epock is a period of time in history, isn't it?" said Gonzalo.

"It's a point in time," said Rubin, "marked by some significant historical event and later used as a reference, but it's spelled e-p-o-c-h. It ends with an 'h.' "

"Making a mistake in spelling under the conditions isn't surprising," said Gonzalo defensively. "The man was dying and maybe he could hardly see. Maybe the 'k' looked like an 'h' to him. Besides, he was a Russian, and he might not have known how to spell the word."

Pentili said, with a trace of impatience, "That is not really the point. 'Epock' or 'epoch,' 'k' or 'h,' what does it mean?"

Avalon said, "Actually, Tom is the code expert. . . ."

Trumbull shrugged. "Larry has come to *you* men. You work at it. If anything occurs to me, I'll interrupt."

Avalon said, "Would you have a code book, Mr. Pentili, in

which 'epock' stands for some phrase or sentence? Is it a recognized code?"

"I assure you that neither 'epock' nor 'epoch' means anything in any code of which Stepan had knowledge. No, the answer had to be in the sports page, and if the letters had any meaning it was in connection with the sports page."

"Why do you say that?" asked Halsted.

"Let me explain further," said Pentili—then interrupted himself to say, "I *will* have a little more brandy, Henry, if you don't mind. You're listening to all this, I hope."

"Yes, sir," said Henry.

"Good!" said Pentili. "Now in the ordinary course of events, Stepan might have, in an emergency, transmitted information more densely—that is, with the greatest information per symbol—by transmitting a number. Each number could represent a given phrase. That's an inflexible message, of course, since the proper phrase might not exist, but a number might give a fair approximation, and in the extremity of approaching death, he could do no more. He opened the paper to a page on which there were numbers and where one number might be significant."

Halsted said, "He might merely have wanted a sheet of paper to write on."

"He had nothing to write with," said Pentili.

"His blood."

Pentili twisted his mouth distastefully. "He might have done that but he didn't. He might not even have been aware he was bleeding. And if he wanted to do that, why open the paper? The front page would have been enough."

"He might have opened it at random," said Halsted stubbornly.

"Why? He was a professional. He had lived with death for years and he knew that the information he carried was more important than his life. What he did would have to be to pass on that information."

Trumbull said, "Come on, Roger, you're being trivial."

Pentili said, "It's all right, Tom. As a matter of fact, the general opinion in the department was that there was no puzzle; that Gregory's attempt at the point of death meant nothing; that whatever he tried to do had failed. I was the only one who wanted to follow it up, and I must admit I never succeeded in translating the message.

"The trouble was, you see, that he had opened to the sports page. About the only page in the paper that could have been more littered with numbers was the financial page. How can we look at all the numbers on the sports page and select the one that was significant?"

Avalon said, "If we assume that Gregory knew what he was doing, then despite all the numbers, the particular significant number must have been obvious, or should have been. For instance, all the numbers on the page may have had no meaning at all. It may have been the number of the page that counted."

"First thought! However, it was page 32, and 32 stood for 'Cancel previous message.' There was no previous message, and that was not it."

Avalon said, "What was on the sports page?"

"I can't reproduce it from memory, of course, and I don't have a Xerox copy to show you. That page dealt with baseball almost entirely, for the baseball season was in its last few weeks. It had baseball standings on it, the box scores of particular games, some pitching statistics."

"And was Stepan knowledgeable about baseball?"

"To a limited extent," said Pentili. "He was professionally interested in America, reading American history avidly, for instance, so he would be interested in the national game. You remember World War II movies with their cliché that any Nazi spy, no matter how cleverly schooled, would always give himself away by his ignorance of last year's World Series? Stepan intended not to be caught in this fashion, but he could scarcely make himself an expert."

"Well," said Avalon stiffly, "if ignorance of baseball is the hallmark of the Nazi spy, I had better turn myself in. I know nothing of the game."

"Nor I," said Drake, shrugging.

Gonzalo said, "Come on, nobody can read the papers, watch television, or talk to people without knowing something about the game. You guys are just indulging in snobbery. Why don't we figure this out? What kind of a number ought it to be? How many digits?"

Pentili said, "At least two digits, possibly three. Not more than three."

"All right. If Gregory was no baseball expert, he would have to pick something simple and obvious. Batting averages are in three digits. Maybe there was some batting average that made the headlines."

Pentili shook his head. "There were no numbers in the headlines. We would have been on to that like a shot. I assure you that nowhere on the page, *nowhere*, was there any one number that stood out from the rest. No, gentlemen, I am quite convinced that the sports page by itself was insufficient, that Gregory in his last moments used it only because there was nothing else he could do. The number was there but there was no way of picking it out without a hint—so he prepared one."

Rubin said, "You mean the Scrabble letters? 'Epock'?"

"Yes."

"I don't see what kind of hint that might be."

Gonzalo said, "He might not have finished, you know. He managed to get five letters out and then died. Maybe he gave up on the sports page and was trying to spell out the number, only he didn't finish. If he wanted to write 'one hundred twenty-two,' for instance, that would take a lot more than five letters."

Rubin said, "Are you telling us there's a number that begins with 'epock'?" He rolled his eyes upward in exasperation.

Gonzalo said, "The letters don't have to be in order. In Scrabble, you're always arranging and rearranging your letters—like in anagrams. After he had all the letters he wanted, he'd have rearranged them into the number he was spelling. He died too soon."

Halsted said, "Sorry, Mario, that's not possible. The written forms of the numbers have an odd distribution of letters. For instance" (his mathematician's eyes gleamed), "do you know that you can write all the numbers from zero to nine hundred ninety-nine without using the letter 'a'?"

"So?" said Gonzalo. "There's no 'a' in 'epock.'"

"No, but there's a 'p' and a 'c'. Write out the numbers in order and you won't come to a 'p' till you reach—uh—one heptillion, which has twenty-four digits. And you won't reach a 'c' till one octillion, which has twenty-seven. Of course, that's in the American system of numeration. In the British system . . ."

"You made your point," growled Trumbull.

Rubin said, "He could still have been incomplete, though.

He may have given up on the sports page altogether, started fresh, and intended to take out those five letters plus a 't,' rearranging the whole to spell 'pocket.' There may have been something in his pocket that carried the message. . . ."

"There wasn't," interposed Pentili curtly.

"It may have been removed after the knifing and he was too far gone to realize it."

"That's a second-order conjecture. You assume an additional 't' and then a pocket-picking as well to account for it. Unlikely!"

"Might 'pocket' have been a code word?" said Rubin.

"No!" Pentili waved his hand left and right, palm outward, in a gesture of impatience. "Gentlemen, it is amusing to listen to your conjectures but you are moving in the wrong direction. Habit has a firm hold even at the moment of death. Stepan was a neat person, and when death came he had his hand on the top of the Scrabble box and was clearly making an effort to replace it. There is no question in my mind that he had taken out all the tiles he was going to. We have these five letters, no more."

Halsted said, "He would not have had time to rearrange the letters."

Pentili sighed. "There are exactly 120 different ways in which 5 different letters can be arranged. Not one of the rearrangements is an English word, any more than 'blain' is," he smiled briefly. "One arrangement is 'kopec,' which is a small Russian coin usually spelled 'kopek,' but that has no significance that any of us could see. No, there must be a reference to a number."

Avalon said suddenly, "Was there anything on the sports page besides sports? I mean, were there advertisements, for instance?"

Pentili looked with concentration into the middle distance as though he were concentrating on an invisible sheet of paper. He said, thoughtfully, "No advertisements. There was, however, a bridge column."

"Ah, could the letters have referred to that? See here, Mr. Pentili, I am not a bridge buff in the real sense, but I play the game and sometimes read a bridge column. They invariably have a hand shown under the heads, 'north,' 'south,' 'east,' and 'west.' Each hand has its cards listed according to suit, 'spades,' 'hearts,' 'diamonds,' 'clubs,' and under each suit the cards are listed in descending order of value."

"Well?" said Pentili stonily.

"So consider 'epock.' The 'e' may stand for 'east,' the 'c' for 'clubs.' East's hand may have five clubs, which may, as an example, be J, 8, 4, 3, 2. The Jack and the 3 are excluded because they are occupied by letters that do not stand for digits. That leaves 842 as your code."

Pentili looked at him with some surprise. He said, "I must admit that I've never thought of this. When I am back in my office I will look at the bridge hand. Amazing, Mr. Avalon, I would not have thought a new notion could have been advanced at this stage of the game."

Avalon said, flushing a little, "I can but do my poor best, sir."

"However," said Pentili, "I don't believe your suggestion can be useful. Poor Stepan was not, to my knowledge, a bridge player, and it seems to me only a monomaniac on the subject would have tried to use bridge for a code like that at the point of death. It has to be very simple. He might have used the page number as the code, but I suspect he could no longer see the tiny symbols on the newspaper page. He recognized the sports page as a whole and he could still see the large letters of the Scrabble set. And we can find nothing simple there."

Gonzalo said, "Unless Henry has a suggestion."

"Ah," said Pentili, "then it comes to Henry in the end. What does all this mean, Henry?"

Henry, who had been remaining silently at the sideboard throughout the discussion, said, "I cannot say, sir, unless the number 20 would be of signifi—"

He was interrupted by a suddenly frowning Pentili. "Twenty! Is that a guess, Henry?"

"Not entirely, sir. Is it significant, then?"

"Significant? I've spent years gloomily suspecting he was trying to tell us twenty. Twenty meant 'Government in firm control.' I haven't mentioned twenty in the course of the story, have I?"

There was a chorused negative.

"If I could have shown," said Pentili, "that Stepan was trying to tell us twenty, I might have been able to stop the Bay of Pigs. At least I would have tried; God, I would have tried. But I don't see how you get twenty out of this, Henry."

"Why, sir, if it is true that Mr. Stepan was only moderately knowledgeable in baseball, then he would see on the sports page only what other moderately knowledgeable people would see—like myself, for instance. As Mr. Gonzalo would say, I speak from ignorance when I say that all I see on the sports page is the result of the games—the *score* in other words—and that brings 'twenty' rather forcibly to mind."

Avalon, possibly smarting at the failure of his own suggestion, said, "I don't think much of that, Henry. 'Score' is rather an archaic word. Would Stepan have known it?"

"I imagine he would, Mr. Avalon," said Henry, "Mr. Pentili has said that Stepan was an avid reader of American history, and one of the best known historical phrases is 'Fourscore and seven years ago . . .' "

Pentili looked disappointing, "It's a clever notion, Henry, but not convincing. Too bad."

"It becomes convincing, sir, when you realize that the Scrabble letters also signify twenty."

"In what way?"

"When Mr. Gonzalo asked his question about 'blain' he specifically asked if it were an *English* word. No one has specified that 'epock' must be English."

Gonzalo said delightedly, "You mean it's Russian for twenty?"

Pentili said, "No, it is *not* Russian for twenty. I've already mentioned the 'kopec' 'kopek' possibility, but that has nothing to do with twenty, surely."

"I'm not thinking of Russian words," said Henry. "As you have said, habits are hard to break even at the point of death, and Mr. Stepan must have found himself using Russian letters. . . ."

"The Cyrillic alphabet," said Rubin.

"Yes, Mr. Rubin. Now I have seen the USSR written in Russian in letters that look like CCCP. I suspect therefore that the Russian 'c' is equivalent to our 's' and the Russian 'p' is equivalent to our 'r.' "

"Quite so," said Pentili, looking dumbfounded.

"And the Russian 'k' is equivalent to our hard 'c' so that in *our* letters, 'epock' becomes 'erosc,' and that can be rearranged to read 'score.' "

Pentili seemed overcome by a deep depression. "You win,

Henry. Why couldn't you have told me all this in 1960?"

"Had I but known, sir," said Henry."

"The Sports Page"—Afterword

In some ways, there is a certain inflexibility about my scheme for writing Black Widower stories. There is always the banquet and the general conversation; then the grilling and the presentation of a mystery; then the discussion and solution.

But there is a certain flexibility as well, for the mystery itself can be anything at all. It can be a murder, or a theft, or a spy story, or a missing-will story.

It can even, on occasion, be that hoariest of devices, the dying-clue mystery. Why not? They're always fun.

"The Sports Page" appeared in the April 1977 *EQMM*.

By the way, readers occasionally write me to offer alternative solutions to my Black Widowers. In the case of this story, two readers came up with identical alternate solutions that were (in my opinion) cleverer than the one I had constructed. One was Dan Button, editor of *Science Digest*, and the other was Paul Edwin Kennedy, a Boston lawyer. Let me quote the latter: "He [Stepan] left us the cryptic message 'epock.' Any person 'moderately familiar' with baseball is familiar with the box scores. To him, the letters 'e,' 'po,' and 'k' stand for 'error,' 'put out,' and 'strike,' respectively. We can then translate 'epock' as "error put out c strike.' Surely it's obvious then that 'c' stands for Cuban."

Dan Button, using identical reasoning, interprets the message as either "You will strike out (suffer disaster) if you go ahead with the plan," or "The strike (invasion) is out, because of the erroneous information you've received."

Unbelievable that, without knowing it, while constructing one solution, I had laid the groundwork for another that was even more subtle.

4.

Second Best

When the Black Widowers opened the new season with their September banquet, following hard upon the national conventions, it was not surprising that the talk turned to politics.

Emmanuel Rubin, who was host, had (as might be expected) considerable fault to find with both candidates, and a minute analysis of their shortcomings left each sounding highly unacceptable.

Thomas Trumbull scowled. He said, "Who's your write-in candidate, then?"

"Himself," said Mario Gonzalo quickly, smoothing the lapel of a jacket that bore the pattern of a patchwork quilt of the louder sort. "Manny has voted the straight Rubin ticket for years."

Rubin said, "It certainly doesn't make sense to vote for someone I *know* to be less capable than I am. If, for the sake of argument, I admit I lack the capacity to be President of the United States, then any lesser man, *ipso facto*, should not get my vote, or anyone's."

Geoffrey Avalon, sipping slowly at his second drink, which had not yet reached the midpoint at which he automatically stopped, said austerely, "All things being equal, I don't think it good practice to oust a sitting President. Experience and continuity count for a great deal."

James Drake, peering through cigarette smoke, cleared his throat and said softly, "How much experience did he have two years ago when . . ."

Rubin interrupted and overrode Drake. "Don't reason with him, Jim. Geoff voted for Nixon in '72." His straggly beard lifted and he glared through the thick lenses of his eyeglasses.

Avalon stood more stiffly than usual and a faint flush rose to his cheeks. "I'm not ashamed of that. The chief issue in '72 was foreign policy, and I believe to this day that Nixon's foreign policy was a rational and useful one."

"He was corrupt," said Rubin.

"That was not known at the time. I cannot vote on the basis of future knowledge."

"What future knowledge? I've known he was not to be trusted ever since he entered Congress in 1947."

"We don't all have your 20-20 hindsight vision, Manny," said Avalon with wounded dignity.

"Hindsight, hell," said Rubin. "I can produce a hundred witnesses who heard me denounce Nixon over a period of thirty years."

"We all heard you many times right here at the Black Widowers," said Roger Halsted, looking over the *hors d'oeuvres* tray critically.

Avalon, reaching the halfway mark of his drink, put it down firmly and said, "I believe we're allowed our political differences, Manny. Membership in the Black Widowers does not deprive me of my civil rights."

"Vote as you please," said Rubin, "but I would like to remind you that you were the only Black Widower to vote Republican that year."

Avalon touched his neat graying mustache as though to convince himself his drink had not wetted it and said, "Does that include Henry?"

Gonzalo said eagerly, "Whom did you vote for in '72, Henry?"

Avalon said, "You needn't answer, Henry. Your political opinions are your own."

Henry, the invaluable waiter at the Black Widower banquets, was putting the final touches at the table. He said, "I have no reason to keep it secret, Mr. Avalon. Like Mr.

Rubin, I distrusted the President and so, with some misgiving, I voted for the other man."

"Six to one against you, Geoff," said Rubin, grinning widely.

Avalon said, "What about your guest?" With perhaps just a touch of spite, he added, "For whom, after all, you're putting on this show."

"Because he's interviewing me?" began Rubin indignantly.

The guest closed his notebook with a snap, loudly enough to draw all eyes, and said, in a surprisingly gentle voice, "Actually, I voted for Nixon. I'm not really keyed into politics, but I generally vote Republican."

"Six to two," said Avalon, in low-voiced satisfaction, shooting a swift glance at Rubin, who looked a little put out.

Gonzalo said, looking up from the portrait he was quickly sketching of the guest, "How can you be a reporter and not be keyed in to politics?"

"I'm not exactly a . . ."

Trumbull lifted his voice. "Save it for the grilling, Mario, damn you. If you'd come on time, you could have been introduced to Mr. Gardner."

"I don't have to take lessons in early arrival from *you*, Tom," said Gonzalo, hurt. "They're paving Park Avenue, and my taxi . . ."

Henry, waiting patiently, sent his voice through a momentary hole in the conversation. "Gentlemen, at the request of Mr. Rubin, tonight's host, our chef has been pleased to prepare a smorgasbord. If you will all be kind enough to help yourselves from the dishes on the sideboard . . ."

They lined up with the avidity of healthy trenchermen and Halsted, whose incipient paunch was eloquent evidence of his brotherly affection for calories, said, "We've never had a smorgasbord before, Manny."

"Nothing wrong with trying something new," said Rubin.

"Oh I approve—I approve." Halsted's eyes wandered avidly over the selection.

Gonzalo said, "That leaves you only semi-employed tonight, Henry."

Henry smiled paternally and said, "I shall try to keep myself occupied, Mr. Gonzalo."

The sideboard's contents had been reduced to fragments,

coffee was at its second cup, and brandy was being served, when Rubin clattered spoon on water glass and said, "Brother Black Widowers, it is time for the grilling, and Mario has clamored for the chance. Very much against my better judgment, I'm going to let him. Mario . . ."

Gonzalo smiled and leaned back in his seat, draping an arm negligently over the back. He said, "Mr. Gardner, I apologize for having been late. Park Avenue was being paved. . . ."

"We know all that," said Rubin. "Get on with it."

"I managed to catch up over the meal, however. You are Arthur Gardner, and you work on a free-lance basis for *Personalities* magazine. Am I correct so far?"

"Yes, sir." Gardner's gray hair, thick, moderately long, and well arranged, made him look the fiftyish he was, but none of his other features concurred. With a bit of hair dye he could easily have passed for something under forty. His teeth were good but his smile was uneasy. He didn't seem quite at home with the company.

Gonzalo said, "I further gather that your current assignment is that of interviewing Manny Rubin for a piece in *Personalities*."

"That's right. Front-of-the-book piece."

"And you've come to this dinner, as Manny's guest, as part of the assignment."

"Yes," said Gardner. "I do not conduct a simple interview. I try to sample Mr. Rubin's activities, so to speak."

"Ah," said Gonzalo, "that brings us to the key question. If your activities are concerned with presenting Manny to the public, how can you possibly justify your existence?"

Gardner said, "If Mr. Rubin can justify his, then mine is automatically justified."

Avalon laughed loudly. "That's a good answer. You're squelched, Mario."

"He was primed," said Gonzalo indignantly, "but never mind. Mr. Gardner, before dinner you said you weren't familiar with politics. Isn't that a handicap in your line of work?"

"No, sir. If I were a political reporter, it would be, but I deal with personalities."

"What if your personality is a politician?"

"I know enough for that."

"Have you ever messed up an assignment because of your ignorance of politics?"

"I'm not *ignorant* of politics," said Gardner softly, and not noticeably annoyed. "I have never needed more than I have, even when—I have done an interview, for instance, with Hubert Hum—"

Trumbull broke in, "Hold it, Mario. Mr. Gardner, we of the Black Widowers have grown sensitive over small things. You said, 'even when—' then paused, and changed subjects on us. Please unchange. Even when *what*?"

Gardner looked genuinely puzzled, "I don't understand."

"You were about to say something and didn't. Now, what were you about to say?"

Gardner comprehended. "Oh—that's a war story that seems to bother me a bit every presidential election year. It's not important."

"Could you tell us just the same?"

"But it happened a quarter of a century ago. It's all over."

"Even so, that's the turn the grilling has taken. I'm afraid it's part of the requirements of the game that you must answer. I assure you everything said here is confidential."

Gardner looked about him, rather helplessly. "There's nothing confidential about it. It was the winter of 1950. In Korea, the army under General MacArthur had reached the Manchurian border in late November and we were all going to be home by Christmas."

"I know," said Drake, with dry reminiscence. "Then the Chinese came pouring south and caught us with our pants down."

"You're so right," said Gardner bitterly. "To this day, I don't know how we could have been caught so flat-footed. Anyway, the South Korean divisions just melted away. After all, they could become part of the countryside. Take off the uniform and each of them is just another local peasant. For Americans and the few western Allies, it was another thing. We just had to scurry south as fast as we could and stay together as best we could till we had built a line that would hold.

"Lots of us were separated from our units. I was. For five days I made my way southward wondering when some Chinese unit might spot me or when some Korean peasants might trap me for what I wore and carried.

"I hid by day and moved on by night. My rations were gone and after a while I went hungry. I didn't know what was ahead or if there was an American army anywhere at all. It was the worst defeat in the field an American army had ever suffered since the Civil War.

"The third day I came across another American soldier. I nearly shot him before I recognized him as one of us. He nearly shot me, for that matter. He was wounded and had difficulty moving. I helped him along but that slowed me down quite a bit and a dozen times I thought of leaving him behind. I couldn't quite make myself do that. I'd like to say it was a humanitarian impulse but he was another pair of eyes and he might see something that I alone would see too late. Besides that, he was company. God, I would do anything for company.

"The fifth night, he was dying. I knew it and he knew it. I didn't know what to do to help him, or to just make it easier for him. So I stayed with him and he talked. I didn't really listen, you know. I just kept trying to watch all sides at once and was half wishing he would die so that I could move on, and half wishing he wouldn't die and leave me alone.

"He was lightheaded and rambled on from topic to topic. He talked American politics. He said Truman was through and the Republicans would probably put Taft in the White House in '52. I remember he said that would be the fourth set of relatives to become Presidents and the second father-son combination. That rather stuck in my mind—I don't know why—but everything else he said is just gone, except that it was all about Presidents. I think he must have been a presidential buff and that he knew everything about them.

"Just before the end, he talked about himself and his family. He was married and had a kid, a little girl two months old whom he had never seen. He managed to get something out of a pocket and give it to me. 'Get it to her,' he said, 'please. She'll know I at least saw her holding the little girl; that I thought of them at the last.' He tried to kiss it. It was the photograph of a woman and a baby and I suppose it had reached him just before the army had fallen apart.

"I said, 'Okay. What's your name? Where do you live?' In the two days we had been together, we hadn't exchanged names. Names hadn't been important those two days.

"His eyes were glazing and he was mumbling. He said, 'My

name? A good name. Presidential name. No relative, of course. Second-best vote-getter on the list. They love him.' His voice trailed away, but I remember his exact words. I thought of it a lot, you see.

"I shook him, but he was dead. Well, what could I do? I certainly wasn't going to linger behind to give him a Christian burial or anything like that. I just wanted out. But I did try to reach for his dog tags so I could hand them in if I ever got back to any American line. Also to get his name so I could deliver the photo. I thought that if I ever got back I had the obligation to try to do that.

"My hand never touched him. I heard the sound of Chinese—I guess it was Chinese—and someone was on top of me. I think he tripped over me. I tore away, using my rifle as a club, and then I ran. I heard shots but nothing hit me, and I kept running. Then up ahead I heard someone swearing in English and I raised my hand, shouting, 'American! American!'

"I was with an American company and that was it. It was two more days before I got my thoughts sorted out, and part of that time I think I was on a stretcher."

There was a pause and Halsted said, "So you never got the soldier's dog tags."

"No, sir," said Gardner emphatically. "We were *retreating*. We didn't stop and turn till we were well south of Seoul, and then we came back only to the boundary between the two Koreas more or less. My buddy, whoever he was, died deep in North Korea, and he remains in North Korea to this day."

"Then you couldn't deliver the photo?" said Halsted.

Gardner said, "I tried. The trouble was I didn't even know what his unit was and we lost a great many men in that retreat. I checked as far as I could. I suppose I could have run a copy of the picture in some national magazine and waited for a woman to come and claim it, but that took more money than I was willing to spend.

"It bothers me a bit. His daughter should be in her late twenties now, and his wife should be my age. His wife might be dead or married again; his daughter may be a mother herself and she may never give a thought to a father she's never seen. Still—it's just possible it might be nice for them to have *some* little thing he touched as he was dying, *some* assurance they filled his dying thoughts. But what can I do? Still, when presidential elections are in the air, I think of it more than I usually do."

Avalon said, "One can't blame one's self for something that is completely outside one's control."

Halsted said, "But you said you tried, Mr. Gardner. How could you possibly have tried? You had nothing to go on."

Gardner said, "Sure I did. He said he had the name of one of the American Presidents. It was probably the accident of his name that made him such a presidential buff. And he said the President was the second-best vote-getter in the list and that the people loved him. That seemed clear enough to me. After I got out, I wrote to Washington and I was able to have them run a check on the names of those missing in action in the course of the retreat. It seemed certain to me that his body was never recovered so he wouldn't be listed as killed in action, and that cut down on the numbers a bit."

"I take it you didn't find anything," said Drake, lighting a fresh cigarette."

"Nothing. There wasn't a single Roosevelt on the list."

Rubin exploded. "Roosevelt? Why Roosevelt?"

Gardner looked surprised. "Why not Roosevelt? It's the *only* name considering what he said. The *only* name. I don't know why there wasn't someone by that name missing in action. It could be typical Army snafu, but since there wasn't I came to a dead end."

"How do you make out Roosevelt?" said Rubin.

"Surely you're old enough to remember the 1936 election. I was ten years old then, but I remember the fuss it made. Franklin Roosevelt carried forty-six of the forty-eight states and left poor Alf Landon with Maine and Vermont only—eight electoral votes."

"And that made him second best?"

"Well, Washington was elected twice by unanimous vote of the electoral college, in 1788 and in 1792. That put him in first place. You can't do better than unanimous. And FDR is in second place."

Avalon, sitting bolt upright, his neat little pepper-and-salt beard giving him the air of a sage whenever he drew his eyebrows together and grew portentous, said, "Actually not. In 1820, James Monroe, our fifth President, was running for re-election. The United States was practically a one-party nation at the time. The Federalist Party had virtually committed suicide by engaging injudiciously in what came to be considered treasonable activity during the War of 1812. Everyone who counted politically, therefore, called himself a Democratic-Republican. Later on new factions and new parties formed about several of the dominant personalities, but that time had not yet come. Therefore, Monroe ran for re-election with no formal opposition." He paused and gazed about at the others with a touch of complacence.

Tom Trumbull said, "Come on, Geoff, you just happened to read all about this recently, so don't make it sound as though you're dredging it up from some deep well of remembered knowledge. What are you getting at?"

"I did *not* read about it recently. These are facts every schoolchild knows, or would know if schools were worth anything these days. The point is that Monroe got every electoral vote but one. The lone dissenter—from New Hampshire, I believe—cast his vote for John Quincy Adams, for the express purpose of keeping it from being unanimous. No man but Washington, he said, should be elected unanimously.

"You see, then," Avalon continued, "that if Washington is in first place as a vote-getter, Monroe is in second place, F.D.R. is only in third. That is why you found no Roosevelts among the missing in action. The dead soldier's name must have been Monroe. . . ."

Gardner stared about him with astonishment. "Incredible!" he said. "I can't believe it. I never thought for one minute there was anyone other than Roosevelt that it could be. Are you sure?"

Avalon shrugged. "We can look it up. We have a couple of almanacs on the reference shelf."

"Don't bother to get the almanac, Henry," said Rubin. "Geoff is right; at least in this case."

Gardner said, "I suppose I can get back to Washington on this. The army must keep its records forever. You know, I feel rotten. If I hadn't been so cocksure, I might have found the wife and child a quarter of a century ago."

"I don't know," said Drake thoughtfully. "It seems to me there are two parts to the identification. The President was the second-best vote-getter, and the people loved him. I'll grant Roosevelt's popularity, but how did Monroe stand?"

"Nowhere," said Rubin at once. "Nowhere. He inherited

the presidency because it had become almost traditional at the time to have it go to a Virginian. He was the fourth Virginian out of five Presidents, the four being Washington, Jefferson, Madison, and Monroe. Monroe was the last and the least of them. His only great accomplishment was the Monroe Doctrine, and that was really the product of John Quincy Adams, his Secretary of State."

"Well, then, was it Monroe or wasn't it Monroe?" said Gardner. "You've got me completely mixed up. What's the answer?"

"I'm not sure," said Rubin, "but I'm positive it wasn't Monroe. Look, the Constitution gives the right to elect the President to the electoral college, and for the first eight elections or so there aren't even any records of any popular vote. No presidential candidate had to squeeze votes out of the general public in those early years; he had to intrigue for the votes of a few electors. That wasn't vote-getting in our modern sense and if we're going to try to figure out first and second place in vote-getting, we'll have to eliminate the early Presidents. I'm sure the soldier never thought of either Washington or Monroe in any vote-getting capacity."

Gardner rubbed the line of his jawbone. "When did the vote-getting start?"

Rubin said, frowning, "The first modern election campaign, a libelous circus featuring dirty tricks, was in 1840. That was William Henry Harrison winning over Martin Van Buren. I suspect we ought to start with him."

Avalon said, "No, Manny. The 1840 election may have set the style but I think we've got to start with Andrew Jackson back in 1832."

"All right," said Rubin, casting his right hand upward as though negligently tossing away a point. "Start with Andy Jackson."

Drake, sitting back in his chair, peered at the rest out of his contact lenses and said, "Johnson got a landslide vote in 1964 and Nixon got one in 1972, but the soldier died in late 1950. . . ."

"Right," said Gardner. "Truman was President then, so we have to stop with him."

Avalon said, "I'm pretty sure that if we restrict ourselves to the Presidents between Jackson and Truman, both included, then the greatest vote-getter was Roosevelt in 1936 and the second greatest—and I'm certain of this—was Warren Harding over James Cox in 1920."

Gardner said, "Are you saying then it's Harding?"

"No, we're not," said Rubin quickly. "No one in their right mind can possibly suppose that your soldier friend would be proud of the presidential aspect of his name if he were named Harding."

Drake said, "If Geoff is right and Harding won by the second biggest landslide in terms of percentages, then Harding it is. You can't argue with figures."

"Yes, you can," said Rubin. "You can deny that one particular set of figures is the basis of the judgment. The fact is that in all the history of the presidency no one can possibly be considered for the top mark as a vote-getter but Roosevelt; that's why I was so astonished when Gardner decided on him as second-best. But *why* is Roosevelt considered tops? Not through percentage points, but because he was elected in four successive presidential years, 1932, 1936, 1940, and 1944, and no other President has been elected more than twice. It's the number of elections that counts."

Gardner said, "That doesn't do any good. Who's in second place, then?"

Rubin said, "Well, I don't know. It should be one of the two-term Presidents, but how can we say which? It depends on your soldier friend's prejudices and predilections."

"Perhaps not," said Avalon. "If he was a presidential buff, he must have had some logical criterion for his choice and we ought to be able to find it."

Gonzalo said, "There's the bit about his being loved. Which President was most loved by the people after Roosevelt? That should tell us."

Rubin said, "I don't think so. All Presidents were loved by most of those who voted for him. It's a kind of automatic reflex. Hell, I would say that right now there is a quarter of the electorate that think Nixon was done dirt and that love him still. I think we ought to be careful how we use that criterion."

Avalon said, "Well, let's not talk aimlessly. Roosevelt was our only four-term winner and there were no three-term winners. Therefore we have to pick our second-best vote-getter out of those Presidents who won two elections. From Jackson to Truman there were six two-election winners, if I count

correctly. I'll name them and you check me off, Manny, and if
we get into an argument, we'll refer to the almanac. The two-
term winners are Andrew Jackson, Abraham Lincoln, Ulysses
S. Grant, Grover Cleveland, William McKinley, and Woodrow
Wilson.

"Now we can start eliminating, and Manny, you continue
to correct me, if necessary. Lincoln's first election in 1860
was a fluke and no tribute really to his vote-getting ability. It
so happened that he faced a disunited Democratic Party,
which ran both Stephen Douglas and John Breckenridge
against him. I think a fellow called Bell also ran. Had
Lincoln faced a united opposition, he'd have been snowed
under. As it was, he managed to get a majority of the
electoral votes with a minority of the popular vote.

"The same is true of Woodrow Wilson, who faced both
Theodore Roosevelt and William Howard Taft in 1912. If the
Republican Party had been united, Wilson would have been
badly beaten. As for Grover Cleveland, he won twice but not
in successive election years. He beat James Blaine in 1884
and Benjamin Harrison in 1892, but was defeated in 1888.
That makes him both twenty-second and twenty-fourth President, the only man in American history to get two presidential numbers.

"That leaves just three Presidents who won two successive
elections without benefit of a major split in the opposition,
and they were Jackson, Grant, and McKinley. The second
best has to be one of them."

Avalon stopped for a few minutes, then said, "Only I'm not
sure which."

Trumbull said, "What's the good of an analysis that leaves
us with three candidates?"

Gonzalo said, "I still say we've got to remember that the
soldier said the people loved him. It has to play some part."

Rubin shrugged. "I don't know; I mistrust that. But let's
see. For instance, McKinley was a gentle and lovable soul in
his private life, but he was a weak President and stirred few
hearts. In fact, it was his losing opponent, William Jennings
Bryan, who received the fanatical adoration of his followers."

Gonzalo said, "That makes McKinley all the better as a
vote-getter, if he ran against a strong opponent."

"Maybe," said Rubin, "but we're working now on the sup-
position that the man we're after won *and* was loved. So it's

not McKinley. Grant was a war hero, so there were plenty of people to idolize him. However, his victories were over another part of the nation, and they didn't love him in the southern states."

"Besides, he was corrupt, wasn't he?" said Gonzalo.

"Not he himself. Those around him. And that was not fully realized till after the re-election victory of 1872, so it has nothing to do with the case. That leaves us Andrew Jackson, a strong vote-getter, idolized by many of those who were for him and with his popularity spread widely over the nation."

"He was well hated by some," growled Trumbull.

"Every President is. Even F.D.R. No, I'm pretty sure that second best would have to be Jackson. And it's a common name, too. I'll bet there were a number of Jacksons missing in action in that winter retreat in Korea."

There was a longish silence, and then Gardner said, "Well, I'll try to track down the Jacksons. Maybe to play if safe I ought to get names and addresses on the Hardings and Monroes and McKinleys too."

Avalon said, "Maybe you'll have to make a list of anyone with a presidential name. Manny's argument is ingenious, but it's too refined to carry conviction. I suspect Manny realizes that, too."

Rubin was stung into instant defense. "No such thing. There is no other sensible way of working out the problem, given the data. If anhone can supply one, I should like to hear it, that's all."

"Is that a general challenge?" said Gonzalo.

"It is," said Rubin.

"Even to Henry?"

"Even to Henry," said Rubin, after a slight hesitation. "I don't see how he can improve it."

"That's your cue, Henry," said Gonzalo, grinning. "Knock him dead."

Henry, who had long since cleared the sideboard and who had been listening with the greatest interest, said, "I can scarcely claim to know more of American history than Mr. Rubin or Mr. Avalon."

Gonzalo said, "Come on, Henry, they'll tell you any history you want to know. Just improve on Manny's argument."

"I'm not sure that I can," said Henry cautiously, "but I have a question of Mr. Gardner, if I may."

Gardner, who looked puzzled at the sudden entry of the waiter into the argument, said, "Yes, of course."

"Several of the gentlemen, and you yourself, have spoken of the second-best vote-getter having been loved by the people. That, however, is not my recollection of the wording in your account. Did the dying soldier say, 'The people loved him'?"

Gardner thought for a moment. "No. He said, 'They love him.'"

"Are you sure, sir? It was years ago."

"I admit that. But I thought about it a lot that first year and it was 'They love him.'"

Gonzalo said, "I see what Henry's driving at. The 'they' doesn't refer to people generally, and once we figure out to whom it does refer, we've got it. Right, Henry?"

"Well, no, Mr. Gonzalo," said Henry. "I rather imagine it *does* refer to the people; I just wanted to get the exact wording. Mr. Gardner, was it a complete statement, or was the soldier trying to add something to it?"

"There you've got me, Henry. I don't know."

"But it was the last thing he said. 'They love him.' He didn't say anything after that? He might have intended to say something more, to add to the statement, but couldn't make it?"

"I suppose so, but I don't know."

Trumbull said impatiently, "What's all this about, Henry?"

Henry said, "I'm not quite certain, yet. I am curious, however, about something Mr. Rubin said. Sir, did you say that Grover Cleveland was elected for two nonconsecutive terms?"

"That's right, Henry," said Rubin, "in 1884 and 1892."

"And he was defeated in 1888?"

"Yes, by Benjamin Harrison, on whom he turned the tables in 1892. It was very unusual. A President in office was defeated for re-election in two elections running, and the same two candidates in those elections swapped victory and defeat."

Henry said patiently, "Yes, Mr. Rubin, but the point is that Grover Cleveland ran as a candidate of one of the major parties three times in succession."

"So he did. But he only won twice."

"I understand. Of the other five two-term candidates, did any other run a third time?"

"Andrew Jackson did. He ran three times and was elected only twice."

Avalon said, "Henry Clay and William Jennings Bryan ran three times each and each lost every time. Henry Clay . . ."

Trumbull overrode him hastily, "Nixon ran three times and won twice but that was after Truman."

Henry said, "How did Cleveland do in the middle race? The one he lost?"

Rubin said, "I can't give you the exact figures, but I think it was a narrow loss."

Henry said, "Perhaps we should now turn to the almanac." He went to the reference shelf and brought it back.

Rubin said, "Let me look it up. I know about where it is."

He riffled the pages, then ran his fingers down one page, whistling softly. "Here it is. Oh good God, he lost in the electoral college 233 to 168 but he had the lead in the popular vote. He was nearly 400,000 votes ahead of Harrison. Not an absolute majority because there were a couple of minor candidates in the field, Prohibitionists and Laborites."

Henry said, "Then it seems to me that if Franklin D. Roosevelt led the field in four successive elections, Grover Cleveland led the field in three successive elections and he can be considered the second-best vote-getter."

Avalon, however, said, "Hold on." He had been riffling through the alamanac's pages. "Manny said Jackson ran a third time, too. He ran and was defeated in 1824, but he had the plurality in that year. Jackson also led the field in three successive elections." He held the page up before Henry's eyes.

"That is so, sir," said Henry, "but Mr. Rubin had discarded victories over a split opposition. In 1824, Jackson ran against three major opponents. Cleveland led the field three times in a row against a single unified opposition each time. He's still second best."

Rubin said, "Well, Henry, you convince me. But how did you know? Did you just happen to know that Cleveland led Harrison in the popular vote the time Cleveland lost?"

Gonzalo said, "It's no mystery. While we were all arguing,

Henry just looked up all the statistics in the almanac. Right, Henry?"

"No, sir," said Henry, "it wasn't necessary to go to the almanac."

"Frankly," said Gardner impatiently, "I don't think that Henry's analysis is any more convincing than the others."

"It would not be," said Henry, "if it depended on the election statistics, but I just used those to confirm a decision made on other grounds."

"On what other grounds, Henry?" said Avalon sternly. "Don't play games with us."

"It did occur to me, Mr. Avalon, when Mr. Gardner told his story, that it was possible the dying soldier was not merely making a statement when he said, 'They love him,' but was attempting to complete a quotation. This is especially so since, if Mr. Gardner's memory is right, he used the present tense."

"Well, Henry?"

"I seemed to recall that there is a well-known quotation in the history of politics that goes, 'They love him most for the enemies he has made.' I thought the reference might have been to Franklin Roosevelt, but I didn't really know. While you were arguing, therefore, I consulted Bartlett. The remark was made on July 9, 1884, by one Edward Stuyvesant Bragg, who was, at the time, seconding the nomination of Grover Cleveland."

And the awed silence that followed was broken by Gardner, who said softly, "You've sold me, Henry. Mind if I do an article on you someday?"

Henry smiled and shook his head. "I'd rather you didn't, sir. I value my anonymity."

"Second Best"—Afterword

"Second Best" was written in August 1976 in the heat of a presidential campaign. I suppose it was inevitable that, with my mind on what was taking place, I would do a Black Widowers story that dealt with elections.

That was not very bright of me. I am experienced enough to understand that one should not deal with things that are topical at the time of writing—but at the time of publishing.

After all, it takes about nine months between the time a story is accepted by *EQMM* and the time it is published.

Though I submitted the story quite confidently (since I was fond of it), Fred Dannay shot it right back. It would have to appear *after* the election, and the readers would be sated with the subject by then.

It was embarrassing to make so elementary a mistake, but it had its advantage, too. In each of the first two books of this series, I included three stories that had not appeared in any form prior to book publication, and I intended to have three such stories in this third book as well. "Second Best" was filed away cheerfully as the first of them.

5.

The Missing Item

Emmanuel Rubin, resident polymath of the Black Widowers Society, was visibly chafed. His eyebrows hunched down into the upper portion of his thick-lensed spectacles and his sparse gray beard bristled.

"Not true to life," he said. "Imagine! Not true to life!"

Mario Gonzalo, who had just reached the head of the stairs and had accepted his dry martini from Henry, the unsurpassable waiter, said, "What's not true to life?"

Geoffrey Avalon looked down from his seventy-four inches and said solemnly, "It appears that Manny has suffered a rejection."

"Well, why not?" said Gonzalo, peeling off his gloves. "Editors don't have to be stupid all the time."

"It isn't the rejection," said Rubin. "I've been rejected before by better editors and in connection with better stories. It's the reason he advanced! How the hell would he know if a story were true to life or not? What's he ever done but warm an office chair? would he . . ."

Roger Halsted, whose career as a math teacher in a junior high school had taught him how to interrupt shrill voices, managed to interpose. "Just what did he find not true to life, Manny?"

Rubin waved a hand passionately outward. "I don't want to talk about it."

"Good," said Thomas Trumbull, scowling from under his neatly waved thatch of white hair. "Then the rest of us can hear each other for a while. Roger, why don't you introduce your guest to the late Mr. Gonzalo?"

Halsted said, "I've just been waiting for the decibel level to decrease. Mario, my friend Jonathan Thatcher. This is Mario Gonzalo, who is an artist by profession. Jonathan is an oboist, Mario."

Gonzalo grinned and said, "Sounds like fun."

"Sometimes it almost is," said Thatcher, "on days when the reed behaves itself."

Thatcher's round face and plump cheeks would have made him a natural to play Santa Claus at any Christmas benefit, but he would have needed padding just the same, for his body had that peculiar ersatz slimness that seemed to indicate forty pounds recently lost. His eyebrows were dark and thick, and one took it for granted that they were never drawn together in anger.

Henry said, "Gentlemen, dinner is ready."

James Drake stubbed out his cigarette and said, "Thanks, Henry. It's a cold day and I would welcome hot food."

"Yes, sir," said Henry with a gentle smile. "Lobster thermidor today, baked potatoes, stuffed eggplant . . ."

"But what's this, Henry?" demanded Rubin, scowling.

"Hot borscht, Mr. Rubin."

Rubin looked as though he were searching his soul and then he said grudgingly, "All right."

Drake, unfolding his napkin, said, "Point of order, Roger."

"What is it?"

"I'm sitting next to Manny, and if he continues to look like that he'll curdle my soup and give me indigestion. You're host and absolute monarch; I move you direct him to tell us what he wrote that isn't true to life and get it out of his system."

"Why?" said Trumbull. "Why not let him sulk and be silent for the novelty of it?"

"I'm curious, too," said Gonzalo, "since nothing he's ever written has been true to life. . . ."

"How would you know, since you can't read?" said Rubin suddenly.

"It's generally known," said Gonzalo. "You hear it everywhere."

"Oh God, I'd better tell you and end this miasma of pseudowit. Look, I've written a novelette, about fifteen thousand words long, about a world-wide organization of locksmiths. . . ."

"Locksmiths?" said Avalon, frowning as though he suspected he had not heard correctly.

"Locksmiths," said Rubin. "These guys are experts, they can open anything—safes, vaults, prison doors. There are no secrets from them, and nothing can be hidden from them. My global organization is of the cream of the profession and no man can join the organization without some document or object of importance stolen from an industrial, political, or governmental unit.

"Naturally, they have the throat of the world in their grip. They can control the stock market, guide diplomacy, make and unmake governments and, at the time my story opens, they are headed by a dangerous megalomaniac. . . ."

Drake interrupted even as he winced in his effort to crack the claw of the lobster. "Who is out to rule the world, of course."

"Of course," said Rubin, "and our hero must stop him. He is himself a skilled locksmith. . . ."

Trumbull interrupted. "In the first place, Manny, what the hell do you know about locksmithery or locksmithmanship or whatever you call it?"

"More than you think," retorted Rubin.

"I doubt that very much," said Trumbull, "and the editor is right. This is utter and complete implausibility. I know a few locksmiths, and they're gentle and inoffensive mechanics with IQ's . . ."

Rubin said, "And I suppose when you were in the army you knew a few corporals and, on the basis of your knowledge, you'll tell me that Napoleon and Hitler were implausible."

The guest for that evening, who had listened to the exchange with a darkening expression, spoke up. "Pardon me, gentlemen, I know I'm to be grilled at the conclusion of dinner. Does that mean I cannot join the dinner conversation beforehand?"

"Heavens, no," said Halsted. "Talk all you want—if you can get a word in now and then."

"In that case, let me put myself forcefully on the side of Mr. Rubin. A conspiracy of locksmiths may sound implausible to us who sit here, but what counts is not what a few rational people think but what the great outside world does. How can your editor turn down anything at all as implausible when everything . . ." He caught himself, took a deep breath, and said, in an altered tone, "Well, I don't mean to tell you your business. I'm not a writer. After all, I don't expect you to tell me how to play the oboe," but his smile as he said it was a weak one.

"Manny will tell you how to play the oboe," said Gonzalo, "if you give him a chance."

"Still," Thatcher said, as though he had not heard Gonzalo's comment, "I live in the world and observe it. *Anything* these days is believed. There is no such thing as 'not true to life.' Just spout any nonsense solemnly and swear it's true and there will be millions rallying round you."

Avalon nodded magisterially and said, "Quite right, Mr. Thatcher. I don't know that this is simply characteristic of our times, but the fact that we have better communications now makes it easier to reach many people quickly so that a phenomenon such as Herr Hitler of unmourned memory is possible. And to those who can believe in Mr. von Däniken's ancient astronauts and in Mr. Berlitz's Bermuda Triangle, a little thing like a conspiracy of locksmiths could be swallowed with the morning porridge."

Thatcher waved his hand. "Ancient astronauts and Bermuda Triangles are nothing. Suppose you were to say that you frequently visited Mars in astral projection and that Mars was, in fact, a haven for the worthy souls of this world. There would be those who would believe you."

"I imagine so," began Avalon.

"You don't have to imagine," said Thatcher. "It *is* so. I take it you haven't heard of Tri-Lucifer. That's t-r-i."

"Tri-Lucifer?" said Halsted, looking a little dumbfounded. "You mean three Lucifers. What's that?"

Thatcher looked from one face to another and the Black Widowers all remained silent.

And then Henry, who was clearing away some of the lobster shells, said, "If I may be permitted, gentlemen, I have heard of it. There were a group of them soliciting contributions at this restaurant last week."

"Like the Moonies?" said Drake, pushing his dish in Henry's direction and preparing to light up.

"There is a resemblance," said Henry, his face a bit thoughtful, "but the Tri-Luciferians, if that is the term to use, give a more other-worldly appearance."

"That's right," said Thatcher, "they have to divorce themselves from this world so as to achieve astral projection to Mars and facilitate the transfer of their souls there after death."

"But why—" began Gonzalo.

And Trumbull suddenly roared out with a blast of anger, "Come on, Roger, make them wait for the grilling to start. Change the subject."

Gonzalo said, "I just want to know why they call them..."

Halsted sighed and said, "Let's wait a while, Mario."

Henry was making his way about the table with the brandy when Halsted tapped his water glass and said, "I think we can begin the grilling now, and Manny, since it was your remark about true-to-lifeness that roused Jonathan's interest over the main course, why don't you begin."

"Sure." Rubin looked solemnly across the table at Thatcher and said, "Mr. Thatcher, at this point it would be traditional to ask you how you justify your existence, and we would then go into a discussion of the oboe as an instrument of torture for oboists. *But* let me guess and say that at this moment you would consider your life justified if you could wipe out a few Tri-Luciferians. Am I right?"

"You are, you are," said Thatcher, energetically. "The whole thing has filled my life and my thoughts for over a month now. It is ruining..."

Gonzalo interrupted. "What I want to know is why they call themselves Tri-Luciferians. Are they devil worshipers or what?"

Rubin began, "You're interrupting the man...."

"It's all right," said Thatcher. "I'll tell him. I'm just sorry that I know enough about that organization to be able to tell him. Apparently, Lucifer means the morning star, though I'm not sure why...."

"Lucifer," said Avalon, running his finger about the lip of his water glass, "is from Latin words meaning 'light bringer.' The rising of the morning star in the dawn heralds the soon-following rising of the Sun. In an era in which there were no clocks that was an important piece of information to anyone awake at the time."

"Then why is Lucifer the name of the devil?" asked Gonzalo.

Avalon said, "Because the Babylonian King was apparently referred to as the Morning Star by his flattering courtiers, and the Prophet Isaiah predicted his destruction. Can you quote the passage, Manny?"

Rubin said, "We can read it out of the Bible, if we want to. It's the Fourteenth Chapter of Isaiah. The key sentence goes, 'How art thou fallen from heaven, O Lucifer, son of the morning!' It was just a bit of poetic hyperbole, and very effective too, but it was interpreted literally later, and that one sentence gave rise to the whole myth of a rebellion against God by hordes of angels under the leadership of Lucifer, which came to be considered Satan's name while still in heaven. Of course, the rebels were defeated and expelled from heaven by loyalist angels under the leadership of the Archangel Michael."

"As in *Paradise Lost*?" said Gonzalo.

"Exactly as in *Paradise Lost*."

Thatcher said, "The devil isn't part of it, though. To the Tri-Luciferians, Lucifer just means the morning star. There are two of them on Earth, Venus and Mercury."

Drake squinted through the curling tobacco smoke and said, "They're also evening stars, depending on which side of the Sun they happen to be. They're either east of the Sun and set shortly after sunset, or west of the Sun and rise shortly before sunrise."

Thatcher said, with clear evidence of hope, "Do they have to be both together, both one or both the other?"

"No," said Drake, "they move independently. They can be both evening stars, or both morning stars, or one can be an evening star and one a morning star. Or one or the other or both can be nearly in a line with the Sun and be invisible altogether, morning or evening."

"Too bad," said Thatcher, shaking his head, "that's what *they* say. Anyway, the point is that from Mars you see *three* morning stars in the sky, or you can see them if they're in the right position; not only Mercury and Venus, but Earth as well."

"That's right," said Rubin.

"And," said Thatcher, "I suppose then it's true that they can be in any position. They can all be evening stars or all morning stars, or two can be one and one can be the other?"

"Yes," said Drake, "or one or more can be too close to the Sun to be visible."

Thatcher sighed. "So they call Mars by their mystic name of Tri-Lucifer—the world with the three morning stars."

"I suppose," said Gonzalo, "that Jupiter would have four morning stars, Mercury, Venus, Earth, and Mars, and so on out to Pluto, which would have eight morning stars."

"The trouble is," said Halsted, "that the farther out you go, the dimmer the inner planets are. Viewed from one of the satellites of Jupiter, for instance, I doubt that Mercury would appear more than a medium-bright star, and it might be too close to the Sun for anyone ever to get a good look at it."

"What about the view from Mars? Could you see Mercury?" asked Thatcher.

"Oh yes, I'm sure of that," said Halsted. "I could work out what the brightness would be in a matter of minutes."

"Would you?" said Thatcher.

"Sure," said Halsted, "if I've remembered to bring my pocket calculator. Yes, I have it. Henry, bring me the Columbia Encyclopedia, would you?"

Rubin said, "While Roger is bending his limited mathematical mind to the problem, Mr. Thatcher, tell us what your interest is in all this. You seem to be interested in exposing them as fakers. Why? Have you been a member? Are you now disillusioned?"

"No, I've never been a member. I . . ." He rubbed his temple hesitantly. "It's my wife. I don't like talking about it, you understand."

Avalon said solemnly, "Please be assured, Mr. Thatcher, that whatever is said here never passes beyond the bounds of this room. That includes our valued waiter, Henry. You may speak freely."

"Well, there's nothing criminal or disgraceful in it. I just don't like to seem to be so helpless in such a silly . . . It's breaking up my marriage, gentlemen."

There was a discreet silence around the table, broken only by the mild sound of Halsted turning the pages of the encyclopedia.

Thatcher went on. "Roger knows my wife. He'll tell you she's a sensible woman. . . ."

Halsted looked up briefly and nodded. "I'll vouch for that, but I didn't know you were having this . . ."

"Lately, Carol has not been social, you understand, and I certainly haven't talked about it. It was with great difficulty, you know, that I managed to agree to come out tonight. I dread leaving her to herself. You see, even sensible people have their weaknesses. Carol worries about death."

"So do we all," said Drake.

"So do I," said Thatcher, "but in a normal way, I hope. We all know we'll die someday and we don't particularly look forward to it, and we may worry about hell or nothingness or hope for heaven, but we don't think about it much. Carol has been fascinated, however, by the possibility of demonstrating the actual existence of life after death. It may have all started with the Bridey Murphy case when she was a teen-ager—I don't know if any of you remember that . . ."

"I do," said Rubin. "A woman under hypnosis seemed to be possessed by an Irishwoman who had died a long time before."

"Yes," said Thatcher. "She saw through that, eventually. Then she grew interested in spiritualism and gave that up. I always relied on her to understand folly when she finally stopped to think about it—and then she came up against the Tri-Luciferians. I never saw her like this. She wants to join them. She has money of her own and she wants to give it to them. I don't care about the money—well, I do, but that's not the main thing—I care about *her*. You know, she's going to join them in their retreat somewhere, become a daughter of Tri-Lucifer, or whatever they call it, and wait for translation to the Abode of the Blessed. One of these days, she'll be gone. I just won't see her anymore. She promised me it wouldn't be tonight, but I wonder."

Rubin said, "I take it you suppose that the organization is just interested in her money."

"At least the leader of it is," said Thatcher grimly. "I'm sure of it. What else can he be after?"

"Do you know him? Have you met him?" said Rubin.

"No. He keeps himself isolated," said Thatcher, "but I hear he has recently bought a fancy mansion in Florida, and I doubt that it's for the use of the membership."

"Funny thing about that," said Drake. "It doesn't matter how lavishly a cult leader lives; how extravagantly he throws money around. The followers who support him and see their money clearly used for that purpose never seem to mind."

"They identify," said Rubin. "The more he spends, the more successful they consider the cause. It's the basis of ostentatious waste in governmental display, too."

"Just the same," said Thatcher, "I don't think Carol will ever commit herself entirely. She might not be bothered by the leader's actions, but if I can prove him *wrong*, she'll drop it."

"Wrong about what?" asked Rubin.

"Wrong about Mars. This head of the group claims he has been on Mars often—in astral projection, of course. He describes Mars in detail, but can he be describing it accurately?"

"Why not?" asked Rubin. "If he reads up on what is known about Mars, he can describe it as astronomers would. The Viking photographs even show a part of the surface in detail. It's not difficult to be accurate."

"Yes, but it may be that somewhere he has made a mistake, something I can show Carol."

Halsted looked up and said, "Here, I've worked out the dozen brightest objects in the Martian sky, together with their magnitudes. I may be off a little here and there, but not by much." He passed a slip of paper around.

Mario held up the paper when it reached him. "Would you like to see it, Henry?"

"Thank you, sir," murmured Henry, and as he glanced at it briefly, one eyebrow raised itself just slightly, just briefly.

The paper came to rest before Thatcher eventually and he gazed at it earnestly. What he saw was this:

Sun	—26
Phobos	—9.6
Deimos	—5.1
Earth	—4.5
Jupiter	—3.1
Venus	—2.6
Sirius	—1.4
Saturn	—0.8
Canopus	—0.7
Alpha Centauri	—0.3
Arcturus	—0.1
Mercury	0.0

Thatcher said, "Phobos and Deimos are the two satellites of Mars. Do these numbers mean they're very bright?"

"The greater the negative number," said Halsted, "the brighter the object. A —2 object is 2½ times brighter than a —1 object, and a —3 object is 2½ times brighter still, and so on. Next to the Sun, Phobos is the brightest object in the Martian sky, and Deimos is next."

"And next to the Sun and the two satellites, Earth is the brightest object in the sky, then."

"Yes, but only at or near its maximum brightness," said Halsted. "It can be much dimmer depending on where Mars and Earth are in their respective orbits. Most of the time it's probably less bright than Jupiter, which doesn't change much in brightness as it moves in its orbit."

Thatcher shook his head and looked disappointed. "But it *can* be that bright. Too bad. There's a special prayer or psalm or something that the Tri-Luciferians have that appears in almost all their literature. I've seen it so often in the stuff Carol brings home, I can quote it exactly. It goes, 'When Earth shines high in the sky, like a glorious jewel, and when the other Lucifers have fled beyond the horizon, so that Earth shines alone in splendor, single in beauty, unmatched in brightness, it is then that the souls of those ready to receive the call must prepare to rise from Earth and cross the gulf.' And what you're saying, Roger, is that Earth *can* be the brightest object in the Martian sky."

Halsted nodded. "At night, if Phobos and Deimos are below the horizon, and Earth is near maximum brightness, it is certainly the brightest object in the sky. It would be 3½ times as bright as Jupiter, if that were in the sky, and 6 times as bright as Venus at its brightest."

"And it could be the only morning star in the sky."

"Or the only evening star. Sure. The other two, Venus and Mercury, could be on the other side of the Sun from Earth."

Thatcher kept staring at the list. "But would Mercury be visible? It's at the bottom of the list."

Halsted said, "The bottom just means that it's twelfth brightest, but there are thousands of stars that are dimmer and still visible. There would be only four stars brighter than Mercury as seen from Mars: Sirius, Canopus, Alpha Centauri, and Arcturus."

Thatcher said, "If they'd only make a mistake."

Avalon said in a grave and somewhat hesitant baritone, "Mr. Thatcher, I think perhaps you had better face the facts. It is my experience that even if you *do* find a flaw in the thesis of the Tri-Luciferians it won't help you. Those who follow cults for emotional reasons are not deterred by demonstrations of the illogic of what they are doing."

Thatcher said, "I agree with you, and I wouldn't dream of arguing with the ordinary cultist. But I know Carol. I have seen her turn away from a system of beliefs she would very much like to have followed, simply because she saw the illogic of it. If I could find something of the sort here, I'm sure she'd come back."

Gonzalo said, "Some of us here ought to think of something. After all, he's never *really* been on Mars. He's got to have made a mistake."

"Not at all," said Avalon. "He probably knows as much about Mars as we do. Therefore, even if he's made a mistake it may be because he fails to understand something we also fail to understand and we won't catch him."

Thatcher nodded his head. "I suppose you're right."

"I don't know," said Gonzalo. "How about the canals? The Tri-Luciferians are bound to talk about the canals. Everyone believed in them and then just lately we found out they weren't there; isn't that right? So if he talks about them, he's caught."

Drake said, "Not everybody believed in them, Mario. Hardly any astronomers did."

"The general public did," said Gonzalo.

Rubin said, "Not lately. It was in 1964 that Mariner 4 took the first pictures of Mars and that pretty much gave away the fact the canals didn't exist. Once Mariner 9 mapped the whole planet in 1969 there was no further argument. When did the Tri-Luciferians come into existence, Mr. Thatcher?"

"As I recall," said Thatcher, "about 1970. Maybe 1971."

"There you are," said Rubin. "Once we had Mars down cold, this guy, whoever he is who runs it, decided to start a new religion based on it. Listen, if you want to get rich quick, no questions asked, start a new religion. Between the First Amendment and the tax breaks you get, it amounts to a license to help yourself to everything in sight. I'll bet he talks about volcanoes."

Thatcher nodded. "The Martian headquarters of the astral

projections are in Olympus Mons. That means Mount Olympus, and that's where the souls of the righteous gather. That's the big volcano, isn't it?"

"The biggest in the solar system," said Rubin. "At least, that we know of. It's been known since 1969."

Thatcher said, "The Tri-Luciferians say that G. V. Schiaparelli—he's the one who named the different places on Mars—was astrally inspired to name that spot Olympus to signify it was the home of the godly. In ancient Greece, you see, Mount Olympus was . . ."

"Yes," said Avalon, nodding gravely, "we know."

"Isn't Schiaparelli the fellow who first reported the canals?" asked Gonzalo.

"Yes," said Halsted, "although actually when he said *canali* he meant natural waterways."

"Even so, why didn't the same astral inspiration tell him the canals weren't there?" asked Gonzalo.

Drake nodded and said, "That's something you can point out to your wife."

"No," said Thatcher, "I guess they thought of that. They say the canals were part of the inspiration because that increased interest in Mars and that that was needed to make the astral-projection process more effective."

Trumbull, who had maintained a sullen silence through the discussion, as though he were waiting his chance to shift the discussion to oboes, said suddenly, "That makes a diseased kind of sense."

Thatcher said, "Too much makes sense. That's the trouble. There are times when I want to find a mistake not so much to save Carol as to save myself. I tell you that when I listen to Carol talking there's sometimes more danger she'll argue me into being crazy than that I'll persuade her to be rational."

Trumbull waved a hand at him soothingly. "Just take it easy and let's think it out. Do they say anything about the satellites?"

"They talk about them, yes. Phobos and Deimos. Sure."

"Do they say anything about how they cross the sky?" Trumbull's smile was nearly a smirk.

"Yes," said Thatcher, "and I looked it up because I didn't believe them and I thought I had something. In their description of the Martian scene, they talk about Phobos rising in the west and setting in the east. And it turns out that's true.

And they say that whenever either Phobos or Deimos cross the sky at night, they are eclipsed by Mars's shadow for part of the time. And that's true, too."

Halsted shrugged. "The satellites were discovered a century ago, in 1877, by Asaph Hall. As soon as their distance from Mars and their period of revolution were determined, which were almost at once, their behavior in Mars's sky was known."

"*I* didn't know it," said Thatcher.

"No," said Halsted, "but this fellow who started the religion apparently did his homework. It wasn't really hard."

"Hold on," said Trumbull truculently, "some things aren't as obvious and don't get put into the average elementary-astronomy textbook. For instance, I read somewhere that Phobos can't be seen from the Martian polar regions. It's so close to Mars that the bulge of Mars's spherical surface hides the satellite, if you go far enough north or south. Do the Tri-Luciferians say anything about Phobos being invisible from certain places on Mars, Thatcher?"

"Not that I recall," said Thatcher, "but they don't say it's always visible. If they just don't mention the matter, what does that prove?"

"Besides," said Halsted, "Olympus Mons is less than twenty degrees north of the Martian equator, and Phobos is certainly visible from there any time it is above the horizon and not in eclipse. And if that's the headquarters for the souls from Earth, Mars would certainly be described as viewed from that place."

"Whose side are you on?" growled Trumbull.

"The truth's," said Halsted. "Still, it's true that astronomy books rarely describe any sky but Earth's. That's why I had to figure out the brightness of objects in the Martian sky instead of just looking it up. The only trouble is that this cult leader seems to be just as good at figuring."

"I've got an idea," said Avalon. "I'm not much of an astronomer, but I've seen the photographs taken by the Viking landers and I've read the newspaper reports about them. For one thing, the Martian sky in the daytime is pink, because of the fine particles of the reddish dust in the air. In that case, isn't it possible that the dust obscures the night sky so that you don't see anything? Good Lord, it happens often enough in New York City."

Halsted said, "As a matter of fact, the problem in New York isn't so much the dust as the scattered light from the buildings and highways, and even in New York you can see the bright stars, if the sky isn't cloudy.

"On Mars, it would have to work both ways. If there is enough dust to make the sky invisible from the ground, then the ground would be invisible from the sky. For instance, when Mariner 9 reached Mars in 1969, Mars was having a globewide duststorm and none of its surface could be seen by Mariner. At that time, from the Martian surface, the sky would have had to be blanked out. Most of the time, though, we see the surface clearly from our probes, so from the Martian surface, the sky would be clearly visible.

"In fact, considering that Mars's atmosphere is much thinner than Earth's, less than a hundredth as thick, it would scatter and absorb far less light than Earth's does, and the various stars and planets would all look a little brighter than they would with Earth's atmosphere in the way. I didn't allow for that in my table."

Trumbull said, "Geoff mentioned the Viking photographs. They show rocks all over the place. Do the Tri-Luciferians mention rocks?"

"No," said Thatcher, "not that I ever noticed. But again, they don't say there aren't any. They talk about huge canyons and dry riverbeds and terraced icefields."

Rubin snorted. "All that's been known since 1969. More homework."

Avalon said, "What about life? We still don't know if there's any life on Mars. The Viking results are ambiguous. Have the Tri-Luciferians committed themselves on that?"

Thatcher thought, then said, "I wish I could say I had read all their literature thoroughly, but I haven't. Still Carol has forced me to read quite a bit since she said I ought not defame anything without learning about it first. "

"That's true enough," said Avalon, "though life is short and there are some things that are so unlikely on the surface that one hesitates to devote much of one's time to a study of it. However, can you say anything as to their attitude toward Martian life from what you've read of their literature?"

Thatcher said, "They speak about Mars's barren surface, its desert aridity and emptiness. They contrast that with the excitement and fullness of the astral sphere."

"Yes," said Avalon, "and of course, the surface *is* dry and empty and barren. We know that much. What about microscopic life? That's what we're looking for."

Thatcher shook his head. "No mention of it, as far as I know."

Avalon said, "Well, then, I can't think of anything else. I'm quite certain this whole thing is nonsense. Everyone here is, and none of us need proof of it. If your wife needs proof, we may not be able to supply it."

"I understand," said Thatcher. "I thank you all, of course, and I suppose she may come to her senses after a while, but I must admit I have never seen her quite like this. I would join the cult with her just to keep her in sight but, frankly, I'm afraid I'll end up believing it, too."

And in the silence that followed, Henry said softly, "Perhaps, Mr. Thatcher, you need not go to that extreme."

Thatcher turned suddenly. "Pardon me. Did you say something, waiter?"

Halsted said, "Henry is a member of the club, Jonathan. I don't know that he's an astronomer exactly, but he's the brightest person here. Is there something we've missed, Henry?"

Henry said, "I think so, sir. You said, Mr. Halsted, that astronomy books don't generally describe any sky but Earth's, and I guess that must be why the cult leader seems to have a missing item in his description of Mars. Without it, the whole thing is no more true to life than Mr. Rubin's conspiracy of locksmiths—if I may be forgiven, Mr. Rubin."

"Not if you don't supply a missing object, Henry."

Henry said, "On Earth, Mercury and Venus are the morning and evening stars, and we always think of such objects as planets, therefore. Consequently, from Mars, there must be three morning and evening stars, Mercury, Venus, plus Earth in addition. That is memorialized in the very name of the cult and from that alone I could see the whole thing fails."

Halsted said, "I'm not sure I see your point, Henry."

"But, Mr. Halsted," said Henry, "where is the Moon in all this? It is a large object, our Moon, almost the size of Mercury and closer to Mars than Mercury is. If Mercury can be seen from Mars, surely the Moon can be, too. Yet I noticed it was not on your list of bright objects in the Martian sky."

Halsted turned red. "Yes, of course. The list of planets

fooled me, too. You just list them without mentioning the Moon." He reached for the paper. "The Moon is Smaller than Earth and less reflective, so that it is only one seventieth as bright as the Earth, at equal distance and phase, which means—a magnitude of 0.0. It would be just as bright as Mercury and in fact it could be seen more easily than Mercury could be because it would be higher in the sky. At sunset, Mercury as evening star would never be higher than 16 degrees above the horizon, while Earth could be as much as 44 degrees above—pretty high in the sky."

Henry said, "Mars, therefore, would have four morning stars, and the very name Tri-Lucifer is nonsense."

Avalon said, "But the Moon would always be close to Earth, so wouldn't Earth's light drown it out?"

"No," said Halsted. "Let's see now—never get a pocket calculator that doesn't have keys for the trigonometric functions—the Moon would be, at times, as much as 23 minutes of arc away from Earth, when viewed from Mars. That's three quarters the width of the Moon as seen from Earth."

Henry said, "One more thing. Would you repeat that verse once again, Mr. Thatcher, the one about the Earth being high in the sky?"

Thatcher said, "Certainly. 'When Earth shines high in the sky, like a glorious jewel, and when the other Lucifers have fled beyond the horizon, so that Earth shines alone in splendor, single in beauty, unmatched in brightness, it is then that the souls of those ready to receive the call must prepare to rise from Earth and cross the gulf.' "

Henry said, "Earth may be quite high in the sky at times, and Mercury and Venus may be on the other side of the Sun and therefore beyond the horizon—but Earth cannot be 'alone in splendor.' The Moon has to be with it. Of course, there would be times when the Moon is very nearly in front of Earth or behind it, as seen from Mars, so that the two dots of light merge into one that seems to make Earth brighter than ever, but the Moon is not then beyond the horizon. It seems to me, Mr. Thatcher, that the cult leader was never on Mars, because if he had been he would not have missed a pretty big item, a world 2,160 miles across. Surely you can explain this to your wife."

"Yes," said Thatcher, his face brightening into a smile, "she would have to see the whole thing as a fake."

"If it is true, as you say," said Henry quietly, "that she is a rational person."

"The Missing Item"—Afterword

A few of the stories in the first two volumes of Black Widowers stories did *not* appear in *EQMM*, but in *The Magazine of Fantasy and Science Fiction* (*F & SF*) instead. This was a bit difficult, for I couldn't make a Black Widowers tale an outright fantasy or science fiction.

Once in a while, though, I, being what I am, constructed one of the stories in such a way that it dealt at least tangentially with science fiction or fantasy, and then *F & SF* would get it.

Or did get it, anyway. In 1977, a new magazine reached the newsstands, a sister magazine of *EQMM*. The new magazine was *Isaac Asimov's Science Fiction Magazine* (*IASFM*), and, of course, it was thereafter no longer cricket for me to give a story to any science-fiction magazine unless it had first been offered to *IASFM*.

In fact, I deliberately tried to construct as distinct a science-fiction mystery as I could for my own magazine, and "The Missing Item" was the result. It appeared in the Winter 1977 issue of *IASFM*. (The magazine was a quarterly in its first year.)

6.

The Next Day

Emmanuel Rubin's glasses always gave the illusion of magnifying his eyes with particular intensity when he was aroused. He said, in an intense whisper, "You brought an *editor* as your guest?"

James Drake's train from New Jersey had arrived late and he had, in consequence, almost committed the solecism of being late to his own hostship over the monthly banquet of the Black Widowers. He was in an uncharacteristically snappish mood therefore and said, "Why not?"

He flicked the ash from his cigarette and added, "If we can have writers for guests, and even as members, Zeus help us, why not editors?"

Rubin, a writer, of course, said haughtily, "I wouldn't expect a chemist to understand." He looked briefly in the direction of the guest, who was tall and spare, with longish red-blond hair and with the kind of abbreviated mustache and beard that gave him a Robin Hood air.

Drake said, "I may be a chemist to you, Manny, and to all the world besides, but I'm a writer to him." Drake tried to look modest, and failed signally. "I'm doing a book."

"You?" said Rubin.

"Why not? I can spell and, judging by your career, that's the only requirement."

"If your guest thinks it is, he has about the mental equipment needed for an editor. What's his name again?"

"Stephen Bentham."

"And what firm is he with?"

Drake stubbed out his cigarette. "Southby Publications."

"A *shlock* outfit," said Rubin, with contempt. "They're a sex-and-sensation house. What do they want with you?"

Drake said, "I'm doing a book on recombinant DNA, which is a sensational subject these days—not that you know anything about it."

Mario Gonzalo had just entered, brushing at his brown velvet jacket to remove the city fly-ash. He said, "Come on, Jim, all the papers are full of it. That's the stuff they're going to make new disease germs with and depopulate the world."

Rubin said, "If Mario's heard about it, Jim, you'll have to admit I have, too—and everyone else in the world has."

"Good. Then my book is what the world needs," said Drake.

Gonzalo said, "The world needs it about as much as it needs air pollution. I've seen two books on the subject advertised already."

"Ha," said Drake, "they're talking about the controversy, the politics. I'm going to talk about the chemistry."

"Then it will never sell," said Rubin.

It was at this point that Henry, that paragon of waiters, without whom no Black Widowers banquet could endure, announced softly to Drake that the gentlemen might seat themselves.

Geoffrey Avalon drifted toward Henry, having now had the pleasure of a sedate conversation with the guest—with whom he had talked eye to eye, something which, from his 74 inches of height, he could not often do.

"I detect a fishy aroma, Henry," he said. "What has been planned for this evening?"

"A bouillabaisse, sir," said Henry. "An excellent one, I believe."

Avalon nodded gravely, and Roger Halsted, smiling, said, "Even an average bouillabaisse is excellent, and with Henry's encomium, I stand ready to be delighted."

Avalon said, "I hope, Mr. Bentham, that you have no objection?"

"I can't say I've ever eaten it." Bentham spoke in a distinct, but not exaggerated, English accent, "but I'm prepared to have a go at it. A French dish, I believe."

"Marseillaise in origin," said Halsted, looking as though he were coming very close to licking his chops, "but universal in appeal. Where's Tom, by the way?"

"Right here," came an exasperated voice from the steps. "Damn taxi driver. Thanks, Henry." Thomas Trumbull, his tanned forehead creased and furrowed into fifty lines of anger, gratefully took the scotch and soda. "You haven't started eating, have you?"

"Just about," said Gonzalo, "and if you hadn't arrived, Roger would have had your share of the bouillabaisse, so it would have been a silver lining for someone. What was with the taxicab?"

Trumbull seated himself, took another invigorating sip of his drink, buttered a roll, and said, "I told the idiot to take me to the Milano and the next thing I knew I was at some dive movie on West Eighty-sixth Street called the Milano. We had to make our way through four extra miles of Manhattan streets to get here. He claimed he had never heard of the Milano Restaurant, but he did know that flea dive. It cost me three bucks extra in taxi fare."

Rubin said, "You're pretty far gone, Tom, if you couldn't tell he was going northwest when you wanted to go southeast."

"You don't think I was watching the streets, do you?" growled Trumbull. "I was lost in thought."

Avalon said austerely, "You can't rely on the local wisdom of the New York taxi driver. You ought to have said explicitly, 'Fifth Avenue and Thirteenth Street.'"

"Thanks a lot," said Trumbull. "I shall instantly turn the clock back and say it."

"I presume there'll be a next time, Tom, and that you're capable of learning from experience," said Avalon, and received a scowl for his pains.

After the bouillabaisse arrived, there was a lull in the conversation for a while as the banqueters concentrated on the evisceration of mussels and the cracking of lobster shells.

It was Drake who broke it. He said, "If we consider recombinant DNA . . ."

"We aren't," said Rubin, spearing a scallop neatly.

". . . then what it amounts to is that the whole argument is about benefits that no one can demonstrate and dangers that no one can really pinpoint. There are only blue-sky probabilities on either side, and the debaters make up for their lack of hard knowledge by raising their voices. What I propose to do is to go into the chemistry and genetics of the matter and try to work out the real chances and significance of specific genetic change. Without that, both sides are just searching in a dark room for a black cat that isn't there."

Avalon said, "And all this for the general public?"

"Certainly."

"Isn't that rather heavy going for the general public?"

"It isn't for the comic-book audience, but I think I can manage the *Scientific American* to *Natural History* range. Tell them, Bentham," said Drake, with perhaps a trace of smugness, "you've seen the sample chapters."

Bentham, who had tackled the bouillabaisse with a certain tentativeness but had grown steadily more enthusiastic, said, "I can only judge by myself, to be sure, but I suspect that since I follow the line of argument, the average college man ought to."

"That still limits your audience," said Gonzalo.

Bentham said, "We can't say that. It's a very hot subject and, properly promoted . . ."

"A Southby specialty," muttered Rubin.

"It could cach on," Bentham said. "People who don't really understand might nevertheless buy it to be in fashion; and who knows, they might read it and get *something* out of it."

Drake tapped his water glass as Henry doled out the brandy. Drake said, "If everyone is sufficiently defishified and if Henry will remove the towels and finger bowls, I think we may start to grill our guest. Mr. Stephen Bentham. Tom, will you do the honors?"

"Glad to," said Trumbull. "Mr. Bentham, it is our custom, ordinarily, to inquire as to how a guest may justify his existence. In this case, I suppose we can allow the fact that you are involved with the production of a book by our esteemed colleague, Dr. Drake, to speak for you. We will therefore pass on to more mundane questions. You seem young. How old are you?"

"Twenty-eight."

"I have the feeling you have not been long in the United States. Am I right?"

"I've been living and working here for about five months now, but I have been here on brief visits before. Three times."

"I see. And what are your qualifications for your post; as editor, that is?"

"Not overwhelming." Bentham smiled suddenly, an oddly charming and rueful smile. "I have done some editing with Fearn and Russell in London. Rather happy with them—low-key concern, you know, but then, British publishing generally is low-key."

"Why throw that over to take a job with an American firm where the pressures are bound to be greater? They are greater, I assume."

"Very much so," again the rueful smile, "but there's no mystery as to why I came. The explanation is so simple that it embarrasses me to advance it. In a word—money. I was offered three times my British salary, and all moving expenses paid."

Halsted intervened suddenly. "Are you a married man, Mr. Bentham?"

"No, Mr. Halsted. Quite single, though not necessarily celibate. However, single men can use money, too."

Rubin said, "If you don't mind, Tom, I would like to add the reverse of the question you asked. I can see why you've joined Southby Publications. Money is a potent argument. But why the hell did that *shlock* concern hire you? You're young, without much experience, and they're not the kind of firm to hire promising young men out of benevolence. Yet they triple your salary and pay moving expenses. What have you got on them?"

Bentham said, "I met Mr. Southby on one of my earlier trips and I think he was rather taken with me." His fair skin turned a noticeable pink. "I suspect it was my accent and my appearance. Perhaps it seemed to him I would lend an air of scholarship to the firm."

"A touch of class," murmured Avalon, and Bentham turned pinker still.

Trumbull resumed the questioning, "Manny calls Southby Publications a *shlock* concern. Do you agree with that?"

Bentham hesitated. "I don't know. What does the expression mean?"

Rubin said, "Cheap, worthless books, sold by high-pressure campaigns hinting at sex and sensationalism."

Bentham remained silent.

Drake said, "Go ahead, Bentham. Anything you say here will never go beyond these walls. The club observes complete confidentiality."

"It isn't that, Jim," said Bentham, "but if I were to agree, it might wound your feelings. You're an author of ours."

Drake lit another cigarette. "That wouldn't bother me. You're hired to give the firm a touch of class and you'll do my book as another touch of class."

Bentham says, "I grant you that I don't think much of some of the books on the list, but Dr. Drake is right. Mr. Southby doesn't object to good books if he thinks they will sell. He is personally pleased with what he has seen of Dr. Drake's book; even enthusiastic. Perhaps the firm's character can be improved."

Avalon said, "I would like to put in my oar, Tom, if you don't mind. Mr. Bentham, I am not a psychologist, or a tracer of men's thoughts through their expressions. I am just a humble patent attorney. However, it seems to me that you have looked distinctly uneasy each time you mentioned your employer. Are you sure that there is nothing you are keeping from Dr. Drake that he ought to know? I want an unequivocal answer."

"No," said Bentham quickly, "there is nothing wrong with Dr. Drake's book. Provided he completes the book and that the whole is of the quality of the parts we have seen, we will publish and then promote it adequately. There are no hidden reservations to that statement."

Gonzalo said, "Then what are you uneasy about? Or is Geoff all wrong about your feelings in the first place?" He was gazing complacently at the caricature of Bentham he had produced for the guest galley that lined the walls of the meeting room. He had not missed the Robin Hood resemblance and had even lightly sketched in a feathered hat in green, of the type one associated with the Merry Men.

Bentham said, in sudden anger, "You could say I'm uneasy, considering that I'm about to be bloody well slung out on my can."

"Fired?" said Gonzalo, on a rising note.

"That's the rough one-syllable version of what I have just said."

"Why?" said Drake, in sudden concern.

"I've lost a manuscript," said Bentham. "Not yours, Dr. Drake."

Gonzalo said, "In the mails?"

"No. Through malice, according to Southby. Actually, I did every ruddy thing I could do to get it back. I don't know *what* was in that man's mind."

"Southby's?"

"No, the author's. Joshua Fairfield's his name."

"Never heard of him," said Rubin.

Trumbull said, "Suppose you tell us what happened, Mr. Bentham."

Bentham said, "It's a grim, stupid thing. I don't want to cast a pall over a very pleasant evening."

Trumbull said, "Sorry, Mr. Bentham, but I think Jim warned you that answering our questions was the price of the meal. Please tell us exactly what happened."

Bentham said, "I suppose the most exciting thing that can happen in a publishing house is to have something good come in over the transom; something good that has not passed through the hands of a reputable agent and is not by a recognized author; something that has reached you by mail, written by someone whom no one has ever heard of.

"Aside from the sheer pleasure of the unexpected windfall, there is the possibility that you have a new author who can be milked for years to come, provided the product is not that of a one-book author—which is not an unheard-of phenomenon."

Rubin began, "Margaret Mitchell . . ." and stopped when Trumbull, who sat next to him, elbowed him urgently.

"Anyway," said Bentham, jarred only momentarily by the interruption, "Southby thought he had one. One of the readers brought it to him in excitement, as well he might, for readers don't often get anything that's above the written-in-crayon-on-lined-paper level.

"He should have gone to an editor—not necessarily me—with the manuscript, but he chose to go directly to Southby. I presume he felt there might be a deal of credit for the discovery and he didn't want Southby to be unaware of the discoverer. I can't say I blame him.

"In any case, Southby was infatuated with the manuscript, called an editorial conference, said he was accepting the book and had notified the author. He explained, quite enthusiastically, that it was to get the full Southby treatment. . . ."

Rubin said indignantly, "Up to and including cooking the best-seller lists. Tom, if you give me the elbow again, I'll break it off."

Bentham said, "I dare say you're right, Mr. Rubin, but this book deserved all it could get—potentially. Southby said he thought it needed work and he gave it to me to edit. That struck me as a remarkable sign of confidence and I was rather gung-ho on the matter. I saw quick promotions on the horizon if I could manage to carry it off. The other editors didn't seem to mind, though. One of them said to me, 'It's your butt that's in the sling if this doesn't work, because Southby's never wrong.' "

Avalon said gravely, "It sometimes happens that when the boss makes a mistake, the underling tabbed to reverse the mistake is fired if he fails."

Bentham nodded. "The thought occurred to me, eventually, but it excited me further. The scent of danger sharpens the desire to be in at the kill, you know.

"You can see, then, that I went over the manuscript in a painstaking manner. I went through it once at moderate speed to get a sense of the whole and was not displeased. Southby's description of it was not, on the whole, wrong. It had a good pace and was rich in detail. A long family saga—a rough and domineering father, a smooth and insinuating mother in a rather subtle battle over the sons, their wives, and their children. The plot was interlocking, never halting, and there was enough sex to be suitable for Southby, but the sex *worked*. It fit the story.

"I turned in a favorable report of my own on the book, indicating its chief flaws, and how I proposed to handle them. It came back with a large 'very good' on it, so I got to work. It had to be tightened up. The last thing any beginner, however talented, learns is to tighten. Some scenes were misplaced or misemphasized, and that had to be corrected.

"I am not myself a great writer and could never be, but I've studied writing that *is* great sufficiently closely to be able to amend and improve what is already written well, even if, from a cold start, I could not produce anything nearly as good. It took me some six weeks of intense work to complete the job. I knew that my head was on the line and I was not about to lose the war for lack of a horseshoe nail.

"It wasn't till after I had done a thorough piece of work that I called in the author, Joshua Fairfield. I thought it better that way. Had I called him in en route, so to speak, there would have been bound to be acrimonious arguments over the changes, and much time would be wasted on trivial points. If he could see the revisions as a whole, I felt he would be satisfied. Any minor disagreements could be easily settled.

"Or so I reasoned, and perhaps I had need of a little experience myself. The author arrived and we met, actually, for the first time. I can't say I particularly liked his looks. He was about my age but he had a rather somber cast of countenance, small, dark eyes—almost beady—and poor teeth.

"I went through the amenities. We shook hands. I told him how pleased we all were with the book; how well it was going to do; the promotion we would give it; and so on.

"I then said, rather casually, in order to emphasize the minor nature of the changes—compared to what was not changed, you know—that I had taken the liberty of introducing some small emendations here and there. At that, he sat upright and his small eyes bulged. He seized the manuscript, which was on the table before us, shook some of it out of one of the boxes, riffled through the pages where I had made the necessary changes in a fine-point pencil, done quite lightly to allow of further chánges, and *shrieked*.

"He really did. He screamed that I had written something on every page and that he would have to get the whole thing retyped and that the bill would go straight to me. Then he seized the boxes and was gone. I couldn't stop him. I swear to you, I couldn't move, I was that thunderstruck.

"But not panicky, either. The manuscript was photocopied and I had made copious notes of the changes I had made. Since he was under contract—or so I assumed—we could publish over his objections. He might proceed to sue us, but I don't think he could have won, and the publicity, I couldn't help but think, would simply sell more books.

"The trouble is that when I went to see Southby to tell him what had happened, it turned out there was no contract and everything came apart. It seemed that Southby and Fairfield were haggling over the advance. I suppose I might have been more diplomatic when I heard this. It was *not* a good idea to ask Southby if, in view of the advertising budget being planned, it made much sense to haggle over a matter of two thousand dollars in the advance."

Rubin grunted. "Well, now you know something about Southby."

"I know he didn't like to have it made to look as though it were his fault. He ordered me to get that manuscript back and he made it pretty clear that I was in for it if I did not.

"It proved difficult from the start. I tried Fairfield at his apartment, I tried him on the phone. It took me three days and then he finally answered the phone. I managed to keep him on the phone. I told him he could have the advance he wanted. I told him that every change was negotiable and that we could go over the book line by line—which was exactly what I had tried desperately to avoid in the first place—and I warned him that no publisher would take it precisely as it was.

"He said, with a rather snide and unpleasant snicker, that that was not so, that another publisher *would* take it exactly as was. He had still not turned it over to that other publisher, but he hinted that he might.

"I took that as a bluff and didn't let it rattle me. I just told him quietly that no firm could guarantee a best seller as Southby could, reminded him of some of our other books . . ."

Rubin said, "Sure. Trash like *Dish for the Gods*."

Avalon said, "Let him speak, Manny."

"Well," said Bentham, "we were on the phone for over an hour and he finally put it to me straight. Would I publish it as written? I said, just as straight, that we could negotiate every change, but that there would have to be some—for his own good.

"He remained truculent and nasty, but he gave in, just like that. He said he would deliver it the next day and I said enthusiastically—and trying to hide my relief—that that was top hole, and that he was to go to it, the sooner the better, and I would send a messenger if he'd like. He said, no, he didn't want any stinking messenger, and hung up."

Halsted said, "Happy ending."

"No, because he never delivered the manuscript. We waited a week and then Southby finally got him on the phone and all he got out of Fairfield were snarls to the effect that his paid monkey, Bentham, could keep his stinking sarcasm and shove it and we would get no manuscript from him on any terms, or words to that effect.

"That's where it stands. Needless to say, I was *not* sarcastic. I was perfectly reasonable and diplomatic at all times. I was firm on the key point of revision, but not offensively so. In fact, he had agreed to deliver it the next day. As far as Southby was concerned, however, I had lost the manuscript through my malicious treatment of the man, and he's out of his mind with rage."

Drake said, "But he hasn't fired you yet, Bentham. And if he hasn't, maybe he won't."

"No, because he still has hopes. I told him that Fairfield was probably bluffing and was probably psychotic, but he's not listening to me these last few days.

"In fact, I may soon be sliding along the street with Southby's boot-marks clearly imprinted on my rear end. This is all the more certain since he must realize that none of this would have happened if he had not played silly haggling games over pin money. He would certainly have had the man under contract otherwise. Firing me will be the evidence he needs for all the world, and most of all for himself, to see that I was to blame and not he."

Halsted said, "But it would be difficult for you to work for Southby after this anyway, wouldn't it? You'd be better off somewhere else."

Bentham said, "Unquestionably—but in my own time and at my own resignation. After all, the editorial field is not exactly wide open now, and I might have difficulty finding a new position, and with an as-yet thin reserve of savings, that prospect does not fill me with delight. Southby might well try to see to it that my chances were even less than normal."

Rubin said, "You mean, he would try to blacklist you? I wouldn't put it past him."

Bentham's gloom showed him to be in full agreement. He said, "Still, what's worst is that with my editing we would have had a good book there. It would be something we could be proud of. Southby and Fairfield could make a fortune and I could make a reputation that would move me on to a much better position elsewhere. And the world would have a whacking good first novel with the promise of better things to come.

"Fairfield has the makings of a great novelist, blast his soul, and I have my editorial pride and wanted to be part of that greatness. And I was *not* sarcastic and he *did* give in. He *did* say he'd deliver it the next day. Why in the devil's name didn't he? That's what bothers me. Why didn't he?"

There was a rather dank pause. Avalon finally said, "There may be an explanation for this. There have been first-class men of genius who have been monsters of villainy in their private lives. Richard Wagner was one; Jean-Jacques Rousseau was another. If this man, Fairfield, is bluffing, and I rather guess he is, too, then he may simply have judged Southby to be a kindred soul and he feels that you will be fired. It's what he would do in Southby's place. Then, when you are gone, he will show up with the manuscript."

"But why?" said Bentham.

"No puzzle there, I think," said Avalon. "In the first place, you dared tamper with his manuscript and he feels you must be punished. In the second, once you are gone he can be reasonably certain that Southby, after all this, will publish his manuscript as written."

"Then why did he say he would deliver it the next day?"

Avalon bent his formidable eyebrows together for a moment and said, "I suppose he felt you would tell Southby, ebulliently, that the thing was in the bag—as you did—and that Southby's anger, sharply intensified by falsely raised hopes, would explode and make certain your rapid firing."

"And all that stuff about my sarcasm would then just be designed to further infuriate Southby?"

"I should think so. Yes."

Bentham thought about it. "That's a pretty dismal picture you've painted. Between Fairfield and Southby there's no escape."

Avalon looked uneasy. "I'm sorry, Mr. Bentham, but that's the way it looks to me."

Bentham said, "I can't believe it, though. I spoke to the man for an hour or more on the phone. He did not *sound* vindictive. Stubborn and nasty, yes, but not personally vindictive."

Avalon said, "I hate to be the insistent advocate of a solution personally abhorrent to me, but surely you were not looking for vindictiveness and would not be expected to see it if it were not absolutely in plain view."

Bentham said desperately, "But there's more. I have read his book and you have not. I believe no one, however skillful, can write a book alien to his own philosophy and . . ."

"That's nonsense," said Rubin. "I can write a piece of fiction hewing to any philosophy you please. I could write one from the Nazi point of view if I were of a mind to, which I'm not."

"You couldn't," said Bentham. "Please don't interpret that as a challenge, but you couldn't. In Fairfield's book there were a variety of motivations, but none was out of the kind of motiveless malignity some people attribute to Iago. There was no unreasoning anger arising over trivial causes."

"But that's the very point," said Avalon. "It seems a trivial cause to you but you don't see through this man's eyes. Changing his novel in even a minor way is to him unforgivable and he'll hound you down over it."

Trumbull said in a troubled voice, "I hate to join in this gallows fiesta, Mr. Bentham, but Geoff sounds as though he might be right."

"Ah," said Rubin suddenly, "but I don't think he is."

Bentham turned in his direction eagerly. "You mean you don't think Fairfield is out to get me?"

Rubin said, "No. He's mad at you, surely, but not to the point of wanting to cut his own throat. What we've got to do is look at this thing carefully with writer psychology in mind. No, Mr. Bentham, I don't mean trying to see a writer's personality in his writing, which I still say can't be done for any really good writer. I mean something that holds for *any* beginning writer.

"I grant that a beginner might feel psychotic enough to fly into a fury at any changes imposed on his golden prose, but even that pales into nothing compared to another need—that of getting into print.

"Remember, this guy was haggling with Southby over a few thousand dollars in advance money, and what was that to him? We sneer at Southby for sticking at a small sum when millions might be in view. Isn't it queerer that the author should do so and risk not only millions, but publication altogether? Is it conceivable that a beginner who must have worked on his book for years would even dream of chancing failure to publish by haggling over the advance?"

Avalon said, "If he were the semipsychotic individual whom Mr. Bentham has described, why not?"

Rubin said, "Isn't it much more likely that he *already* had another publisher on the string, and that he tried Southby only because of the firm's reputation for turning out best sellers? His quarrel over the advance was his effort to make the two firms bid against each other in an auction they didn't know was taking place. Then, when Bentham tried to make changes, he turned back to the other publisher, who perhaps was willing to make fewer changes, or even none."

Bentham said, "Do you mean, Mr. Rubin, that Fairfield originally went to some publisher—call him X? X read the manuscript, suggested a revision, and Fairfield took it back, presumably to revise, but brought it to us instead. When we offered a lower advance and suggested greater revision, he took it back to X?"

"Yes, and you marked up his copy," said Rubin. "I think that annoyed him more than the revision itself had. It meant he had to have the copy retyped *in toto* before submitting it. Even erasing the pencil marks would leave some marks, and he might be a little shy of letting X know he was playing tricks with the manuscript.

"After all, you got him on the phone three days after he had stormed out and he already had another publisher on the hook. After three *days*?"

Bentham said, "That's why I assumed he was bluffing."

"And risk publication? No, Publisher X exists, all right."

Trumbull said, "I must be going crazy, but I've switched sides. You've convinced me, Manny."

Bentham said, "Even if you're right, Mr. Rubin, I'm still in a hopeless position."

"Not if you can prove this Fairfield was playing games. Once Southby sees that, he'll be furious with the author, not with you. Then you can bide your time and resign at such time as suits yourself."

Bentham said, "But for that I would have to know who Publisher X is, and I don't. And without that, he simply won't believe the story. Why should he?"

Rubin said, "Are you sure Fairfield didn't mention the publisher?"

"I'm sure."

Halsted said, with a mild stutter, "How would you know? You've only been in the country a few months and may not know all the publishers."

"There are hundreds in New York and surrounding areas and I certainly don't know them all," said Bentham. "I know the larger ones, though. Surely X would be among the larger ones."

Rubin said, "I should think so. No hint at all?"

"If there was, it whizzed by me."

Rubin said, "Think. Go over the conversation in your mind."

Bentham closed his eyes and sat quietly. No one else made a noise except Drake, whose bolo-tie tip clinked against his water glass when he reached forward to stub out a cigarette.

Bentham opened his eyes and said, "It's no use. There's nothing there."

Drake looked leftward toward the sideboard where Henry was standing. "This is a serious situation, Henry. Do you have any suggestions?"

"Only the publisher's name, sir."

Bentham looked around in astonishment, "What?"

Trumbull said hastily, "Henry is one of us, Mr. Bentham. What are you talking about, Henry? How can you know?"

"I believe the author, Mr. Fairfield, mentioned it in his phone conversation with Mr. Bentham."

Bentham said, on the edge of anger, "He did *not!*"

Henry's unlined face showed no emotion. "I beg your pardon, sir, I do not mean to offend you, but you inadvertently omitted an important part of the story. It was rather like Mr. Trumbull's misadventure in the cab when he left out an important part of the direction. Or like Dr. Drake's point that those who argue about recombinant DNA do so without adequate knowledge of the fundamentals."

Gonzalo said, "You mean we're looking in a dark room for a black cat that *is* there?"

"Yes, sir. If Mr. Bentham had told his story otherwise, the whereabouts of the black cat would be obvious."

"In what way could I have told the story otherwise?" demanded Bentham.

"You told the story with indirect quotations throughout, sir, and thus we never got the exact words anyone used."

"For a very good reason," said Bentham. "I don't remember the exact words. I'm not a recording device."

"Yet sometimes in indirect quotation, a person is reported as saying something he could not possibly have said in direct quotation."

"I assure you," said Bentham coldly, "my account was accurate."

"I'm sure it is, within its limitations, sir. But if there is a Publisher X, why did Mr. Fairfield promise to deliver the manuscript the next day?"

Bentham said, "Oh God, I forgot about that. Are we back to motiveless malignity?"

"No, sir. I would suggest he didn't say that."

"Yes, he did, Henry," said Bentham. "I'm unshakable in that."

"Do you wish to put his remark into direct quotations and maintain that he said, 'I will deliver the manuscript the next day'?"

Bentham said, "Oh, I take your meaning. 'The next day' *is* a paraphrase, of course. He said, 'I will deliver the manuscript tomorrow.' What's the difference?"

Henry said, "And then you agreed enthusiastically, urged him to do so at once, and offered to place a messenger at his service. You don't think that sounded like sarcasm, sir?"

"*No.* He said, 'I will deliver the manuscript tomorrow' and I was enthusiastic. Where's the sarcasm?"

"To Morrow," said Henry carefully, pronouncing it as two words.

"Good God," said Bentham blankly.

Rubin brought his fist down on the table, "Damn! William Morrow & Company," he said, "one of New York's larger publishing houses."

"Yes, sir," said Henry. "I looked it up in the telephone book, to make certain, immediately after Mr. Bentham's account of the phone conversation. It is at 105 Madison Avenue, about a mile from here."

Gonzalo said, "There you are, Mr. Bentham. Just tell your boss that it's with William Morrow & Company and that the author had it in to them first."

"And he can then fire me for stupidity. Which I deserve."

"Not a chance," said Gonzalo. "Don't tell him the literal truth. Tell him that as a result of your own clever detective work you uncovered the facts of the case through a confidential source you cannot reveal."

Henry said, "After all, sir, confidentiality is the policy of the Black Widowers."

"The Next Day"—Afterword

I had a mild coronary on May 18, 1977, and you'd think the world was coming to an end the way Janet carried on. In July of that year, for instance, I wrote "The Next Day," and just because we were having a heat wave with temperatures in excess of a hundred degrees, Janet wouldn't let me leave our air-conditioned apartment to take it down to the *EQMM* offices. I had to mail it in.

This was a horrible blow because whenever I submit a story to *EQMM*, I always spend some time chaffing with the beautiful Eleanor Sullivan, managing editor of the magazine. (By chaffing, of course, I mean chasing her around and around the desk—and Janet thought that wouldn't be good for my heart, either.)

Fortunately, Eleanor bore up under the horror of being deprived of my company and sent on the story to Fred anyway. He took it and it appeared in the May 1978 *EQMM*.

I sometimes wonder on how small an ambiguity it is possible to hang a Black Widower plot. This story may represent the record.

7.

Irrelevance!

"I think," said Mario Gonzalo, "that I know Henry's secret; how he gets the answer when we don't." Gonzalo nodded in the direction of the waiter, who was quietly serving the drinks that were prelude to the monthly banquet of the Black Widowers.

James Drake stubbed out his cigarette and said, "I've known it all along. He's smarter than we are."

"Sure," said Gonzalo, flicking tobacco ash from the sleeve of his velvet jacket and helping himself to some Brie on a cracker, "but being smarter isn't enough."

"Being dumber isn't enough, either," broke in Emmanuel Rubin, glowering through his thick-lensed glasses, "so what good will the secret do you, Mario?"

"Being really dumb," said Gonzalo coolly, "is to be afraid to listen for fear of learning something. So I suppose you're not interested, Manny."

"What, and miss a good laugh?" said Rubin. "Go ahead, Mario."

Geoffrey Avalon, having accepted his drink from Henry, approached and said, "A good laugh about what?"

"About Mario's idea as to how Henry manages to come up

with solutions," said Rubin. "Henry, you can listen, too. Mario has your secret."

Henry smiled discreetly. "I have made no secret of what I do. The gentlemen of the Black Widowers analyze the problems carefully, remove all the useless adornments, and leave a plain picture for me to describe."

"Not at all," said Gonzalo, "not at all. You just say that to throw us off. The secret is—irrelevance!"

There was a short pause. Then Rubin's scanty beard bristled and he said in high-pitched disbelief, "Is *that* what I'm supposed to listen to so that I can learn something?"

"Sure," said Gonzalo. "We're all of us reasoning men—even you, sometimes, Manny—and we try to solve any little puzzle presented to us by catching at all the relevant angles. But if it were the relevant matters that mattered, so to speak, there'd be no puzzle. Anyone would then see the answer. It's Henry's trick of seeing the irrelevant that gives him the answer."

Drake said, "This is a contradiction in terms, Mario. Something that is irrelevant has nothing to do . . ."

Gonzalo interposed patiently, "Something that *seems* irrelevant but isn't. We see that it seems irrelevant; Henry sees that it really isn't irrelevant. Right, Henry?"

Henry's face showed no expression beyond a general benevolence. "It is certainly an interesting suggestion," he said.

Avalon drew his formidable eyebrows together. "It is surely more than that, Mario. Henry sees what we do not, because he looks clearly at life while the rest of us do not have his direct and simple honesty and are not capable of doing so. Even if you were to see what Henry does, you would not get the answer."

Gonzalo said, "I bet I can. Five dollars says that if there's a puzzle today, I'll use Henry's technique and get the answer before he does."

"You're on," said Rubin at once.

"Good," said Mario. "Geoff, you hold the stakes. But remember, no bet if there's no problem."

Drake said, "Oh there'll be a problem. Personally, I think we're each of us deliberately choosing our guests for their problematical content."

"And yet perhaps not this time," said Avalon, "since the

guest has not arrived—nor tonight's host, either, unless the steps on the stairs . . . No, it's Tom."

Thomas Trumbull's white and crisply waved hair made its appearance, followed by the rest of his body as he mounted the stairs.

He said, "If you're worried about the host's whereabouts, Geoff, Roger Halsted's just arrived downstairs with a stranger who, I presume, is our guest for tonight. I raced ahead since I am a dying man who needs a dr— Ah thank you, Henry."

Gonzalo had taken his seat next to Halsted and, spreading out his napkin with a practiced flick, said, "We almost thought we would have to start without a host or a guest, Roger. What happened? Decided you couldn't stand the expense?"

Halsted reddened and his mild stutter seemed a shade more pronounced. "Not my fault, really. Burry was delayed; Dan Burry, my guest. His phone rang just as I was picking him up and he grew very upset. I couldn't very well press him too hard and urge him to hang up. For a while, in fact, I thought I'd have to leave without him."

"What was it about, do you know? The phone call, I mean."

Halsted looked in the direction of his guest. "I don't know. Something involving one of his students. He's a school principal, you know."

"Your school?"

"No, but why don't you save your questions for the grilling?"

"Do you mind letting me start it?"

"Not at all," and Halsted turned his attention to the crabmeat soup.

Dan Burry was a rather large man with dark hair as crisply waved as Trumbull's and with a brief mustache of the kind Adolf Hitler had put out of fashion for at least a generation. His jowled face bore a worried look and he tackled his roast duck with an enthusiasm dulled by absence of mind.

He did not participate in the general conversation and seemed to listen only distantly as Rubin and Drake debated the respective values of nuclear fusion and solar power as the ultimate energy source.

Burry seemed unprepared, therefore, for the suddenness with which the focus of attention suddenly shifted. While Henry freshened the coffee and produced brandy, Gonzalo said, "Mr. Burry, how do you justify your existence?"

Burry looked at Gonzalo with what seemed a momentary flash of indignation but then muttered in a depressed sort of way, "Ah yes, Roger warned me that there would be a question-and-answer period."

"Yes," said Gonzalo, "and in return for the dinner, you are expected to answer frankly and fully, under terms of strict confidentiality, of course. So how do you justify your existence?"

Burry said, "I try to maintain an atmosphere and organization at a city high school such that at least some of the student body can gain an education and a respect for learning. That is justification enough, I think, whenever I succeed."

"Do you succeed often?"

"Not often."

Avalon cleared his throat. "The education of the young of any species begins with discipline."

"Those who believe so," said Burry, "all too frequently believe it ends with discipline, too, and confuse the purpose of a school with the purpose of a prison."

Gonzalo said, "I understand that just as you were leaving for dinner tonight, you received an unsettling phone call. Did that involve school business?"

Burry cast a hard glance in Halsted's direction. Halsted reddened and said, "I was explaining why we were late, Dan."

Gonzalo said, "What was the phone call about?"

Burry shook his head. "It is not something I should discuss. It is an unfortunate matter that involves a minor."

"A minor what?"

"I'm using the word as a noun, Mr. Gonzalo, not as an adjective. It involves a human being who is only seventeen."

Gonzalo said, "We understand your reluctance to discuss the matter, but I assure you, the fact that a minor is involved is irrelevant." He paused and seemed to savor the word for a moment. "The terms of the dinner are that you answer our questions. Roger should have explained that to you."

"May I stress again," interrupted Avalon, "the confidentiality of our proceedings."

"Including the waiter," said Trumbull, scowling, "who is a valued member of this organization."

Burry glanced briefly at Henry, who had now taken up his post at the sideboard with his usual look of quiet attention, and said, "I won't deny, gentlemen, that I'd welcome a discussion of the matter, for I have been very frustrated over it. Still, I cannot use the name of the young man. Will it suit the rules of your organization if I refer to him only as John?"

Rubin said, "It's our experience, Mr. Burry, that that kind of subterfuge always fails. You'll slip and use his real name."

"John is his real name, Mr. Rubin, and is as nearly anonymous as a given name can be. I will merely refrain from using his full name."

Halsted said, "I think we can allow that."

Burry said, "Let me tell you about John first. He's a good-looking young man, a bit undersized but keen, quick, and intelligent. His intelligence attracted the attention of his teachers at once and I, of course, am always on the lookout for such things. All students are, in theory, of equal importance and all deserve the best education we can give them, but the unusually bright ones are, of course, our special delight and, too often, our special heartbreak."

"Why heartbreak?" asked Gonzalo quickly.

"Because very often a bright child is as much the victim of his social handcuffs as he would be if he had not a brain in his head. It's a mistake to think that intelligence alone can lift you out of the mud, and there is no use in citing examples to the contrary. It may happen, given special circumstances; in most cases, it does not happen."

"I presume," said Rubin sardonically, "John is a child of the ghetto—as was my father in his time."

Burry said in a deliberate and even tone, "John is a child of the ghetto, but not as your father was, Mr. Rubin. Your father and you can, if you are circumspect, hide your origin. You may change your name, be careful with your speech, abandon your idiosyncrasies, and you might pass. It would take a special law to pin an identifying badge on you. John and others like him, however, are born with the identifying badge, and long before you can know them as individuals you recognize them as blacks."

Rubin looked uncomfortable. "I meant no offense."

"None taken. Some blacks do need identification, I might say. By the convention of our society a single black ancestor makes one black. A man might therefore be apparently white but socially black. As myself. I am black."

"That makes no difference to us, sir," said Avalon austerely.

"Why should it?" said Burry. "Nor does it seem to make a difference to some of the students. One prominent nonobscene graffito in the fourthfloor toilet reads, 'Burry is five fourths white.' Just the same, my one ancestor does make a difference in my attitude toward John.

"I'm desperate to give a youngster like that the kind of chance he might have if he looked like me. In the gathering crisis of our times, the human species cannot afford to waste brains, and this one may be wasted."

"Drugs?" asked Trumbull.

Burry shrugged. "Pot, of course. That's a rite of passage with kids these days—like smoking a pipe was to Tom Sawyer, or to Mark Twain, for that matter. And then for all the talk about the damage done by marijuana, the evidence is not as strong as for the damage done by tobacco, yet not only is tobacco smoking legal and socially acceptable, but also the government subsidizes the tobacco growers."

"You start with pot and you go on to heroin," said Avalon dryly. "Another rite of passage."

"Sometimes—especially if you make both equally illegal, so that the pot smoker fails to see much difference—but only sometimes. One can go from social drinking to alcoholism, a condition as dangerous as heroin and far more common, yet society does not for that reason condemn or outlaw social drinking.

"In any case," Burry went on, "John is not deeply involved in pot and does not have the makings of a heroin addict. No, I'm afraid John's temptations lie in another direction—crime."

Avalon said, "What kind of crime, Mr. Burry?"

"Nothing exceedingly dramatic. I suspected him of being a purse snatcher, a shoplifter, a petty thief. It was only a suspicion, until tonight. Now, I'm afraid, it's a certainty."

"Is that what the phone call was about?" asked Gonzalo.

"It was about John," said Burry despondently. "It was, indeed, from him. He was in trouble and he turned to me. There is some small satisfaction in that. I managed to obtain a lawyer for him and I promised to supply reasonable bail, if necessary. It was that which delayed our arrival. And yet I can take only minimal satisfaction from being of help now. I suspect I failed him to begin with."

"In what way?" asked Gonzalo.

"If I had been more ingenious, I might have persuaded him to cooperate with the police."

"Not much chance of that, Dan," said Halsted. "Anyone who's a schoolteacher knows that in the bright lexicon of youth, there is no such word as 'squeal.' The guys who keep their mouths shut go to jail, but they are heroes and are taken care of. The squealers may stay out of jail but they're ostracized and very likely beaten up."

"I know that, Roger," said Burry, "I need no education in the mores of the street, but I might have done it if I were smart enough. I'll see him tonight after this meal—if you won't mind my leaving by ten-thirty at the latest—and if he'll co-operate, I'll get him out of the city. There are agencies who will help in this respect and I've used them before. These people we're after won't mount an intercity hunt for him. It isn't the Syndicate we're talking about."

Avalon twiddled his empty brandy glass and said, "What *are* we talking about, Mr. Burry?"

"A burglary ring organized by medium-sized racketeers who employ high-school students as their field operatives. The kids bring in their takings and receive a percentage. It saves them the trouble of trying to peddle the goods themselves—but if they hold out for their own profit, and are caught at it, they are beaten up."

Trumbull said, "It sounds very much like a Fagin operation."

"It's *exactly* a Fagin operation," said Burry. "You don't suppose the practice died out with Oliver Twist, do you?"

"And you're after Fagin himself, I take it," said Trumbull.

Burry said, "It certainly does no good to pick up the kids. They're eventually let go and the game goes on. Even if they were not let go, replacements are easily obtained, and the game still goes on. You've got to get the corrupters themselves. And beyond that," he added sadly, "the quirks in our society that make such things possible."

"If you can cure those quirks," said Avalon, "you will have achieved a first for our ten thousand years of so-called civilization."

"Then at least the corrupters," said Burry. "If I were smart enough to see my way into persuading John to go in with me . . ."

Gonzalo interrupted. "That's twice now you've said you needed to be smart enough. Why smart enough? Persuasive enough, I can see; eloquent enough; unscrupulous enough; threatening enough. Why smart enough?"

Burry hesitated and rubbed his chin, as though wondering what to say. He decided, apparently, and said, "The police have been after the burglary ring and, among others, they have consulted me. They had reason to think that some of the students at my school were involved and they wanted me to co-operate with them in finding the students. To be truthful, I wasn't anxious to do this."

"To squeal?" asked Drake, stony-faced.

For a moment, Burry stiffened with quite apparent indignation. Then he relaxed. "You're right. I don't want to squeal, but that's just a gut reaction. There's more to it than that. As I told you, picking up the youngsters does not solve the problem, but it may manufacture hardened criminals. Were I to find some youngster I suspected of being involved, what I would hope to do would be to obtain the necessary information from him and turn over the information, not the youngster, to the police."

Avalon said, "I don't think you would get the necessary information by kindly persuasion, Mr. Burry. The police might have better arguments than you have."

Trumbull slapped the table with the palm of his hand. "Geoff, that's stupid. Those kids are heroes to their peers if they resist the police, and if any police officer tried to beat anything out of them, not only is any information he gets inadmissible as evidence, but also the policeman involved will be up on charges."

"I call that hobbling the police to the cost of the honest citizen," said Avalon.

"I call it forcing the police to a single standard of conduct and having them treat the poor, the ill-educated, the unpopular as circumspectly as they would treat those with money and lawyers," said Trumbull.

"Why not enforce the single standard by treating the well-to-do criminal as roughly as the poor ones, then?" demanded Avalon.

Trumbull said, "Because they're only *suspected* criminals. The state of actual criminality comes only after trial and judgment, and until then the person in custody has all the rights and privileges of a free American, including decent treatment at the hands of the guardians of the very law that says so. Mr. Burry, I think your attitude is a good one."

Burry said, "Thank you, but good or not, it didn't work. What the police need is evidence. They have suspicions as to the identity of the ringleaders, the Fagins, but until they can find them in action, surrounded by their stolen goods, they aren't likely to be able to prove it. One of the difficulties appears to be that the criminals change their base of operation frequently, and are never in one place long enough to leave a clear trail. Of course, if we knew in advance where they would be, we would have a chance. And that is the kind of information the youngsters would have, for they have to know where to bring the loot.

"Without that—well, the poorer sections of New York are an incredible rabbit-warren that could swallow up an army of police searchers who would encounter frozen-faced inhabitants denying all knowledge of anything. From the pattern of the robberies, the police suspect the scene of operations must be on Manhattan's West Side somewhere between Eightieth Street and 125th Street, but that's not much of a hint. But I had my eye on John."

"Why him?" asked Drake.

"Money," snapped Burry. "It comes to that. We live in a society that measures all values by money, and that delivers unending pressures by advertising in every medium urging the possession of material things that can be had only for money. Sex standards are set by the beautiful people, and those can be met only with money. Well, then, if you don't have money, what do you do? Devote your life to gaining those skills that will make money in the end. What if you firmly believe that the disadvantages you were born with will make it impossible for you to make money even if you gain those skills? You give up, perhaps, and get the money by the shortest route—and another youngster is lost both to himself and to society."

Drake said, "Yes, but this is true for many of the students at the school, I'm sure. Why John?"

"Of course, it's true of many. That's why the youngsters are so easily recruited. But I have been interested in John, so my eye has been on him, and in recent months he has shown money."

"In what way?" asked Rubin, who had been absently doodling dollar signs on his napkin.

"Better clothes, for one thing; an air of self-confidence, for another. Something amounting almost to arrogance in his attitude toward girls. There's no point in having money if you don't show it, and I know the signs. I had no proof, of course, no real evidence, and I didn't want to confront John with my suspicions if, by any chance, I happened to be wrong.

"Then last Monday, I passed him in the hall, quite by accident, and he had a piece of paper in his hand. It seemed to me it had been passed to him. I had not been looking in his direction; it had been an impression out of the corner of my eye. I certainly didn't see who had done the passing, for it was between periods and the halls were quite crowded. It's good to be in the halls at unpredictable intervals at such times, by the way. The possible presence of authority does impose some sense of discipline at such times, however minimal." Burry sighed, and smiled rather weakly.

Gonzalo said, "But what about the paper?"

"I had no reason to think the paper had anything to do with the robberies, but it seemed unusual, and I have learned to respond at once to anything unusual. 'What's that paper you're holding, John?' I asked in what I hoped was a friendly tone.

" 'The paper, Mr. Burry?' he asked, and my suspicions were aroused at once. To repeat a question is almost invariably a play for time. So I asked to see it; I held out my hand for it. By now, the main flood of students had passed, though some turned for a quick look backward."

Trumbull said, "Could you force him to hand over the paper? He has a right to his personal property, hasn't he?"

Burry said, "I would not have used force, naturally, but within the school my powers to enforce discipline are, in theory, considerable. I might have suspended him from his classes for failure to comply, and that would have been an unhappy position for John. He enjoyed his classes. In any case, he complied.

"He hesitated, said, 'It's just a piece of paper I picked up, Mr. Burry,' glanced at it carelessly, and handed it over, saying with an air of mocking virtue, 'I was going to put it in a wastebasket, Mr. Burry. You wouldn't want the halls all littered.'

"I resisted the temptation to point out that one more piece of paper would have made no difference in the extent of litter and said, 'I am pleased at your thoughtfulness. I'll see to it that this is thrown away,' and put it in my pocket without looking at it. I then asked him how he was doing with his schoolwork and he answered easily enough. He seemed in no way perturbed at my having the paper in my possession.

"I waited till I was back in my office before I looked at it, and I must say I was disappointed. It was a typewritten sheet, Xeroxed, not very professionally done, and it urged students to demand decent educational facilities, a message I wholeheartedly agreed with.

"But there was nothing conspiratorial about it—or at least I could see nothing as conspiratorial. I didn't trust my own judgment in the matter, so I called the detective lieutenant who had approached me on the matter of the burglary ring. He visited me after hours; in plainclothes, of course; and I showed him the letter without telling him the name of the youngster from whom I had obtained it."

Trumbull said, "Surely, he asked the name?"

Burry said, "I told the story in such a way that no one youngster of whatever name was implicated."

Trumbull who, as a cryptographer by profession, might have been particularly interested, said, "By withholding information, you may have deprived the lieutenant of crucial clues in the understanding of the message."

"He didn't think so," said Burry. "He laughed, and told me it was nonsense. I think he would have torn it up if I hadn't rescued it—perhaps out of disappointment, for when I called him, I may have given him the impression I had something. I've kept studying it myself the past few days. Heaven help me, I even tried warming it over a hot plate in case invisible ink showed up.

"Now it is too late. Young John was arrested in what must have been the central clearing place; taken in clear guilt, with identifiable stolen goods in his possession. John called me from the police station; that was the phone call. And I've spoken to my detective friend. And if I had been clever enough to understand the letter, I might have stopped John."

Avalon said, "*If* the letter had significance. Not every piece of innocent literature conceals a guilty secret."

"This one does, though," said Rubin, his eyes flashing, his voice strident. "Let me ask you a few questions, Mr. Burry. You say *John* was taken. You mentioned no one else, not even by inference. Was he alone?"

"It's my understanding he was."

"And had John been holding the paper for some indefinite period when you first became aware of it, or had he just received it?"

"I can't answer that question definitely, Mr. Rubin," said Burry, "but it was my impression that it had been passed to him even as I watched. I wish I had seen who it was who passed it, but I didn't."

Rubin said triumphantly, "Then the passer was there and watched you ask John to hand over the paper and watched him do so. The passer turned that information to the higher-ups of the burglary ring, and they had to take into account the possibility that John might talk. If the letter gave some sort of information that told John where to take the stolen goods, that information was quickly changed. John, being no longer trustworthy, would not be told of the change and he would walk in alone to the meeting place that was no longer to be a meeting place and was taken."

Trumbull said, "Wait. Hold on. How had the police known about the meeting place, old or new?"

Burry studied his fingers and said, "According to my detective friend, to whom I also talked before coming here, John had been under quiet surveillance for some time. Through nothing *I* said," he added hurriedly. "He had been identified at the scene of a burglary—not with certainty, you understand, but they were keeping an eye on him. I hadn't known that."

Trumbull said, "Then if you hadn't taken that paper and roused suspicion—assuming Manny Rubin's notion is correct—John would have led the police to an active clearinghouse, and right to some of the controlling figures."

Burry nodded. "The thought had occurred to me."

Gonzalo said hotly, "How the devil could Mr. Burry know this, Tom?"

"I'm returning to an earlier point," said Trumbull. "Our guest showed the letter to the detective and it was ignored. He did *not* mention the name of the young man involved and I said that might be vital evidence. I was right. If the detective had known it was taken from a young man who was under surveillance, he would have treated it much more seriously."

"You're right," said Burry. "I'll have to tell them now."

"Wait," said Gonzalo. "I have a better idea. Why not tell them what the letter means? If you could be of help to them, they might be willing to go a bit easier on John if you asked them to."

"John," rumbled Avalon, "may think he's been double-crossed already. He may think the burglary ring deliberately let him walk into a trap to pay him back for handing over the piece of paper. He may be willing to cooperate now."

"The catch is," said Burry, "that I don't know what the letter means, so I can't use it to win either consideration from the police or co-operation from John."

Gonzalo said eagerly, "Do you remember what the letter said, Mr. Burry? Can you repeat it?"

"I don't have to," said Burry. "I have it with me. I've been carrying it in my pocket since I got it—and taking it out to stare at it now and then, for all the good it did me."

He took it out. It was tightly creased and dog-eared. He unfolded it, flattened it out, and passed it to Gonzalo. It made its way about the table and after it reached Drake, that gentleman passed it on to Henry, even as Burry's hand had reached out to take it. Henry glanced at it quickly and then returned it to Burry.

The typewriting did not have a professional touch, nor did the Xeroxing. It had an all-capital headline:

PROTEST NATIONAL DISCRIMINATION AGAINST NEW YORK.

Underneath, it said, "Join the march on City Hall on October 20. Demand that Congress recognize the rights of the poor to a quality education. There is no disgrace in being a New Yorker. We are Americans, every bit as much Americans as the people of Tar Heel, North Carolina, and we want our rights as Americans. No more, but certainly no less."

"Is that all?" said Avalon in astonishment.

"That's all," said Burry.

"What a remarkably stupid message," said Avalon. "Why march on City Hall? City Hall is helpless. What's more, no one is ever going to get much sympathy from small-town America by making fun of them. Tar Heel, North Carolina! I admit that 'tarheeler' is a nickname for a North Carolinian because of the early production of rosin and tar from pine trees in that state, but that kind of name only sounds well when used by those who are so named. To make up a name like Tar Heel, North Carolina, is a deliberate insult. It would be like having a Southerner refer to the town of Damyankee, Massachusetts. What do they hope to gain?"

"Nothing," said Rubin, smiling, "because it's not a call to action. I'll bet there isn't any march scheduled for October 20, is there, Mr. Burry?"

"I don't know," said Burry. "I haven't heard of one."

"Then it's a message, all right," said Rubin.

Burry said, "Where? I tried looking at initial letters, final letters, every other word, ever third word. I can't find anything."

Mario Gonzalo shook his head slowly and with a moderately insufferable air of superiority. "It couldn't possibly be any of those things, Mr. Burry. I could have told you that before I ever saw the letter."

There was a moment's complete silence and every other Black Widower turned to stare at Gonzalo. "Good God," said Drake, blinking through cigarette smoke, "he sounds like Sherlock Holmes."

Gonzalo said, "If you don't mind, there's five dollars riding on this, so just listen." He put aside the free-flowing caricature of Burry that he had drawn in the course of the discussion and said, "John got the mesasage as Mr. Burry was watching, and he handed it over promptly. But he looked at it first, isn't that right, Mr. Burry? Just a glance?"

Burry hesitated and said, "Yes, just a quick look."

"Exactly! If it was a message, he had to see what it was before he handed it over, and if a quick look was enough, then he had no time to match up first letters or last letters or skip words. And if we take just a glance at the letter we'll see what he saw."

Rubin said with elaborate politeness, "And would you kindly tell us what *you* see?"

Gonzalo said, "I told you what to look for at the start of the evening. Look for the irrelevancy. Tar Heel, North Carolina, is irrelevant. They could have made up the name of any other town—Jet Air, Utah, or Lollipop, South Dakota. Why insist on Tar Heel? Because it's the key. John took one quick look at the letter to see the name of the town, and once he had it, that was all he needed, and he could give the paper away."

Avalon said thoughtfully, "Well, you know, there's something to that."

"Nothing much," said Rubin, "unless Mario can tell us what Tar Heel, North Carolina, means."

"It could be an anagram."

"Like what?"

Gonzalo said, "I've been working on one: 'Al, the not real corn hair.' "

There was a sticky silence, and then Trumbull brought his fist down on the table. "Damn it, Mario, what does that mean?"

"I don't know. There could be other anagrams. Or it could be a cryptogram. Or there could be a book somewhere that has a list of words equivalents. Maybe it means, 'Cheese it, the cops.' I don't know. But it means something."

Rubin said, "That's a big help, telling us it means something."

Gonzalo said, in an aggrieved tone, "Then let's do some thinking. It won't hurt if we spend a few minutes trying to anagram it, or something, and maybe work out what it means."

The minutes passed in a dead silence and finally Burry looked at his watch and sighed. He said, "I really must get down to the police station. I suppose the letter is really meaningless."

"Well, now, Dan," said Halsted, stroking his hair back from his receding hairline, "we can't really say that till we've asked Henry."

"The waiter?"

"Why, yes. He has an uncommon knack for seeing the obvious. Except that I don't see *him*. Henry!"

Henry's head appeared as he climbed the stairs with a rapidity quite different from his usual gentle flow. "I beg your pardon, Mr. Halsted," he said, "I did not intend to be gone long. May I ask Mr. Burry a question?"

Burry had risen and was clearly on his way to the cloakroom. He said, "Well, yes, but nothing too complicated, I hope."

"Unless you said something about it during the brief interval in which I was absent, sir, I believe you did not mention the actual place—the address—at which the student was apprehended."

"No, I did not."

"Do you know the place?"

Burry sucked his lower lip inward and bit at it thoughtfully, "It was mentioned. Yes. But don't think I remember it."

Henry said, "Was it, by any chance, 283 West 92nd Street?"

Burry stared at Henry for a moment, then sat down. "Yes, it was, now that you mention it. That was precisely the address. How did you know?"

"It's in the letter, sir."

"Where?" said Avalon. "Show us where."

Henry said, "Mr. Gonzalo's reasoning seemed to me perfectly correct in every detail when he pointed out the irrelevance and, therefore, the importance of the town of Tar Heel, North Carolina. There seemed to be a general impression that it was a manufactured name, but it occurred to me that it might be a real one. There are very many peculiar names among the small towns of the United States; Tar Heel would be sedate and conservative compared to some. And if it were real, it would have unmistakable significance, so I went down to look it up."

Avalon said, "You mean there *is* a Tar Heel, North Carolina?"

"There is, Mr. Avalon."

"And it's listed in the gazetteer?"

"It may be, but I tried another source. The all-inclusive recording of all the inhabited places in the United States large enough to include a post office is in a Zip Code directory, and we have one downstairs. Tar Heel, North Carolina, *is* included, and, of course, so is its Zip Code. The directory is the book that Mr. Gonzalo referred to when he spoke of a list of word equivalents."

"I was thinking of phrases," said Gonzalo.

"It is numbers, but that's a mere detail. The number equivalent is, of course, unique. Tar Heel has a Zip Code of 28392 and no other, and if the clearinghouse is on the Upper West Side, 283 West 92nd Street would seem the likely interpretation. Undoubtedly, there are ways of coding for the East Side or the West Side, or if not all the numbers are used, as in 2 West 92nd Street, or if a named street such as Amsterdam Avenue is used. Still, the prevalence of numbered streets and avenues in Manhattan make a Zip Code code, if I may use the phrase, particularly useful."

Burry said blankly, "How could I miss that?"

Drake grunted. "We always ask ourselves that after Henry sees whatever there is to see."

Burry said, "If I show this to the police, they'll see that the correspondence between the Zip Code and the address *can't* be a coincidence. And if they know that much, then they may learn more."

"If they concentrate on the letter," said Rubin, "they might learn something about the typewriter, the Xeroxing, and so on. And if you confront John with what you know and indicate that the gang will assume the information came from him, he might be willing to tell more. He can be in no worse trouble with them and he might improve his standing with the police."

Burry had his coat and hat on. "Thank you, all of you. Thank you, Henry." He whirled out.

Avalon said, "Happy ending."

"Not for everyone," said Henry.

"What do you mean?"

Henry said, "Mr. Gonzalo clearly had the answer, all but the trivial final step. In my opinion, Mr. Rubin owes him five dollars."

"Irrelevance!"—Afterword

In late January 1978, I attended a convention of mystery fans at Mohonk Mountain House (near New Paltz, New York). It was the second of what had been planned to be annual affairs, and it was every bit as much fun as the first had been.

At the end, there was an auction to raise money for the Mohonk Trust Fund, and one of the items auctioned off was the privilege of having one's name used in a Black Widowers tale.

The high bidder was one Dan Burry, and three months

later, when I wrote "Irrelevance!" I had the guest at the banquet named Dan Burry. I used only the name, of course, and not the appearance, the job, or anything else about the auction winner.

The story appeared in the March 1979 *EQMM* under the title of "A Matter of Irrelevance" but, as usual, I prefer the shorter title and restore my own.

The story came out just in time for the third annual meeting of mystery readers at Mohonk, and Dan Burry was beaming. He said that by an odd coincidence the views of the fictional Dan Burry bore a close resemblance to his own.

8.

None So Blind

Roger Halsted, normally soft-spoken, did on occasion become emphatic when the matter under discussion was something that struck at the inner core of his affections.

He said, "You're quite wrong, Manny. Not only is the limerick an authentic and respectable verse form, it is to the English language what the *haiku* is to Japanese, an authentic and peculiar possession."

Halsted's high forehead was pink and his slight stammer was emphasized as he grew, for him, passionate. The others present at the preprandial stage of the monthly banquet of the Black Widowers fell briefly silent in astonishment at Halsted's single-handed bearding of Emmanuel Rubin.

Rubin, who grew passionate even over weather announcements, seemed afire with contradiction. "Are you trying to tell me, Roger, that limericks can't be written in any language?"

"Of course not," said Halsted. "I know a number of limericks in French and German. It's just that it doesn't come natually to those languages or to any other than English. They're not designed for it. For heaven's sake, you can write *haikus* in English; it's just a matter of counting syllables; but it doesn't have the same *effect* as in Japanese."

"Subjective nonsense," said Rubin, his sparse gray beard bristling belligerently. "It's what you're used to. Teach American children *haiku* in grade school and they'll appreciate it in English as Japanese children learn to appreciate it in Japanese."

"You underestimate the difference involved in the fact that syllables in Japanese are more regular in sound than those in English. And where limericks are concerned, what counts is the anarchy of the English language."

"You call it anarchy, Roger, because you know no grammar."

"That's my point," said Halsted. "English grammar is incredibly loose. It consists almost entirely of a collection of exceptions. And the English vocabulary, through a succession of historical accidents, is far larger than that of any other language. Every word in English has twenty synonyms, no two of which are exactly alike in meaning."

"I grant the flexibility of English," said Rubin.

"Then you grant my argument. A limerick is made up of thirteen metrical feet divided into five lines with three, three, two, two, three feet each. There are two unaccented syllables between each accented one in each line, one or two unaccented syllables at the start of each line, and zero, one, or two unaccented syllables at the end of each line. If . . ."

At this point, Mario Gonzalo, the Black Widowers' resident artist, who had been following the argument over a martini and was smacking his lips over both, said, "Come on, Roger, we all know what a limerick is."

Halsted said, "The point I'm trying to make is that the rules for a limerick are rigid and allow almost no leeway. We can get away with it in English because we can shift from a word to its synonym, we can alter word order, use a noun for an adjective, and so on. In other languages, you are not so free—there are too few synonyms, too fixed a word order, too inflexible a set of word properties."

At this point, the one nonmember of the club, the guest brought in by the host of the evening, broke in eagerly. He had been hovering at the edge of the argument waiting for a chance to insert himself, and he now said, "My favorite limerick goes: 'From a crypt in the church of St. Giles . . .'"

Halsted said, "Good! Take that one. I've often heard the second line given as 'Came a scream that rang out for a mile.'"

Now that's wrong! Between the two accented syllables 'scream' and 'rang' there is only one unaccented syllable."

"Not so," said James Drake, touching his small gray mustache as though to reassure himself of its microscopic presence. "You can say it, 'Came a *scream* that rang *out* for a *mile.*'"

Halsted looked annoyed, "That defies the ordinary rhythm of English speech. If you were to read the line as prose, you would sound illiterate if you placed the accent on 'out.' You could say 'Came a *screaming* that *rang* out for a *mile,*' but now you have three unaccented syllables between 'rang' and 'mile,' and that's impermissible too. So you change it to 'Came a *screaming* that *rang* out for *miles,*' which sounds better and which, incidentally, preserves the rhyme, a matter that most amateur limericists are very cavalier about. However, the phrase 'came a screaming,' while permissible English—almost anything is—is a trifle unnatural. So you change it to 'Came a *scream* that *resounded* for *miles*' and you have a perfect limerick line."

Geoffrey Avalon's deep baritone rolled out, effortlessly rising above the general conversation, "And as Henry is trying to tell you, Roger, we have a perfect banquet waiting for us if you'll only shut up and let everyone sit down."

Henry, whose role as waiter at the monthly banquet made him the one indispensable man of the evening, said quietly, "I cannot guarantee perfection, gentlemen, but there will be roast goose that I think you will find acceptable."

Halsted sat down at once. It was widely rumored that the one way to stop him from composing limericks was to place food in front of him, and Halsted had more than once admitted the possibility of there being some truth to that. He was a valiant trencherman, he said.

The guest tried Halsted again after the stuffed mushrooms had been disposed of and bones sprouted from the plates. He said, "I take it you know the St. Giles limerick, then?"

Thomas Trumbull, scowling out of his tanned face under his thatch of white hair, said, "He has heard every limerick invented and, thanks to his insufferable mania and our own incomprehensible tolerance, so have we."

Avalon said, "Since you came late as usual, Tom, I haven't had a chance to introduce my guest to you. This is Ananias

St. John, a cousin of my wife's but a splendid fellow all the same."

"Ananias?" said Trumbull, with a thoughtful look in his eye.

"Ananias," said St. John jovially. "My parents had a perverted sense of humor. However, the Bible is so rarely read these days that the natural allusion is lost. Well, almost so; it wasn't last week, I think. Usually, the trouble I have is in pronunciation. Which reminds me, Geoff, *please* overcome your Anglophilic love of elision and don't pronounce my last name *Sin*jon. Accent the last syllable and make it Sin*john*, or, better yet, give it the full sounding of Saint John."

Halstead said, "Elisions can be useful: 'There was a young fellow named *Sin*jon, Who said to his wife, "Honest Injun" . . .'"

Trumbull shouted, "Damn it, Roger, I'd tell you not to torture us with another limerick, except that you won't find another rhyme for St. John, however execrable."

Halsted said quietly, "'I was having no fling, with that pretty young thing. Just a small bit of fatherly pinchin'.'"

"'Execrable' is the word, all right, Tom," said Avalon.

"Can you do better?" demanded Halsted.

"Who wants to?" said Trumbull. "To want to compose a better limerick is the mark of a man with micro-ambition."

Avalon tapped his water glass with his spoon as Henry passed around the brandy in his usual unobtrusive way.

"Roger," Avalon said, "you were unaccustomedly forward earlier in the evening. Suppose we take advantage of your brashness and ask you to conduct the grilling now."

Trumbull let out a roar of disapproval. "Come on, Geoff. Roger will get this thing turned into a competition of limericks, and I swear I'll leave."

Avalon looked austere. "As host, I make the decisions, and there are no appeals. Roger, you do the grilling, and the subject of limericks is not to be brought up."

Halsted said, eyebrows lifted, "I wouldn't dream of it. I've had my say. Mr. St. John" (he pronounced the name carefully as two equally stressed words), "it is customary, but not obligatory, to ask each guest to justify his existence, and in this case I choose not to. If I do, we may get off on a tangent and, instead, I want to move directly to a nonlimerical point. . . ."

"Grill! Don't orate!" muttered Trumbull.

"Quiet, Tom," said Avalon, with a stiff gesture.

Halsted said, "Earlier, during the dinner, you said that few people saw the natural allusion to your name, Ananias. You mean, of course, the fact that it is used, metaphorically, to mean a liar."

"That's right," said St. John cheerfully. "Ananias and his wife, Sapphira, tried to withhold property from the common fund by lying about it and were struck dead by Peter in consequence. You'll find it at the beginning of the Fifth Chapter of Acts."

Rubin said, "Have you ever thought of changing your name?"

"Why should I?" said St. John. "I like it. It gives me a bit of individuality. I'm the only Ananias I ever met and that suits me fine."

Halsted said, "Back to the point, though. You also said that there *were* allusions made last week. In other words, someone thought you were a liar. Why?"

St. John frowned and his round face assumed an anxious look. "Did I say anything about last week?"

"You did," said Drake, nodding. "I heard it, too."

"I shouldn't have," said St. John. "I've been asked not to talk about it."

Trumbull leaned forward intently and said, "Wait! Are you the St. John who was connected with the Winston Arms incident?"

St. John said cautiously, as though expecting entrapment, "I live in Winston Arms."

"Okay. All I knew was your initial. If I had known your full first name I would have known on the instant of introduction. Look, Mr. St. John, the incident doesn't exactly fall under my jurisdiction and I know of it only from some distance, but it's all right to talk about it *here*. Everything said here never goes beyond the walls, and that includes Henry, our esteemed waiter."

St. John's caution did not abandon him, "How do I know you have the authority to . . ."

Avalon said, "It's all right, Ni. If Tom says you can go ahead, you can. The only thing is that I do try to pick my guests carefully and avoid these damned puzzles. Ni St. John is an electrical engineer with an unimpeachably quiet life, and now look."

"It only happened last week, Geoff," said St. John weakly. "I'm sorry."

"Would you tell us about it?" said Halsted.

There was one last moment of hesitation and then St. John said, "To make it short, I found a dead man and I'm not sure the FBI doesn't think I may have been the killer."

The company of Black Widowers emitted a collective sigh.

"Murder!" whispered Gonzalo. "We hardly ever get anything like that."

Halsted said, "Let the man speak! Would you start from the beginning, Mr. St. John?"

"There isn't much to tell," said St. John. "Last Friday, I was leaving my apartment at the Winston Arms on a routine errand. I had a day off and my wife thought I ought to do some shopping lest unaccustomed leisure rot my moral fiber, I suppose. I was engaged in locking the door—three locks in New York, of course—when, behind me, I heard the door of the elevator open. That meant someone was getting off or going in, so I shouted, 'Hold it, please,' because one can easily wait five or ten minutes for an elevator, if you've just missed a chance. When I got there, though, all three elevator doors were closed. No one was in sight and in the ten seconds it had taken me to get to the elevator bank, anyone getting off would not have had time to vanish into an apartment door. That meant someone had gotten on."

Rubin, who lived in a large apartment complex of his own, said, "Elevators aren't that faultless. It might have stopped at the floor by way of a misfunctioning signal and no one either got on or off."

"As it happened," said St. John, "there turned out to be every reason to suppose someone had got on—a murderer, in fact, which, selfishly speaking, makes it just as well I had my back to the hall and was delayed by the three locks. If I had seen him and tried to get on the elevator with him, he might have tried to kill me, too."

"What time was it?" asked Halsted.

"About four in the afternoon."

"I should think he took a big chance on being seen."

St. John said, "Not necessarily. The peephole in the door of

the apartment he came out of commands a view of the length
of the hall. I imagine he made sure the hall was empty before
going out to signal for the elevator. Anyway, I knew nothing
of this at the time. I just knew someone hadn't held the door
for me and I chafed quite a bit and walked up and down to
pass the time. The wait for an elevator always seems twice as
long if you just stand there and stare at a closed door.

"At the end of the corridor, the opposite end from my
apartment, there was an apartment door, from within which
I heard a distinct moaning, and the door was just a trifle ajar.
I called out, 'Hi! Something wrong?' and shoved the door open
a bit. The moaning was a bit louder and I thought I did hear
the word 'help.' I went in, very reluctantly. Oh it's easy to
sneer, but getting involved *can* be troublesome and, in fact, it
was.

"There was a dying man in the living room. He had been
knifed and it was sticking out of his chest and you'll excuse
me if I don't go into details, but I don't revel in such things.
He was a man I had seen in the elevator occasionally, and we
had waited for it together once or twice, but we had never
spoken. It's traditional in New York, you know, to ignore
your neighbors.

"I was rather paralyzed. I'm not a doctor; I didn't know
what to do. I might have run out yelling for help, or I might
have run back to my apartment and used the intercom to
alert the doorman. But I just stood there frozen and the man
looked at me and said, quite distinctly, 'the blind man,' and
then his neck tendons just went loose. I had never seen
anyone die, but there was no doubt in my mind that I had just
seen it happen."

St. John paused at this point and said, "Waiter, might I
have a refill on the brandy?"

Henry, as always, seemed to have anticipated the request.

The Black Widowers remained silent and finally St. John
cleared his throat and said, "I didn't know what to do then,
either. How could I be sure he was dead? Was I supposed to
apply first aid to save his life—when I knew nothing about
first aid? Besides, I also thought that if he were dead, I wasn't
supposed to move the body or touch anything. I was afraid of
touching even the phone, but then I picked it up with a
handkerchief at one end and dialed the police.

"I went back to my apartment after that to tell my wife

what had happened, and she took some quieting, you can imagine. Then I returned to the dead man to wait for the police."

Gonzalo said, "How did I come to miss the news story? A murder in a posh apartment house usually makes the lower left-hand corner of the *Times* front page and scare headlines in the *News* and the *Post*."

St. John shrugged. "I suspect there was an attempt to keep it as quiet as possible: It made its way through the apartment house, though, because my wife called the office. The tenants have already had a meeting on the problem of security, but that doesn't really have anything to do with the story.

"The fact is that when the policemen came, there were intelligence agents along with them and it was one of those who interviewed me. When I gave him my name, he looked at me sharply and asked if I had my driver's license with me. It seemed to me he thought I was giving him a false name. I produced it, along with a few credit cards, and there it was—Ananias, in clear print.

" 'How well did you know this man?' he asked.

"I said, 'Not at all. I'd see him in the corridor or in the elevator, but I never spoke to him.'

" 'You're neighbors. You live on the same floor.'

"I tried to explain about New York. He listened, showed no expession. He said, 'Did you staighten up in here?'

" 'Not in any way,' I said. 'I touched nothing but the phone, except that I pushed the door open, stepped across the floor, and may have put my hand somewhere on the furniture.' I wasn't trying to be funny. I just wanted to be perfectly honest.

"He said, 'Did you do that?'

"He pointed to the window shade, which hung crookedly as though it were broken, then to some books on a coffee table that seemed disarrayed. I hadn't even noticed that, and I said so. He asked if I had touched one of the ashtrays and I said I hadn't.

"He asked me to tell him what had happened and I did— exactly as I told it to you earlier.

"He said, 'It's your opinion, then, that a blind man came in here and did this?'

"I said I had no such opinion. The dying person had said, 'the blind man,' and that's all. He hadn't said a blind man had knifed him or had come in or anything. Three words and he had died.

"The agent said, 'What do you think he meant?'

"'I don't know,' I said. By now I was pretty wild because it seemed to me I could see how things were going. There was no real sign of a struggle. There seemed to have been no search and maybe nothing was stolen. It looked like a sudden quarrel between friends. There I was on the same floor. I could be the friend. I could have killed him and then tried to cover by calling the police with a story about the murderer going down the elevator and the dead man muttering a senseless phrase.

"They finally let me go, but not until after I had begun to be sure that I was going to be arrested. I'm convinced, though, that if my name had not been Ananias, that agent wouldn't have been half convinced I was lying and he might not have given me such a hard time. Anyway, they warned me not to talk about it, and that's it. The whole story."

Trumbull broke in. "I'm sure your name had nothing to do with it, Mr. St. John. The fact is that there's more to this than you can guess, and that's why it had to be kept reasonably quiet. What I am going to do—if I can get over my astonishment at the coincidence of having you here one week after the event—is to tell you as little as possible, and as much as is necessary.

"The fact is that the dead man, whom we'll call Jones, was an undercover agent. Who and what he was investigating is of no concern to us here, but things were so delicate that he remained completely out of touch with us except on rare occasions and even then only by very tenuous devices concerning which I know no details. As I said, I was not directly concerned. He lived at Winston Arms for two years, had a complicated and thoroughly established cover, and went quietly about his very dangerous business."

Rubin muttered, "That kind of storybook spy activity never rings true to me. Who would want to live such a life?"

"Very few," said Trumbull, "but it has to be done, it's very well paid, and the fringe benefits in the way of early retirement, medical insurance, and pension plans are attractive. But let me go on. . . ."

"Somehow, we now see in hindsight, his cover was blown.

Somehow, he was murdered. It might have been a nonassociated murder, having nothing to do with his job, but we don't believe in pure coincidence in such matters."

Avalon said, "To be dramatic is not always to be correct. Why couldn't it have been someone who came in to burglarize the apartment, found Jones there, knifed him, and then fled in panic without taking anything?"

Trumbull looked scornful. "There was no sign of a forcible entry, and Jones would not be likely to let himself be knifed by a two-bit sneak-thief at four in the afternoon. No; it had to be a carefully planned entry designed to catch Jones off-guard, and it could only have been carried through by a well-organized cabal."

Halsted said, "Why the apartment? Why not arrange an automobile accident? Why not have him mugged in Central Park?"

Trumbull said, "It could be done that way. It has, on occasion. But this was a special case, and it was a matter of psychological warfare, in a way. At least, so we believe. Look at it this way: People living this dangerous life have to be aware of danger at every moment anywhere in the street or in public buildings or in empty places. One's own home, though, is a place of refuge. If there weren't somewhere you could feel safe, the life would become unbearable. To be tracked down, then, and killed in your own apartment, not only gets rid of an important agent but may well demoralize the entire agency.

"The question is not why it was done there, but how. Jones had a gun and it wasn't used. He was a thoroughgoing expert in the various techniques of self-defense, yet there was no sign of a struggle. Combine that with the fact that the killer had gotten into the apartment with every sign of having been invited in.

"To whom could Jones have said, 'Come in'? Jones could not possibly have allowed anyone to enter his apartment under any but the most unambiguous conditions. I doubt that *I* could have gotten into his apartment even if I had flashed my identification. He didn't know me personally and he would have taken into account the fact that my card might have been forged."

St. John said eagerly, "In that case, maybe the agent who

questioned me had the right idea. A blind man could do it."

"Why should he let in a blind man, Ni?" asked Avalon.

"Why not? A blind man isn't dangerous. I know there are stories about blind men being able to get around in the dark when sighted men can't. But this was midafternoon on a sunny day. There was no advantage to being blind."

Avalon said, "But if a blind man isn't dangerous, how could he kill Jones?"

St. John said, "It all works out. Jones would be completely unsuspicious just because the man *was* blind. The blind man would hold out his left hand and Jones would automatically take it. The blind man could have an athlete's grip like Pew in *Treasure Island,* pull Jones off-balance, and before Jones could collect his wits he would be a dead man with a knife between his ribs. Or, actually, almost a dead man."

Avalon said, "Why would a blind man want to get into Jones' apartment? What would be his excuse? A blind man comes to the door, let us say. What does he say to get in?"

St. John said, "He could be collecting for some charity. It's hard to refuse a blind man. If Jones opened the door that might be all the murderer needed. The grip of a hand, a sudden twist, a push inward, the knife, and out again. The whole thing might take no more than fifteen seconds."

"And how," asked Avalon, "would he know the corridor was clear, either when he was trying to get in or trying to get out?"

"A blind man," said St. John, "would have learned to rely on his hearing. People in corridors talk, hum, drum their fingers, shift from foot to foot."

Rubin, with the thick lenses of his glasses magnifying his eyes into orbs of fury, contained himself no longer. "What garbage!" he said. "Jones wouldn't open the door for a blind man under any circumstances. Tom, if he wouldn't let you in because he would suspect a forged identity card, why should he let in a blind man who could be a fraud? What do you need to fake blindness? Dark glasses and a white cane and you've got it. Jones wouldn't fall for that."

"Besides," said Trumbull, "there's no blind man who lives in the apartment house, and no blind man was seen entering or leaving at the time of the murder. The building is high-security, with doormen on duty, of course, and no one is allowed in without being announced."

"Well, if it comes to that," said Rubin, switching sides at once, "I live in an apartment house with a doorman, and that means nothing. A doorman has a thousand jobs. He's on the phone, he rushes out to open a taxi door or help an older resident with her bundles, and a man can slip in. Or else, even with the doorman watching, he just waits for a resident to walk in and then walks in with him, saying cheerfully, 'So how did things go?' The resident, puzzled but polite, says, 'Fine, fine,' and the doorman assumes the invader is a guest of the resident and lets him pass without a word."

Trumbull said sarcastically, "A blind man could pull those clever tricks, could he?"

Rubin shrugged. "I said there was no blind man."

St. John said, his voice squeaking into a higher register, "He *mentioned* a blind man."

"Sure," said Gonzalo. "Someone who *seemed* blind. The murderer sneaks into the apartment house in the way Manny describes. Once inside and up to the right apartment, he puts on the dark glasses and takes out the cane. . . ."

"Where does he get the cane?" demanded Rubin. "They're something like three of four feet long. Does it telescope? If not, how does he hide it while sneaking in?"

Gonzalo said, "All right. Dark glasses, then. He pretends he's blind to get in and then . . ."

Rubin said flatly, "Jones wouldn't open the door to a stranger on the strength of dark glasses, or a cane, either. Right, Tom?"

"Right," said Trumbull. "The whole question hinges on who the hell he could possibly say 'Come in' to. It would have to be someone he knew. A neighbor, perhaps, with whom he'd gotten friendly."

"He wasn't friendly with me," said St. John. "Does that mean, though, that every person living in Winston Arms is going to have to be investigated on suspicion of friendship with intent to kill?"

Trumbull said, "This is not a funny situation, Mr. St. John. But to answer your question, if I were running the investigation, why, yes, that is what I would do."

Gonzalo said, "But Jones mentioned a blind man. How do you get away from that? Do we suppose St. John is lying?"

"My name may be Ananias," began St. John heatedly, "but . . ."

Avalon cut him off with a wave of his hand. He said, "No dying man is going to enunciate clearly or know for sure what he is saying. It could have been anything and it could have meant anything."

St. John said, "Just the same, Geoff, I heard it. The man may not have known what he was saying, but what he said was 'the blind man.' "

Drake lit a cigarette, squinted through the smoke, and said, "Could you swear he didn't say, 'the blond man'?"

St. John looked confounded. " 'Blond man'?"

"Sure. It's not so different from 'blind man.' "

"N-no," said John. "It was 'blind man.' "

Drake said, "Could you swear to it in a court of law, under oath?"

St. John hesitated. "I'm not sure."

Rubin, who for a few moments had seemed withdrawn, said suddenly, "No, it was 'blind man.' "

"Stay on one side, damn it," said Trumbull.

"Listen," said Rubin earnestly, "the problem remains that he said 'Come in' to someone. It couldn't be a neighbor. His apartment had to remain sanctuary. No mere friend could get in. It would have to be something more than that. Think about it. Who are the *only* people he would let in?"

Gonzalo said, with a wide grin, "Women!"

Rubin looked disgusted, "Oh God!"

Gonzalo, galvanized suddenly into seriousness, said, "Why not? You're not trying to tell me Jones is a eunuch. So they got to his girl-friend. He would let *her* in, you bet. They'd embrace and while they're kissing, she slips a nice little blade between his ribs. Do you think it never happened?"

St. John said, outraged, "I've never seen a strange woman on our floor."

"With a little bit of luck, you wouldn't have seen the murder, either," said Gonzalo. "A blond girl, I'll bet. Jim Drake's right. The word was 'blond.' "

St. John said, " 'Blind *man*.' Even if you switch 'blind' to 'blond,' which I don't admit, I stick by 'man.' "

"Besides," said Avalon, whose face had taken on an air of strong disapproval the moment the sex motif had been introduced, "surely he'd know the girl's name. He wouldn't call her 'the blonde.' He would say 'Fifi' or 'Tootsie' or even 'my girl.' "

"If I can get a word in edgewise," roared Trumbull, "I'll be glad to explain that the rules on sexual involvement during the kind of work Jones was doing are strict. The agents have to follow certain well-understood guides. I don't have to give the details, but you can take it as certain there was no light-o-love in Jones' apartment."

Gonzalo said, stubbornly, "People don't always follow rules."

Rubin said, "Back to where I was, then, before Mario introduced nonsense. Who are the *only* ones Jones would admit into the apartment? Who could get close enough to draw a knife? A fellow agent."

"What!" said Trumbull angrily.

"Why not?" demanded Rubin. "If there have been murdering mistresses before this, so have there been traitorous double agents. Besides, Jones said as much."

"When? How?" Trumbull's anger had not abated.

"Think about it. Assuming a traitorous agent, what would have been Jones' last emotion? Maybe not sorrow over dying. He must have made peace with that possibility years before. What must have gotten right into his gizzard was the horror over the betrayal. His trusted coworker, on the inside, burrowing unsuspected. How was it no one had seen it? And as he lay dying, he is conscious of someone bending over him and his last words were a bitter and wondering, "They're *blind*, man." Rubin sat back, triumphant.

There was silence, and St. John said, "That wasn't the intonation of the words. It didn't have the music of that phrase. It was flat—informational, nothing else."

Trumbull said, "I don't believe a traitor was involved."

"Well, of course not," said Rubin, "that's the downfall of half the organizations of your type. By the time you can believe that any of the good old boys are bad old fakes, you've been diddled."

He went on. "Besides, it all makes sense. The guy has been in the apartment before, but he has gotten in without being seen by the doorman in any of a dozen ways. He doesn't want to be seen on the floor either. He knows the elevator can take several minutes to arrive; he's been there before. So he checks the corridor through the peephole, then leaves the door slightly ajar behind him.

"If he hears a noise at any door that signifies someone coming to join him in the corridor, he retreats into the apartment till the coast is clear. If the elevator is about to stop at the floor, he has time to move back, close the apartment door, and still get to the elevator."

Gonzalo said, "What if someone gets off the elevator while he's getting on?"

"Two people passing each other for two seconds isn't the same as having someone wait with you in the corridor and go down the elevator with you. The trouble was that, by a bad coincidence for the murderer, St. John stepped out of his apartment door just as the elevator came.

"If he now dashed back to the apartment he might still be safe, but the elevator door was opening and the temptation was to get in and down while he had the chance. And he did that—a split-second decision that was wrong, for he left the apartment door ajar behind him."

Gonzalo said, "What a lot of horsefeathers. If he didn't want to be associated with the floor, why didn't he just walk down several flights and calmly wait for the elevator on another floor?"

Rubin said sardonically, "The trouble with you, Mario, is that you live in a brownstone. Anyone involved in a high-rise *never* uses the stairs. You don't even let yourself know the stairs are there."

"All very pretty," said Trumbull, "but how do you prove it?"

"I don't have to," said Rubin. "I've presented you with a case that answers every objection you can raise, and it's up to you to prove it. Don't have the organization waste its time checking the apartment-house residents. Let it check its own men. It'll find the culprit—and I hope it's not you, Tom."

Trumbull snarled. "If you think our own men aren't under continuous surveillance, Manny, you're crazier than you're always making yourself sound. We spend too much time trying to corrupt the opposition to suppose that they're not trying to corrupt us. And from the fact that we succeed now and then, we deduce that they succeed now and then. I won't say that it's absolutely certain one of our men didn't do this, but it's a pretty damn close approach to certain. I wouldn't believe in betrayal unless I couldn't think of a single alternative explanation."

"Well, can you?" demanded Rubin. "Can you offer any explanation that will account for Jones saying 'Come in' to someone and for then saying something that sound like 'the blind man'?"

Trumbull said with sudden energy, "Where's Henry?" He shouted, *"Henry!"*

"Yes, sir," came Henry's quiet voice. "Is there anything you wish?"

"Certainly. Have you been listening to the conversation?"

"Yes, sir."

"Then tell Manny he's wrong."

The trace of a smile appeared on Henry's unlined but sixtyish face. "Mr. Rubin is, as always, extremely ingenious and persuasive. I suspect everything he says is correct except for the identity of the murderer."

"That so, Henry?" said Rubin. "Are you telling us you know who did it?"

"I believe the murderer's name is Peter Wanko. That at least is the name he goes under. It would have been unwise for him to disappear immediately after the murder, but I understand he has given notice and . . ."

"Henry!" roared Trumbull. "What the hell are you talking about?"

Henry said, "I'm sorry, sir, but in your anxiety to impress the company with Mr. Jones' intense privacy, you forgot that any apartment resident, however private and however suspicious, will welcome into his apartment, at almost any time, a number of different people."

"And who are those?"

"Why, sir, the service staff. Repairs must be made now and then, and it isn't likely that Mr. Jones will not demand that such repairs be made when they are necessary. If the opposition organization wished to kill Mr. Jones and if they could place one of their own agents on the apartment-house service staff, the rest is a matter of time."

Gonzalo nodded vigorously. "Of course. As soon as Jones needed something repaired . . ."

"Perhaps not that soon, Mr. Gonzalo," said Henry. "The ordinary procedure would be for Jones to call the office and for the office to send a repairman. It would be known where the repairman was and when he was there. The repairman would be under instant and fatal suspicion. Even a dedicated assassin would prefer to escape afterward if he could."

"Well, then?" asked Trumbull.

"I imagine, sir, that this Peter Wanko cultivated a friendship with Mr. Jones—took to greeting him respectfully, asking if all was well. Wanko joined the staff over a year ago and there was ample time for that. As for Mr. Jones, he would be polite, I'm sure, even though he might never have learned the serviceman's name. I imagine when Wanko was in the apartment to do some assigned task, he did it efficiently, was well tipped, and was suitably grateful. It must have seemed natural for him to urge Mr. Jones to call him directly for small jobs and bypass the office. 'I'll take care of you, sir,' he may have said, 'and it will get done sooner.'

"And eventually, Mr. Jones did call Wanko directly. He might have passed him in the lobby and told him he needed something done and would be home at 4 P.M. that day. Wanko went upstairs with no record as to where he would be then, taking care not to be seen. Since he appeared on a legitimate summons, Mr. Jones would not hesitate to let him in. Whereupon Wanko killed him."

The silence was dense until, finally, St. John said, "But this seems more out-of-the-way than Mr. Rubin's theory. I know Peter Wanko and he's a completely harmless person. Where's the evidence?"

Henry said, "There are the last words of Mr. Jones, which you yourself reported. You'll remember that in the argument over limericks before dinner, Mr. Halsted spoke of the flexibility of the English language and of how individual words can serve as different parts of speech. It occurred to me at once, therefore, when you told us of Mr. Jones saying 'the blind man' that while the normal use of 'blind' is an adjective meaning 'unsighted,' it could also be used as a noun. You mentioned a window shade hanging crookedly as though broken, and a blind man could be a man who fixed blinds.

"Toward the end of this evening's discussion, then, I called the Winston Arms, got the evening doorman, said I had an important job that needed good workmanship, and that the man who took care of the window blinds at the Winston Arms had been recommended. 'Oh, you mean Peter Wanko,' said the doorman. 'He's not supposed to do any work outside the building, but he's given notice, so maybe you can use him.' Then he gave me Wanko's phone number and address."

"Good God!" said Trumbull. He leaped for the stairs and was back in just under five minutes. He was grinning broadly. "It's all right, Henry, they got the guy. They arrested him three hours ago—while we were all having our first drinks."

"What gave him away?" asked St. John.

"Apparently," said Trumbull, with satisfaction, "they followed the same line of reasoning Henry used—except that it took them seven days to do it."

"They didn't have the help of the Black Widowers, sir," said Henry.

"None So Blind"—Afterword

As is well known to many people, I don't fly and I don't like to travel by any conveyance. I'm a homebody.

When I take vacations, then, and seize the opportunity to write a Black Widowers tale, I am usually somewhere in upstate New York or in a similar not-very-distant locality.

Every once in a while, though, I do take a cruise; I don't mind going somewhere by ship. In fact, I love being on a ship as long as I can keep my mind off the fact that there is but an inch of steel between myself and a miles-deep stretch of water.

So it happens that "None So Blind" was written in Bermuda. In fact, when the air conditioning on the *Statendam* (our ship on the occasion) was briefly shut down for repairs, Janet and I wandered off to a plush hotel, found an air-conditioned conference room that was not in use, and stayed there a couple of hours in perfect comfort while I finished the story.

"Non So Blind" appeared in the June 1979 issue of *EQMM*.

Just to show you that I don't always turn down Fred's title changes, my own original title was "Come in." As soon as I discovered what Fred was calling it I was overwhelmed at my dullwittedness in not thinking of it myself.

9.

The Backward Look

If Emmanuel Rubin knew how not to be didactic, he never exercised that knowledge.

"When you write a short story," he said, "you had better know the ending first. The end of a story is only the end to a reader. To a writer, it's the beginning. If you don't know exactly where you're going every minute you're writing, you'll never get there—or anywhere."

Thomas Trumbull's young guest at this particular monthly banquet of the Black Widowers seemed all eyes as he watched Rubin's straggly gray beard quiver and his thick-lensed glasses glint; and all ears as he listened to Rubin's firm, decibelic voice.

The guest himself was clearly in his early twenties, quite thin, with a somewhat bulging forehead and a rather diminutive chin. His clothing almost glistened in its freshness, as though he had broken out a brand-new costume for the great occasion. His name was Milton Peterborough.

He said, a small quiver in his voice, "Does that mean you have to write an outline, Mr. Rubin?"

"No," said Rubin emphatically. "You can if you want to, but I never do. You don't have to know the exact road you're going to take. You have to know your destination, that's all. Once that's the case, any road will take you there. As you write you are continually looking backward from that known destination, and it's that backward look that guides you."

Mario Gonzalo, who was quickly and carefully drawing a caricature of the guest, making his eyes incredibly large and filling them with a childlike innocence, said, "Come on, Manny, that sort of tight plotting might fit your cockamamy mysteries, but a real writer deals with character, doesn't he. He creates *people* and they behave in accordance with their characters and that guides the story, probably to the surprise of the author."

Rubin turned slowly and said, "If you're talking about long, invertebrate novels, Mario—assuming you're talking about anything at all—it's possible for an experienced or gifted writer to meander along and produce something passable. But you can always tell the I-don't-know-where-I'm-going-but-I'm-going book. Even if you forgive it its amorphous character for the sake of its virtues, you have to *forgive* it, and that's a strain and a drawback. A tightly plotted story with everything fitting together neatly is, on the other hand, the noblest work of literature. It may be bad, but it never need ask forgiveness. The backward look . . ."

At the other end of the room, Geoffrey Avalon glanced with resignation at Rubin and said, "I think it was a mistake, Tom, to tell Manny at the start that the young man was an aspiring writer. It brings out the worst in him; or, at any rate, the longest-winded." He stirred the ice in his drink with his forefinger and brought his dark eyebrows together forbiddingly.

"Actually," said Thomas Trumbull, his lined face uncharacteristically placid, "the kid wanted to meet Manny. He admires his stories, God knows why. Well, he's the son of a friend of mine and a nice youngster and I thought I'd expose him to the seamy side of life by bringing him here."

Avalon said, "It won't hurt us to be exposed to youth now and then, either. But I hate being exposed to Rubin's theories of literature. Henry."

The quiet and smoothly efficient waiter, who served at all the Black Widowers banquets, was at his side at once without seeming to have moved in order to have achieved that, "Yes, sir?"

"Henry," said Avalon, "what are these strange manifestations?"

Henry said, "Tonight we will have a buffet dinner. The chef has prepared a variety of Indian and Pakistani dishes."

"With curry?"

"Rather heavy on the curry, sir. It was Mr. Trumbull's special request."

Trumbull flared under Avalon's accusing eye. "I wanted curry and I'm the host."

"And Manny won't eat it and will be unbearable."

Trumbull shrugged.

Rubin was not entirely unbearable but he was loud, and only Roger Halsted seemed unaffected by the Rubinian tirade against all things Indian. Halsted said, "A buffet is a good idea," patted his lips with his napkin, and went back for a third helping of everything, with a beatific smile on his face.

Trumbull said, "Roger, if you don't stop eating, we'll start the grilling session over your chewing."

"Go ahead," said Halsted cheerfully. "I don't mind."

"You will later tonight," said Rubin, "when your stomach wall burns through."

Trumbull said, "And you're going to start the grilling."

"If you don't mind my talking with my mouth full," said Halsted.

"Get started, then."

Halsted said thickly, "How do you justify your existence, Milton?"

"I can't," said Peterborough, a little breathlessly. "Maybe after I get my degrees."

"What's your school and major?"

"Columbia and chemistry."

"Chemistry?" said Halsted. "I would have thought it was English. Didn't I gather during the cocktail hour that you were an aspiring writer?"

"Anyone is allowed to be an aspiring writer," said Peterborough.

"Aspiring," said Rubin darkly.

"And what do you want to write?" said Halsted.

Peterborough hesitated and said, with a trace of defensiveness in his voice, "Well, I've always been a science-fiction fan. Since I was nine, anyway."

"Oh God," muttered Rubin, his eyes rolling upward in mute appeal.

Gonzalo said instantly, "Science fiction? That's what your friend Isaac Asimov writes, isn't it, Manny?"

"He's not my friend," said Rubin. "He clings to me out of helpless admiration."

Trumbull raised his voice. "Will you two stop having a private conversation? Go on, Roger."

"Have you written any science fiction?"

"I've tried, but I haven't submitted anything. I'm going to, though. I have to."

"Why do you have to?"

"I made a bet."

"What kind?"

"Well," said Peterborough helplessly, "it's rather complicated—and embarrassing."

"We don't mind the complications," said Halsted, "and we'll try not to be embarrassed."

"Well," said Peterborough, and there appeared on his face something that had not been seen at the Black Widowers banquets for years, a richly tinted blush, "there's this girl. I'm sort of cra—I like her, but I don't think she likes me, but I like her anyway. The trouble is she goes for a basketball player; a real idiot—six-foot-five to his eyebrows and nothing above."

Peterborough shook his head and continued. "I don't have much going for me. I can't impress her with chemistry; but she's an English lit major, so I showed her some of my stories. She asked me if I had ever sold anything, and I said, no. But then I said I intended to write something and sell it, and she laughed.

"That bothered me and I thought of something. It seems that Lester del Rey—"

Rubin interposed. "Who?"

"Lester del Rey. He's a science-fiction writer."

"Another one of those?" said Rubin. "Never heard of him."

"Well, he's no Isaac Asimov," admitted Peterborough, "but he's all right. Anyway, the way he got started was once when he read a science-fiction story and thought it was terrible. He said to his girl, 'Hell, I can write something better than that,' and she said, 'I dare you,' and he did and sold it.

"So when this girl laughed, I said, 'I'll bet I write one and sell it,' and she said, 'I'll bet you don't,' and I said, 'I'll bet you a date against five dollars. If I sell the story, you go with me to a dinner and dance on a night of my choosing.' And she agreed.

"So I've just *got* to write the story now, because she said she'd go out with me if I wrote the story and she liked it, even if it didn't sell—which may mean she likes me more than I think."

James Drake, who had been listening thoughtfully, brushed his gray stub of a mustache with one finger and said, "Or that she's quite confident that you won't even write the story."

"I *will*," said Peterborough.

"Then go ahead," said Rubin.

"There's a catch. I can write the story, I know. I've got some good stuff. I even know the ending so I can give it that backward look you mentioned, Mr. Rubin. What I don't have is a motive."

"A motive?" said Rubin. "I thought you were writing a science-fiction story."

"Yes, Mr. Rubin, but it's science-fiction mystery, and I need a motive. I have the *modus operandi* of the killing, and the way of the killing, but I don't know the why of the killing. I thought, though, if I came here, I could discuss it with you."

"You could *what*?" said Rubin lifting his head.

"Especially you, Mr. Rubin. I've read your mystery stories—I don't read science fiction exclusively—and I think they're great. You're always so good with motivation. I thought you could help me out."

Rubin was breathing hard and gave every appearance of believing that that breath was flame. He had made his dinner very much out of rice and salad, plus, out of sheer famishing, two helpings of *coupe aux marrons* and he was in no mood for even such sweet reason as he was, on occasion, observed to possess.

He said, "Let me get it straight, Joe College. You've made a bet. You're going to get a chance at a girl, or such chance as you can make of it, by writing a story she likes and maybe selling it—and now you want to win the bet and cheat the girl by having me write the story for you. Is that the way it is?"

"No, sir," said Peterborough urgently, "that's *not* the way it is. I'll write it. I just want help with the motive."

"And except for that, you'll write it," said Rubin. "How about having me dictate the story to you? You can still *write* it. You can copy it out in your own handwriting."

"That's not the same at all."

"Yes it is, young man, and you can stop right there. Either write the story yourself or tell the girl you can't."

Milton Peterborough looked about helplessly.

Trumbull said, "Damn it, Manny, why so much on the high horse? I've heard you say a million times that ideas are a dime a dozen; that it's the *writing* that's hard. Give him an idea, then; he'll still have the hard part to do."

"I won't," said Rubin, pushing himself away from the table and crossing his arms. "If the rest of you have an atrophied sense of ethics, go ahead and give him ideas—if you know how."

Trumbull said, "All right, I can settle this by fiat since I'm the host, but I'll throw it open to a vote. How many favor helping the kid if we can?"

He held up his hand, and so did Gonzalo and Drake.

Avalon cleared his throat a little uncertainly. "I'm afraid I've got to side with Manny. It would be cheating the girl," he said.

Halsted said, "As a teacher, I've got to disapprove of outside help on a test."

"Tie vote," said Rubin. "What are you going to do, Tom?"

Trumbull said, "We haven't all voted. Henry is a Black Widower, and his vote will break the tie. Henry?"

Henry paused a brief moment. "My honorary position, sir, scarcely gives me the right to . . ."

"You are not an honorary Black Widower, Henry. You are a Black Widower. Decide!"

Rubin said, "Remember, Henry, you are the epitome of honest men. Where do you stand on cheating a girl?"

"No electioneering," said Trumbull. "Go ahead, Henry."

Henry's face wrinkled into a rare frown. "I have never laid claim to extraordinary honesty, but if I did, I might treat this as a special case. Juliet told Romeo, 'At lovers' perjuries/They say Jove laughs.' Might we stretch a point?"

"I'm surprised, Henry," said Rubin.

Henry said, "I am perhaps swayed by the fact that I do not

view this matter as lying between the young man and the young woman. Rather it lies between a bookish young man and an athlete. We are all bookish men and, in our time, we may each have lost a young woman to an athlete. I am embarrassed to say that I have. Surely, then . . ."

Rubin said, "Well, I haven't. I've never lost a girl to"—He paused a moment in sudden thought, then said in an altered tone—"well, it's irrelevant. All right, if I'm outvoted, I'm outvoted. So what's the story, Peterborough?"

Peterborough's face was flushed and there was a trickle of perspiration at one temple. He said, "I won't tell you any of the story I've been planning except the barest essentials of the point I need help on. I don't want anything more than the minimum. I wouldn't want *that* even, if this didn't mean—so much . . ." He ran down.

Rubin said, with surprising quietness, "Go on. Don't worry about it. We understand."

Peterborough said, "Thanks. I appreciate it. I've got two men, call them Murderer and Victim. I've worked out the way Murderer does it and how he gets caught and I won't say a word about that. Murderer and Victim are both eclipse buffs."

Avalon interrupted, "Are you an eclipse buff, Mr. Peterborough?"

"Yes, sir, I am. I have friends who go to every eclipse anywhere in the world even if it's only a 5 per center, but I can't afford that, and don't have the time. I go to those I can reach. I've got a telescope and photographic equipment."

Avalon said, "Good! It helps, when one is going to talk about eclipses, if one knows something about them. Trying to write on a subject concerning which one is ignorant is a sure prescription for failure."

Gonzalo said, "Is the woman you're interested in an eclipse buff?"

"No," said Peterborough. "I wish she were."

"You know," said Gonzalo, "if she doesn't share your interests, you might try finding someone who does."

Peterborough shook his head. "I don't think it works that way, Mr. Gonzalo."

"It sure doesn't," said Trumbull. "Shut up, Mario, and let him talk."

Peterborough said, "Murderer and Victim are both taking eclipse photographs and, against all expectations, Victim, who is the underdog, the born loser, takes the better photograph, and Murderer, unable to endure this, decides to kill Victim. From there on, I have no trouble."

Rubin said, "Then you have your motive. What's your problem?"

"The trouble is: What *kind* of a better photograph? An eclipse photograph is an eclipse photograph. Some are better than others, but, assuming that both photographers are competent, not *that* much better. Not a murder's-worth better."

Rubin shrugged. "You can build the story in such a way as to make even a small difference murderworthy—but I admit that would take an experienced hand. Drop the eclipse. Try something else."

"I can't. The whole business of the murder, the weapon and the detection, depends on photography and eclipses. So it has to stay."

Drake said softly, "What makes it a science-fiction story, young man?"

"I haven't explained that, have I? I'm trying to tell as little as possible about the story. For what I'm doing, I need advanced computers and science-fictional photographic gimmickry. One of the two characters—I'm not sure which—takes a photograph of the eclipse from a stratospheric jet."

"In that case, why not go whole hog?" said Gonzalo. "If it's going to go science-fictional . . . Look, let me tell you how I see it. Murderer and Victim are eclipse buffs and Murderer is the better man—so make it Murderer who's on that plane, and taking the best eclipse photograph ever seen, using some new photographic gimmick he's invented. Then have Victim, against all expectation, beat him out. Victim goes to the Moon and takes the eclipse photograph there. Murderer is furious at being beaten, goes blind with rage, and there you are."

Rubin said energetically, "An eclipse photo on the *Moon*?"

"Why not?" said Gonzalo, offended. "We can get to the Moon right now, so we can certainly do it in a science-fiction story. And there's a vacuum on the Moon, right? There's no air. You don't have to be a scientist to know that. And you get a better picture without air. You get a sharper picture. Isn't that right, Milton?"

Peterborough said, "Yes, but . . ."

Rubin overrode him. "Mario," he said, "listen carefully. An eclipse of the Sun takes place when the Moon gets exactly between the Sun and the Earth. Observers on Earth then see the Sun blacked out because the opaque body of the Moon is squarely in front of it. We on Earth are in the Moon's shadow. Now, if you're *on* the Moon," his voice grew harsh, "how the hell can you be in the Moon's shadow?"

Avalon said, "Not so fast, Manny, an eclipse is an eclipse is an eclipse. There is such a thing as a lunar eclipse, when the Earth gets between the Sun and the Moon. The Moon is in the Earth's shadow in that case, and the whole Moon gets dark.

"The way I see it, then, is that Murderer takes a beautiful photograph of an eclipse on Earth, with the Moon moving in front of the Sun. He has advanced equipment that he has invented himself so that no one can possibly take a better photo of the Moon in front of the Sun. Victim, however, goes him one better by taking an even more impressive photograph of an eclipse on the Moon, where, as Mario says, there is no air, with the *Earth* moving in front of the Sun."

Peterborough mumbled, "Not the same thing."

"It sure isn't," said Halsted, who had pushed his coffee cup to one side and was doing some quick figuring. "As seen from Earth, the Moon and the Sun have the same apparent width, almost exactly. Pure coincidence, of course; no astronomical necessity at all. In fact, aeons past, the Moon was closer and appeared larger, and aeons future, the Moon will be—well, never mind. The fact is that the Earth is larger than the Moon, and from the Moon you see the Earth at the same distance that you see the Moon when you're standing on Earth. The Earth in the Moon's sky is therefore as much larger than the Moon in appearance as it is in actuality. Do you get that?"

"No," said Gonzalo flatly.

Halsted looked annoyed. "Well, then, don't get it. Take my word for it. The Earth in the Moon's sky is about 3 2/3 as wide in appearance as the Moon is in the Earth's sky. That means the Earth in the Moon's sky is also that much bigger than the Sun, because the Sun looks just the same from the Moon as from the Earth."

"So what's the difference?" said Gonzalo. "If the Earth is

bigger, it gets in the way of the Sun that much better."

"No," said Halsted. "The whole point about the eclipse is that the Moon just fits over the Sun. It hides the bright circle of the gleaming Sun and allows its corona—that is, its upper atmosphere—to shine all about the hidden Sun. The corona gleams out in every direction with the light of the full Moon and does so in beautifully delicate curves and streamers.

"On the other hand, if you get a large body like the Earth in front of the Sun, it covers up the shining sphere and the corona as well. You don't see anything."

Avalon said, "That's assuming the Earth goes squarely in front of the Sun. When you see the eclipse before or after midpoint, at least part of the corona will stick beyond the Earth's sphere."

Peterborough said, "Part isn't the whole. It wouldn't be the same thing."

There was a short silence and then Drake said, "I hope you don't mind if a fellow chemist tries his hand at this, young man. I'm trying to picture the Earth in the sky, getting in the way of the Sun. And if we do that, then there's this to consider: The Earth has an atmosphere and the Moon has not.

"When the Moon moves in front of the Sun, as viewed from the Earth, the Moon's surface is sharp against the Sun. When the Earth moves in front of the Sun, as viewed from the Moon, the Earth's boundary is fuzzy and the Sun shines through Earth's atmosphere. Does that make a difference that you can use in the story?"

"Well," said Peterborough, "I've thought of that, actually. Even when the Sun is completely behind the Earth, its light is refracted through the Earth's atmosphere on every side, and a red-orange light penetrates it and reaches the Moon. It's as though the Moon can see a sunset all around the Earth. And that's not just theory. When there's a total eclipse of the Moon, you can usually see the Moon as a dull brick-red circle of light. It gleams in Earth's sunset atmosphere.

"As the eclipse, as viewed from the Moon, progresses, that side of the atmosphere that has just passed over the Sun is brighter, but grows gradually dimmer while the other side grows brighter. At eclipse midpoint, if you are viewing it from a part of the Moon that sees both Earth and Sun centered with respect to each other, the red-orange ring is evenly bright all the way around—assuming there isn't too much in the way of clouds in Earth's atmosphere at the time."

Drake said, "Well, for God's sake, isn't that a sufficiently spectacular sight for Victim to photograph? The Earth would be a black hole in the sky, with a thin orange rim all around. It would be . . ."

"No, sir," said Peterborough. "It isn't the same thing. It's too dull. It would be just a red-orange ring. Once the photograph is taken the first time, that would be it. It wouldn't be like the infinitely varying corona."

Trumbull said, "Let *me* try! You want the corona visible all around, is that it, Milton?"

"Yes, sir."

"Stop me if I'm wrong, but in my reading, I've been given to understand that the sky is blue because light is scattered by the atmosphere. On the Moon, where there is no atmosphere, the sky is black. The stars, which on Earth are washed out by the scattered light of our blue sky, would not be washed out in the Moon's airless sky. They would be visible."

"Yes, though I suspect the Sun's glare would make them hard to see."

Trumbull said, "That's not important. All you would have to do is cut an opaque circle of metal and hold it up in the air at the proper distance from your photographic equipment in order to just block out the Sun's blazing disc. You can't do that on Earth, because even if you blocked out the Sun, the scattered light of the sky obscures the corona. On the Moon, there's no scattered light in the sky and the corona would shine out."

Peterborough said, "In theory, that's possible. In fact, it can even be done on Earth on mountaintops, making use of a coronagraph. It still wouldn't be the real thing, though, for it's not just a matter of light scattered by the atmosphere. There's light scattered and reflected by the ground.

"The lunar surface would be very brightly lit up and light would be coming in from every angle. The photographs you would take would not be good ones. You see, the reason the Moon does the good job it does here on Earth is that its shadow doesn't just fall on the telescope and camera. It falls on all the surrounding landscape. The shadow of the Moon can, under ideal conditions, be 160 miles wide and cover 21,000 square miles of the Earth's surface. Usually, it's considerably smaller than that, but generally it's enough to cover the immediate landscape—that is, if it happens to be a total eclipse."

Trumbull said, "A bigger opaque object, then . . ."

"It would have to be quite big and quite far away," said Peterborough, "to achieve the effect. That would be too cumbersome."

Halsted said, "Wait, I think I have it. You would need something big for the purpose, all right. Suppose there were spherical space settlements in the Moon's orbit. If Victim is in a spaceship and gets the space settlement between himself and the Sun, that would be exactly what he wants. He could arrange to be close enough to have the shadow—which, of course, is conical and narrows to a point if you get far enough away—to be just thick enough to enclose his entire ship. There would be no world surface to reflect light, and there you are."

Peterborough said uneasily, "I hadn't thought of that. It's possible."

Halsted grinned, and a flush of pleasure mounted to the hairline he had once had. "That's it, then."

Peterborough said, "I don't want to be troublesome, but—but if we introduce the space motif, it's going to create some problems in the rest of the story. It's sort of important that everything stay on or near the Earth and yet that there be something so startling and unexpected that it would . . ."

He paused and Rubin completed the sentence for him, "So startling and unexpected that it would drive Murderer to rage and vengeance."

"Yes."

"Well," said Rubin, "since I'm the master of mystery here, I think I can work it out for you without leaving Earth very far behind, just as soon as I get some points straightened out. You said that Murderer is taking the photographs from a plane. Why?"

"Oh. That's because the Moon's shadow, when it falls on Earth, moves quickly—up to 1,440 miles an hour or about 0.4 mile a second. If you're standing in one place on Earth, the longest possible duration of a total eclipse is 7 minutes and then the shadow has moved beyond you. That's when the

Earth is as deep into the Moon's shadow as it ever gets. When the Earth isn't as deep in and is nearer the final point of the shadow, the total eclipse may last only a couple of minutes, or even only a few seconds. In fact, more than half the time, the Moon's shadow during an eclipse doesn't reach the Earth's surface at all, and when the Moon is squarely in front of the Sun, the Sun overlaps it on all sides. That's an "annular eclipse," and enough sunlight then slips past the Moon to wash out everything. An annular eclipse is no good at all."

"But in the airplane?" prompted Rubin.

"In an airplane, you can race along with the shadow and make the total eclipse last for an hour or more even if it would only endure a very short time on one position on Earth. You have a great deal more time to take photographs and make scientific observations. That's not science-fictional; it's done right now."

"Can you take very good pictures from the plane?" asked Rubin. "Does it allow a steady enough basis for photography?"

"In my story," said Peterborough, "I've got a computer guiding the plane, allowing for wind movements, and keeping it perfectly steady. That's one of the places where the science fiction comes in."

"Still, the Moon's shadow eventually leaves the Earth's surface altogether, doesn't it?"

"Yes, the eclipse track covers a fixed portion of the Earth's surface, and it has an overall starting point and an overall ending point."

"Exactly," said Rubin. "Now, Murderer is confident that his photographs taken from the stratosphere are going to include the best views of an eclipse ever seen, but he doesn't count on Victim's having a spaceship. Don't worry, there's no need to leave Earth very far. It's just that the spaceship follows the Moon's shadow *after* it leaves the Earth. Victim has a still longer chance to take photographs, a steadier base, and no atmospheric interference whatever. Murderer is hoist on his own petard, for he sees that poor simp, Victim, do exactly what he does but go him one better. He snaps and becomes a killer."

Gonzalo waved both arms in the air in excitement. "Wait! Wait! We can do even better than that. Listen, what about that annular eclipse you mentioned a while ago? You said the shadow doesn't reach the Earth."

"It doesn't reach the surface. That's right."

"How high off the surface is it?"

"That depends. Under extreme conditions, the end point of the shadow could miss the Earth by hundreds of miles."

"Yes," said Gonzalo, "but could that end point miss Earth by, say, *ten* miles?"

"Oh sure."

"Would it still be annular, and no good?"

"That's right," said Peterborough. "The Moon would come just barely short of covering the Sun. There would be just the thinnest sliver of Sun around the Moon, and that would give enough light to spoil things. If you took photographs, you'd miss the prominences, the flares, and the corona."

"But what if you went ten miles up into the atmosphere?" said Gonzalo. "Then you'd see it total, wouldn't you?"

"If you were in the right spot, yes."

"There it is, then. One of those annular eclipses comes along, and Murderer thinks he'll pull a fast one. He gets into his stratoplane, goes ten miles up to get into the point of the shadow or just over it, and follows it along. He's going to make a total eclipse out of an annular one—and Victim, the usual loser, does the same thing, except he uses a spaceship and follows it out into space and gets better pictures. What can get old Murderer more torn up than having him play his ace—and getting trumped?"

Avalon nodded his head. "Good, Mario. That *is* an improvement."

Rubin looked as if he had unexpectedly bitten into a lemon. "I hate to say it, Mario . . ."

"You don't have to say it, Manny," said Gonzalo. "I see it all over you. There you are, kid. Write the story."

Peterborough said, with a sigh, "Yes, I suppose that is the best that can be done."

"You don't sound overjoyed," said Gonzalo.

"I was hoping for something more—uh—outrageous, but I don't think it exists. If none of you could think up anything . . ."

"May I interrupt, sir?" said Henry.

"Huh? Oh—no, I don't want any more coffee, waiter," said Peterborough, absently.

"No, sir. I mean concerning the eclipse."

Trumbull said, "Henry's a member of the club, Milton. He broke the tie on the matter of the discussion. Remember?"

Peterborough put a hand to his forehead. "Oh sure. Ask away—uh—Henry."

"Actually, sir, would the photographs be that much better in a vacuum than in the thin air of the stratosphere? Would the difference in quality be enough to result in murder, unless Murderer was a close approach to a homicidal maniac?"

"That's the thing," said Peterborough, nodding. "That's what bothers me. That's why I keep saying I need a motive. These differences in quality of photos aren't big enough."

"Let us consider, then," said Henry, "Mr. Rubin's dictum that in telling a story one should look backward."

"I know the ending," said Peterborough. "I have the backward look."

"I mean it in another sense—that of deliberately looking in the other direction, the unaccustomed direction. In an eclipse, we always look at the Moon—just the Moon in a lunar eclipse, and the Moon covering the Sun in a solar eclipse—and that's what we take photographs of. What if we take a backward look at the Earth?"

"What's to see on the Earth, Henry?" asked Gonzalo.

"When the Moon moves into the Earth's shadow, it is always in the full phase and it is usually completely darkened. What happens to the Earth when it moves into the Moon's shadow? It certainly doesn't darken completely."

"No," said Peterborough emphatically. "The Moon's shadow is thinner and shorter than the Earth's, and the Earth itself is larger than the Moon. Even when Earth passes as deeply as it can into the Moon's shadow, only a tiny bit of the Earth is darkened, a little dot of darkness that makes up, at most, about one six-hundredth of the Earth's circle of light."

"Could you see it from the Moon?" asked Henry.

"If you knew where to look and especially if you had a good pair of binoculars. You would see it start small, move west of east across the face of the Earth, getting bigger, then smaller, and then vanish. Interesting, but certainly not spectacular."

"Not from the Moon, sir," said Henry. "Now suppose we reverse the role of the characters. It is Victim who has the

airplane and who can get a photograph from the stratosphere. It is Murderer who intends to trump his opponent's
ace by taking a better photograph from space—a marginally
better photograph. Suppose, though, that Victim, against all
expectations, from his airplane overtrumps Murderer in his
spaceship."

Avalon said, "How can he do that, Henry?"

"Victim, in his plane, suddenly realizes he needn't look at
the Moon. He looks backward at the ground and sees the
Moon's shadow racing toward him. The Moon's shadow is just
a dark dot when seen from the Moon; it's just the coming of
temporary night as seen from the Earth's surface—but from
a plane in the stratosphere, it is a racing circle of darkness
moving at 1,440 miles an hour, swallowing up the land and
sea—and clouds, for that matter—as it goes. The plane can
move ahead of it, and it is no longer necessary to take single
snapshots. A movie camera can produce the most dramatic
film. In this way, Murderer, having fully expected to outdo
Victim, finds that Victim has captured world attention even
though he had only an airplane to Murderer's spaceship."

Gonzalo broke into loud applause and Trumbull said, "Right
on!" Even Rubin smiled and nodded.

As for Peterborough, he fired up at once, saying, "Sure!
And the approaching shadow would have a thin red rim, for
at the moment the shadow overtakes you, the red prominences cast their light unmasked by the Sun's white light.
That's it, Henry! The backward look does it! If I write this one
properly, I don't care even if it doesn't sell. I won't care even"
(his voice shook) "if—uh—*she* doesn't like it and doesn't go
out with me. The story is more important!"

Henry smiled gently and said, "I'm glad to hear that, sir. A
writer should always have a proper sense of priorities."

"The Backward Look"—Afterword

George Scithers, the clever and efficient editor of *IASFM*
(who won the Hugo as best editor in the 1978 World Science
Fiction convention after having edited only seven issues of
the magazine—a speedy and well-deserved appreciation),
decided that "The Missing Item" had gone over well with the

readers. He therefore asked me for another Black Widowers item relating to science fiction.

I complied with "The Backward Look," which appeared in the September 1979 *IASFM*. (In its second year of existence, *IASFM* rose to bimonthly appearances, and in its third year, it became a monthly.)

In this story, by the way, I have someone refer to Isaac Asimov as a well-known science-fiction writer, and Manny Rubin, as always, reacts with a certain impatience at having Asimov termed a friend of his. I do this every once in a long while, and it is a Trap Door Spiders in-joke.

This is self-indulgence, of course, but the bond between myself and my Gentle Readers is a close and friendly one and I like to think they won't mind an occasional self-indulgence on my part. This time, I made the in-joke a degree of magnitude sharper by bringing in Lester del Rey and having him described as "Well, he's no Isaac Asimov, but he's all right."

Naturally, I wait (in some apprehension) for Lester to decide on a suitable riposte. The fact is that Lester and I are very good friends and have been so for nearly forty years. It's just that we've been baiting each other for nearly forty years, too.

10.

What Time Is It?

The monthly banquet of the Black Widowers had proceeded its usually noisy course and then, over the coffee, there had fallen an unaccustomed quiet.

Geoffrey Avalon sipped at his coffee thoughtfully and said, "It's the little things—the little things. I know a couple who might have been happily married forever. He was a lay reader at an Episcopalian Church and she was an unreformed atheist, and they never gave each other a cross look over that. But he liked dinner at six and she liked it at seven, and that split them apart."

Emmanuel Rubin looked up owlishly from his part of the table, eyes unblinking behind thick lenses, and said, "What's 'big' and what's 'little,' Geoff? Every difference is a little difference if you're not involved. There's nothing like a difference in the time sense to reduce you to quivering rage."

Mario Gonzalo looked complacently at the high polish on his shoes and said, "Ogden Nash once wrote that some people like to sleep with the window closed and some with the window open and each other is whom they marry."

Since it was rather unusual that at any Black Widowers banquet three successive comments should be made without an explosive contradiction, it didn't really surprise anyone when Thomas Trumbull furrowed his brows and said, "That's a lot of horsehair. When a marriage breaks up, the trivial reason is never the reason."

Avalon said mildly, "I know the couple, Tom. It's my brother and sister-in-law—or ex-sister-in-law."

"I'm not arguing that they don't say they've split over a triviality, or even that they don't believe it," said Trumbull. "I just say there's something deeper. If a couple are sexually compatible, if there are no money problems, if there is no grave difference in beliefs or attitudes, then they'll stick together. If any of these things fail, then the marriage sours and the couple begin to chafe at trivialities. The trivialities then get blamed—but that's not so."

Roger Halsted, who had been chasing the last of the apple pie about his plate, now cleansed his mouth of its slight stickiness with a sip of black coffee and said, "How do you intend to prove your statement, Tom?"

"It doesn't require proof," said Trumbull, scowling. "It stands to reason."

"Only in your view," said Halsted, warmly, his high forehead flushing pinkly, as it always did when he was moved. "I once broke up with a young woman I was crazy about because she kept saying 'Isn't it a riot?' in and out of season. I swear she had no other flaw."

"You'd be perjuring yourself unconsciously," said Trumbull. "Listen, Jim, call a vote."

James Drake, host for the evening, stubbed out his cigarette and looked amused. His small eyes, nested in finely wrinkled skin, darted around the table and said, "You'll lose, Tom."

"I don't care if I win or lose," said Trumbull, "I just want to see how many jackasses there are at the table."

"The usual number, I suppose," said Drake. "All those who agree with Tom raise their hands."

Trumbull's arm shot up and was the only one to do so.

"I'm not surprised," he said, after a brief look, left and right. "How about you, Henry? Are you voting?"

Henry, the unparalleled waiter at all the Black Widower banquets, smiled paternally, "Actually, I was not, Mr. Trumbull, but if I had voted, I would have taken the liberty of disagreeing with you." He was passing about the table, distributing the brandy.

"You, too, Brutus?" said Trumbull.

Rubin finished his coffee and put the cup down with a clatter. "What the devil, all differences are trivial. Forms of life that are incredibly different superficially are all but identical on the biochemical level. There seems a world of difference between the worm and the earth it burrows in, but, considering the atoms that make it up, both of them . . ."

Trumbull said, "Don't wax poetical, Manny, or, if you must, wax it in your garage and not here. I suspect jackassery is universal but, just to make sure, I'll ask our guest if he is voting."

Drake said, "Let's make that part of the grilling then. It's time. And you can do the grilling, Tom."

The guest was Barry Levine, a small man, dark-haired, dark-eyed, slim, and nattily dressed. He was not exactly handsome, but he had a cheerful expression that was a good substitute. Gonzalo had already sketched his caricature, exaggerating the good cheer into inanity, and Henry had placed it on the wall to join the rest.

Trumbull said, "Mr. Levine, it is our custom at these gatherings of ours to ask our guest, to begin with, to justify his existence. I shall dispense with that since I will assume that your reason for existence at the moment is to back me up, if you can, in my statement—self-evident, to my way of thinking—that trivialities are trivial."

Levine smiled and said, in a slightly nasal voice, "Trivialities on the human level, or are we talking about earthworms?"

"We are talking about humans, if we omit Manny."

"In that case, I join the jackassery, since, in my occupation, I am concerned almost exclusively with trivia."

"And your occupation, please?"

"I'm the kind of lawyer, Mr. Trumbull, who makes his living by arguing with witnesses and with other lawyers in front of a judge and jury. And that immerses me in triviality."

Trumbull growled, "You consider justice a triviality, do you?"

"I do not," said Levine, with equanimity, "but that is not with what we are directly concerned in the courtroom. In the courtroom, we play games. We attempt to make favorable testimony admissible and unfavorable testimony inadmissible. We play with the rules of questioning and cross-examination. We try to manipulate the choosing of favorable jurors, and then we manipulate the thoughts and emotions of the jurors we do get. We try to play on the prejudices and tendencies of the judge as we know them to be at the start or as we discover them to be in the course of the trial. We try to block the opposition attorney or, if that is not possible, to maneuver him into overplaying his hand. We do all this with the trivia and minutiae of precedence and rationale."

Trumbull's tone did not soften. "And where in all this litany of judicial recreation does justice come in?"

Levine said, "Centuries of experience with our Anglo-American system of jurisprudence has convinced us that in the long run and on the whole, justice is served. In the short run, and in a given specific case, however, it may very well not be. This can't be helped. To change the rules of the game to prevent injustice in a particular case may, and probably will, insure a greater level of injustice on the whole—though once in a while an overall change for the better can be carried through."

"In other words," interposed Rubin, "you despair of universal justice even as a goal of the legal profession?"

"As an attainable goal, yes," said Levine. "In heaven, there may be perfect justice; on Earth, never."

Trumbull said, "I take it, then, that if you are engaged in a particular case, you are not the least interested in justice?"

Levine's eyebrows shot upward. "Where have I said that? Of course I am interested in justice. The immediate service to justice is seeing to it that my client gets the best and most efficient defense that I can give him, not merely because he deserves it, but also because American jurisprudence demands it, and because *he* is deprived of it at *your* peril, for you may be next.

"Nor is it relevant whether he is guilty or innocent, for he is legally innocent in every case until he is proven guilty according to law, rigorously applied. Whether the accused is morally or ethically innocent is a much more difficult question, and one with which I am not primarily concerned. I am secondarily concerned with it, of course, and try as I might, there will be times when I cannot do my full duty as a lawyer out of a feeling of revulsion toward my client. It is then my duty to advise him to obtain another lawyer.

"Still, if I were to secure the acquittal of a man I considered a scoundrel, the pain would not be as intense as that of failing to secure the acquittal of a man who, in my opinion, was wrongfully accused. Since I can rarely feel certain whether a man is wrongfully accused or is a scoundrel past redemption, it benefits both justice and my conscience to work for everyone as hard as I can, within the bounds of ethical legal behavior."

Gonzalo said, "Have you ever secured the acquittal of someone you considered a scoundrel?"

"On a few occasions. The fault there lay almost always in mistakes made by the prosecution—their illegal collection of evidence, or their slovenly preparation of the case. Nor would I waste pity on them. They have the full machinery of the law on their side and the boundless public purse. If we allow them to convict a scoundrel with less than the most legal of evidence and the tightest of cases simply because we are anxious to see a scoundrel punished, then where will you and I find safety? We, too, may seem scoundrels through force of circumstance or of prejudice."

Gonzalo said, "And have you ever failed to secure the acquittal of someone you considered wrongfully accused?"

Here Levine's face seemed to crumple. The fierce joy with which he defended his profession was gone and his lower lip seemed to quiver for a moment. "As a matter of fact," he said, softly, "I am engaged in a case right now in which my client may well be convicted despite the fact that I consider him wrongfully accused."

Drake chuckled and said, "I told you they'd get that out of you eventually, Barry!" He raised his voice to address the others generally. "I told him not to worry about confidentiality; that everything here was *sub rosa*. And I also told him it was just possible we might be able to help him."

Avalon stiffened and said in his most stately baritone, "Do you know any of the details of the case, Jim?"

"No, I don't."

"Then how do you know we can help?"

"I called it a possibility."

Avalon shook his head. "I expect that from Mario's enthusiasm, but not from you, Jim."

Drake raised his hand. "Don't lecture, Geoff. It doesn't become you."

Levine interposed. "Don't quarrel, gentlemen. I'll be pleased to accept any help you can offer, and if you can't, I will be no worse off. Naturally, I want to impress on you the fact that even though confidentiality may be the rule here, it is particularly important in this case. I rely on that."

"You may," said Avalon stiffly.

Trumbull said, "All right, now. Let's stop this dance and get down to it. Would you give us the details of the case you're speaking of, Mr. Levine?"

"I will give you the relevant data. My client is named Johnson, which is a name that I would very likely have chosen if I were inventing fictitious names, but it is a real name. There is a chance that you might have heard of this case, but I rather think you haven't, for it is not a local case and, if you don't mind, I will not mention the city in which it occurred, for that is not relevant.

"Johnson, my client, was in debt to a loan shark, whom he knew—that is, with whom he had enough of a personal relationship to be able to undertake a personal plea for an extension of time.

"He went to the hotel room that the loan shark used as his office—a sleazy room in a sleazy hotel that fit his sleazy business. The shark knew Johnson well enough to be willing to see him, and even to affect a kind of spurious *bonhomie,* but would not grant the extension. This meant that when Johnson went into default he would, at the very least, be beaten up; that his business would be vandalized; that his family, perhaps, would be victimized.

"He was desperate—and I am, of course, telling you Johnson's story as he told it to me—but the shark explained quite coolly that if Johnson were let off then others would expect the same leniency. On the other hand, if Johnson were made an example of, it would nerve others to pay promptly and perhaps deter some from incurring debts they could not repay. It was particularly galling to Johnson, apparently, that the loan shark waxed virtuous over the necessity of protecting would-be debtors from themselves."

Rubin said dryly, "I dare say, Mr. Levine, that if a loan shark were as articulate as you are, he could make out as good a case for his profession as you could for yours."

Levine said, after a momentary pause, "I would not be surprised. In fact, before you bother to point it out, I may as well say that, given the reputation of lawyers with the public, people hearing the defenses of both professions might vote in favor of loan sharks as the more admirable of the two. I can't help that, but I still think that if you're in trouble you had better try a lawyer before you try a loan shark.

"To continue, Johnson was not at all impressed by the shark's rationale for trying to extract blood from a stone, then pulverizing the stone for failure to bleed. He broke down into a rage, screaming out threats he could not fulfill. In brief, he threatened to kill the shark."

Trumbull said, "Since you're telling us Johnson's story, I assume he admitted making the threat."

"Yes, he did," said Levine. "I told him at the start, as I tell all my clients, that I could not efficiently help him unless he told me the full truth, even to confessing to a crime. Even after such a confession, I would still be compelled to defend him, and to fight, at worst, for the least punishment to which he might be entitled and, at best, for acquittal on any of several conceivable grounds.

"He believed me, I think, and did not hesitate to tell me of the threat; nor did he attempt to palliate or qualify it. That impressed me, and I am under the strong impression that he has been telling me the truth. I am old enough in my profession and have suffered the protestations of enough liars to feel confident of the truth when I hear it. And, as it happens, there is evidence supporting this part of the story, though Johnson did not know that at the time and so did not tell the truth merely because he knew it would be useless to lie."

Trumbull said, "What was the evidence?"

Levine said, "The hotel rooms are not soundproofed and Johnson was shrieking at the top of his voice. A maid heard just about every word and so did a fellow in an adjoining room who was trying to take a nap and who called down to the front desk to complain."

Trumbull said, "That just means an argument was going on. What evidence is there that it was Johnson who was shrieking?"

"Oh ample," said Levine. "The desk clerk also knows Johnson, and Johnson had stopped at the desk and asked if the shark were in. The desk clerk called him and sent Johnson up—and he saw Johnson come down later—and the news of the death threat arrived at the desk between those two periods of time.

"Nevertheless, the threat was meaningless. It served, in fact, merely to bleed off Johnson's rage and to deflate him. He left almost immediately afterward. I am quite certain that Johnson was incapable of killing."

Rubin stirred restlessly. He said, "That's nonsense. Anyone is capable of killing, given a moment of sufficient rage or terror and a weapon at hand. I presume that after Johnson left, the loan shark was found dead with his skull battered in; with a baseball bat, with blood and hair on it, lying on the bed; and you're going to tell us that you're sure Johnson didn't do it."

Levine held up his glass for what he indicated with his fingers was to be a touch more brandy, smiled his thanks to Henry, and said, "I have read some of your murder mysteries, Mr. Rubin, and I've enjoyed them. I'm sure that in your mysteries such a situation could occur and you'd find ways of demonstrating the suspect to be innocent. This, however, is not a Rubin mystery. The loan shark was quite alive when Johnson left."

Rubin said, "According to Johnson, of course."

"And unimpeachable witnesses. The man who called down said there was someone being murdered in the next room, and the desk clerk sent up the security man at once, for he feared it was his friend being murdered. The security man was well armed, and though he is not an intellectual type, he is perfectly competent to serve as a witness. He knocked and called out his identity, whereupon the door opened and revealed the loan shark, whom the security man knew, quite alive—and alone. Johnson had already left, deflated and de-energized.

"The man at the desk, Brancusi is his name, saw Johnson leave a few seconds after the security man had taken the elevator up. They apparently passed each other in adjoining elevators. Brancusi called out, but Johnson merely lifted his hand and hurried out. He looked white and ill, Brancusi says. That was about a quarter after three, according to Brancusi— and according to Johnson, as well.

"As for the loan shark, he came down shortly after four and sat in the bar for an hour or more. The bartender, who knew him, testified to that and can satisfactorily enumerate the drinks he had. At about a quarter after five he left the bar and, presumably, went upstairs."

Avalon said, "Did he drink enough to have become intoxicated?"

"Not according to the bartender. He was well within his usual limit and showed no signs of being drunk."

"Did he talk to anyone in particular?"

"Only to the bartender. And according to the bartender, he left the bar alone."

Gonzalo said, "That doesn't mean anything. He might have met someone in the lobby. Did anyone see him go into the elevator alone?"

"Not as far as we know," said Levine. "Brancusi didn't happen to notice, and no one else has admitted to seeing him, or has come forward to volunteer the information. For that matter, he may have met someone in the elevator or in the corridor outside his room. We don't know, and have no evidence to show he wasn't alone when he went into his room shortly after a quarter after five.

"Nevertheless, this two-hour period between a quarter after three and a quarter after five is highly significant. The security guard who encountered the loan shark immediately after Johnson had left at a quarter after three, found the shark composed and rather amused at the fuss. Just a small argument, he said; nothing important. Then, too, the barman insists that the loan shark's conversation and attitude throughout his time in the bar was normal and unremarkable. He made no reference to threats or arguments."

Halsted said, "Would you have expected him to?"

"Perhaps not," said Levine, "but it is still significant. After all, he knew Johnson. He knew the man to be both physically and emotionally a weakling. He had no fear of being attacked by him, or any doubt that he could easily handle him if he did attack.

"After all, he had agreed to see him without taking the precaution of having a bodyguard present, even though he knew Johnson would be desperate. He was not even temporarily disturbed by Johnson's outburst and shrugged it off to the guard. During that entire two-hour interval he acted as though he considered my client harmless and I would certainly make that point to the jury."

Avalon shook his head. "Maybe so, but if your story is going to have any point at all, the loan shark, you will tell us, met with a violent death. And if so, the man who made the threat is going to be suspected of the murder. Even if the loan shark was certain that Johnson was harmless, that means nothing. The loan shark may simply have made an egregious error."

Levine sighed, "The shark did die. He returned to his room at a quarter after five or a minute or two later and, I suspect, found a burglar in action. The loan shark had a goodish supply of cash in the room—necessary for his business—and the hotel was not immune to burglaries. The loan shark grappled with the intruder and was killed before half past five."

Trumbull said, "And the evidence?"

"The man in the adjoining room who had been trying to take a nap two hours before had seethed sufficiently to have been unable to fall asleep until about five and then, having finally dropped off, he was roused again by loud noises. He called down to the desk in a rage, and informed Brancusi that this time he had called the police directly."

Gonzalo said, "Did he hear the same voice he had heard before?"

"I doubt that any voice identification he would try to make would stand up in court," said Levine. "However, he didn't claim to have heard voices. Only the noises of furniture banging, glass breaking, and so on.

"Brancusi sent up the security guard who, getting no answer to his knock and call this time, used his passkey at just about half past five and found the loan shark strangled, the room in wild disorder, and the window open. The window opened on a neighboring roof two stories lower. An experienced cat burglar could have made it down without trouble and might well have been unobserved.

"The police arrived soon after, at about twenty to six."

Trumbull said, "The police, I take it, do not buy the theory that the murder was committed by a burglar."

"No. They could detect no signs on the wall or roof outside the window to indicate the recent passage of a burglar. Instead, having discovered upon inquiry of the earlier incident from the man who had called them, they scorn the possibility of coincidence and feel that Johnson made his way to the room a second time, attacked and strangled the loan shark, knocking the furniture about in the process, then opened the window to make it look as though an intruder had done the job, hastened out of the door, missing the security man by moments, and passing him on the elevator again."

Trumbull said, "Don't you believe that's possible?"

"Oh anything's *possible*," said Levine, coolly, "but it is not the job of the prosecutor to show it's possible. He has to show it's actually so beyond a reasonable doubt. The fact that the police saw nothing on the walls or roof is of no significance whatever. They may not have looked hard enough. A negative never impresses either judge or jury—and shouldn't. And threats at a quarter after three have nothing to do with an act at twenty after five or so unless the man who made the threat at the former time can be firmly placed on the scene at the later time."

Gonzalo was balancing his chair on its back legs with his hands gripping the table. "So what's the problem?"

"The problem is, Mr. Gonzalo," said Levine, "that Johnson *was* placed on the scene of the crime at about the time of the killing."

Gonzalo brought his chair forward with a clatter. "With good evidence?"

"The best," said Levine. "He admits it. Here is what happened: In the two hours after he had left the loan shark, Johnson hurriedly scraped up every bit of money he had, borrowed small sums from several friends, made a visit to a pawnshop, and had raised something like a third of what he owed. He then came back to the hotel hoping for as long an extension as possible through payment of this part sum. He had little hope of success, but he had to try.

"He arrived at the hotel at about a quarter to six, after the murder had been committed, and he noted a police squad car at the curb outside the hotel. Except for noticing its existence, he paid it little attention. He had only one thing on his mind.

"He headed straight for the elevator, which happened to be at the lobby with its door open. As he stepped out of it at the loan shark's floor, he saw a policeman at the door of the room he was heading for. Almost instinctively, he ducked back into the elevator and pushed the lobby button. He was the only man in the elevator and there were no calls to higher floors. The elevator moved downward, stopping at no floors. When he reached the lobby, he hastened out, went home, and stayed there till the police came for him."

A curl of cigarette smoke hung above Drake's head. He

said, "I suppose they learned of the earlier threat and took him in for questioning."

"Right," said Levine.

"But they can't make Johnson testify against himself, so how do they show he was on the spot at the time of the murder?"

"For one thing, Brancusi saw him when he was heading for the elevator. Brancusi called out to head him off and prevent him from running into the police. Johnson didn't hear him and the elevator doors closed behind him before Brancusi could do anything else. Brancusi insists, however, that Johnson was back down again in two minutes or so and hastened out. And he is prepared to swear that Johnson left at precisely ten minutes to six.

Drake said, "Is Brancusi really sure of that?"

"Absolutely. His shift was over at six o'clock and he was furious at the fact that the murder had not taken place an hour later, when he would have been off duty. As it was, he was sure he would be needed for questioning and might be kept for hours. He was therefore unusually aware of the time. There was an electric clock on the wall to one side of his desk, a nice large one with clear figures that was new and had been recently installed. It was accurate to the second and he is absolutely certain it said ten to six."

Avalon cleared his throat. "In that case, Mr. Levine, Brancusi backs up Johnson's story and places your client at the scene not at the time of the murder but afterward."

Levine said, "Here is where the trivialities come in. Brancusi is a bad witness. He has a small stutter, which makes him sound unsure of himself; he has one drooping eyelid, which makes him look hangdog and suspicious; and he has distinct trouble in looking you in the eye. The jury will be ready to believe him a liar.

"Second, Brancusi is a friend of Johnson's, has known him from childhood, and is still a drinking buddy of the man. That gives him a motive for lying, and the prosecution is sure to make the most of that.

"Finally, Brancusi may not want to testify at all. He served six months in jail for a minor offense quite a number of years ago. He has lived a reasonably exemplary life since and naturally doesn't want that earlier incident to be made public. For one thing, it could cost him his job."

Rubin said, "Could the prosecution bring up the matter? It's irrelevant, isn't it?"

"Quite irrelevant, but if the prosecution takes the attitude that it serves to cast a doubt on the reliability of Brancusi as a witness, they might slip it past the judge."

Rubin said, "In that case, if you put neither Johnson nor Brancusi on the stand, the prosecution would still be stuck with the task of proving that Johnson was at the scene at the right time. They can't call Johnson themselves, and they won't call Brancusi to give his evidence because they then can't cross-examine him and bring out that jail term."

Levine sighed. "There's another witness. The man is an accountant named William Sandow. He had stopped at the hotel lobby to buy a small container of breath fresheners, and while he was at the newsstand, he saw Johnson pass him, hurrying out of the hotel. Later in the evening, he read about the murder, and called the police to volunteer the information. His description of the man he saw was a good one and, eventually, he made a positive identification out of a lineup.

"Sandow said that what drew his attention to the man who passed him was the look of horror and anguish on his face. Of course, he can't use terms like that on the witness stand, but the prosecution can get him to make factual statements to the effect that Johnson was sweating and trembling, and this would give him the air of an escaping murderer."

Rubin said, "No, it doesn't. Lots of things could make a man sweat and tremble, and Johnson had good reason to do so short of murder. Besides, Sandow just bears out the story of Brancusi and Johnson."

Levine shook his head. "No, he doesn't. Sandow says he happened to catch a glimpse of the time as Johnson passed him and swears it was exactly half past five, which is just after the murder was committed but *before* the police arrived. If true, that ruins Johnson's story and makes the assumption that he committed the murder a very tempting one."

Rubin said, "Brancusi backs Johnson. It's one man's word against another. You can't convict on that."

"You can," said Levine, "if the jury believes one man and not the other. If Brancusi is bound to make a bad impression, Sandow is bound to make a good one. He is open-faced, clean-cut, has a pleasant voice, and exudes efficiency and honesty. The mere fact that he is an accountant gives him an impression of exactness. And whereas Brancusi is a friend of Johnson and therefore suspect, Sandow is a complete outsider with no reason to lie."

Rubin said, "How sure are you of that? He was very ready to volunteer information and get involved. Does he have some secret grudge against Johnson? Or some connection with the loan shark?"

Levine shrugged his shoulders. "There are such things as public-spirited citizens, even today. The fact that he came forward will be in his favor with the jury. Naturally, my office has investigated Sandow's background. We've turned up nothing we can use against him—at least so far."

There was a short silence around the table, and then finally Rubin said, "Honest people make mistakes, too. Sandow says he just happened to catch a glimpse of the time. Just how did that happen? He just happened to glance at his wristwatch? Why? Brancusi had a good reason to watch the clock. What was Sandow's?"

"He does not claim to have looked at his watch. He caught a glimpse of the same wall clock that Brancusi looked at. Presumably both Brancusi and Sandow were looking at the same clock at the same moment. The same clock couldn't very well tell half past five to one person and ten to six to another at the same time. Clearly, one person is lying or mistaken, and the jury will believe Sandow."

Rubin said, "Brancusi was staring at the clock. Sandow just caught a glimpse. He may have caught the wrong glimpse."

Levine said, "I have considered stressing that point, but I am not sure I ought to. Sandow's statement that he just happened to catch a glimpse sounds honest, somehow. The mere fact that he doesn't claim to see more than he saw, that he doesn't make an undue effort to strengthen his evidence, makes him ring true. And he's an accountant. He says he's used to figures, that he can't help noticing and remembering them. The prosecution will surely have him say that on the stand, and the jury will surely accept that.

"On the other hand, Mr. Rubin, if I try to balance Sandow's cool certainty by having Brancusi become very, very definite and emotional about how certain he is it was ten to six, then he will carry all the less conviction for he will impress the jury as someone who is desperately trying to support a lie.

And if it looks as though he is making a good impression, the prosecution will make a major effort to bring out his previous prison record."

Halsted broke in with sudden animation. "Say, could Sandow see the clock from where he says he was standing at the newsstand?"

Levine said, "A good point. We checked that out at once and the answer is: Yes, he could. Easily."

There was another silence around the table, a rather long one.

Trumbull finally said, "Let's put it as briefly as we can. You are convinced that Johnson is innocent and that Brancusi is telling the truth. You are also convinced that Sandow is either lying or mistaken, but you can't think of any reason he might be or any way of showing he is. And the jury is going to believe Sandow and convict Johnson."

Levine said, "That's about it."

Rubin said, "Of course, juries are unpredictable."

"Yes, indeed," said Levine, "but if that's my only hope, it isn't much of one. I would like better."

Avalon's fingers were drumming noiselessly on the table-cloth. He said, "I'm a patent lawyer myself, and I have just about no courtroom experience. Still, all you need do is cast a reasonable doubt. Can't you point out that a man's liberty rests on a mere glimpse of a clock?"

"I can, and will try just as hard as I can short of pushing the prosecution into attempting to uncover Brancusi's prison record. I would like something better than that, too."

From the sideboard, Henry's voice sounded suddenly. "If you'll excuse me, Mr. Levine—I assume that the clock in question, the one to which both Mr. Brancusi and Mr. Sandow referred, is a digital clock."

Levine frowned. "Yes, it is. I didn't say it was, did I? How did you know?" His momentary confusion cleared, and he smiled. "Well, of course. No mystery. I said it was a new clock, and these days digital clocks are becoming so popular that it is reasonable to suppose that any new clock would be digital."

"I'm sure that is so," said Henry, "but that was not the reason for my conclusion. You said a few moments ago that Mr. Sandow was an accountant and that accountants couldn't help but notice and remember figures. Of course you don't notice and remember figures on an ordinary dial clock—you remember the position of the hands. On a dial clock it is just as easy to tell time when the hour numbers are replaced with dots or with nothing at all."

"Well, then?" said Levine.

"Almost any grown person of reasonable intelligence can tell time at a glance in that way. Accountants have no special advantage. A digital clock is different."

Levine said, "Since it was a digital clock, then accountants *do* have a special advantage. You're not helping me, Henry."

Henry said, "I think I am. You have been unconsciously misleading us, Mr. Levine, by giving the time in the old-fashioned way appropriate to a dial clock. You speak of a quarter after three and a quarter to six and so on. Digital clocks specifically show such times to be three-fifteen and five forty-five. As digital clocks become more and more universal, times will be spoken of in this way exclusively, I imagine."

Levine seemed a little impatient. "How does this change anything, Henry?"

Henry said, "Your statement was that Brancusi was certain that the time at the crucial moment was ten to six, while Sandow was certain it was half past five. If this were so, and if a dial clock were involved, the position of the hands at the two times would be widely different and neither could make a mistake. A deliberate lie by one or the other would have to be involved.

"On the other hand, if it is a digital clock, Brancusi claims he read five-fifty and Sandow claims he read five-thirty, you see."

Levine said, "Ah, and you think that Sandow misread the figure five for a three. No good; it could be maintained with equal justice that Brancusi mistook the three for a five in his annoyance over the fact that the end of his shift was approaching."

Henry said, "It is not a question of a mistake that anyone could make. It is a mistake that an accountant particularly might make. There are fifty cents to half a dollar but thirty minutes to half an hour, and an accountant above all is apt to think of figures in terms of money. To an accountant five-fifty is most likely to mean five and a half dollars. A quick glimpse at a digital clock reading five-fifty might trigger the response five and a half in in accountant's mind, and he will later swear he had seen the time as half past five."

Avalon looked astonished. "You really think Mr. Sandow could have made that mistake, Henry?"

But it was Levine who answered jubilantly, "Of course! It's the only way of explaining how two people could read the same clock at the same time and honestly come up with two different answers. Besides, *there's* the reasonable doubt. Suppose I set up a screen on which I can flash numbers on the pretext that I have to test Sandow's eyesight and memory of numbers, and ask him to detect and identify numbers flashed only briefly on the screen. If I show him five-fifty with a dollar sign before it, he will be bound to say, 'five and a half dollars.' "

Gonzalo said, "He might say 'five-fifty' or something like that."

"If he does, I'll ask him if he means five hundred and fifty dollars or five and a half dollars—after all, does he or does he not see the decimal point?—and he will be sure to say five and a half dollars. He will then repeat that with five-fifty written in other printing styles and with the dollar sign left out. Finally, when I flash the image of a digital clock reading five-fifty and ask whether that is five and a half or ten to six, he won't even have to answer. The jury will get the point."

Levine rose to shake Henry's hand. "Thank you, Henry. I said that cases depend on trivialities, but I never dreamed that this one would rest on something as trivial as the difference between a digital clock and a dial clock."

"But," said Henry, "on that piece of trivia depends the freedom of a man who is presumably wrongfully accused of murder, and that is no triviality at all."

"What Time Is It?"—Afterword

It was almost with disappointment that I noticed that I had completed ten stories toward the twelve I needed for the third book and had managed to compile only one rejection. It meant that I would have to refrain from submitting the last two stories for magazine publication and just write them for the book itself.

Since I had to do it, I did it—and this one was written at the third mystery-fan meeting at Mohonk, which I referred to in the Afterword to "Irrelevance!"

You'll notice that "What Time Is It?" involves a murder, as is rarely the case with my Black Widowers tales. However, it is not a whodunit, or a howdunit, or a whydunit. It's just a matter of explaining a discrepancy—which is what the Black Widowers is all about.

But at least the Black Widowers got an innocent man off the hook.

11.

Middle Name

Roger Halsted looked a bit doleful and said, "I almost didn't get here tonight."

Geoffrey Avalon looked down at him from his straight-backed seventy-four inches and said, "Automobile accident?"

"Nothing so dramatic," said Halsted. "Alice was in one of her feminist moods this afternoon and objected rather strenuously to the fact that the Black Widowers Society is a stag organization."

"But she's known that from the start, hasn't she?" asked Avalon.

"Of course, and it's graveled her from the start, too," said Halsted. "Sometimes it's worse than other times, that's all. And today, well, she may have seen something on TV, read something in the newspapers, had a talk with a friend, or whatever. Anyway, she was upset, and the trouble is, I rather sympathize with her."

Emmanuel Rubin walked over from the other end of the room, where he had been exchanging insults with Mario Gonzalo, host at this month's Black Widowers banquet.

Rubin said, "Are you talking about your wife, Roger?"

"Yes, as a matter of fact."

"I could tell by the troubled look on your face. Bad form. Black Widowers don't have wives."

"Yes?" said Halsted sharply. "Have you told that to Jane?"

"I mean during the banquets, and you know that's what I mean."

"I've heard you mention Jane at the banquets and, besides, my own discussion is germane to the banquets. I would hate to have to give them up."

"Who can make you?" demanded Rubin scornfully, his scanty beard bristling.

Halsted said, "My own conscience, for one thing. And it's not worth breaking up a marriage over."

"Why should it break up a marriage?" said Rubin. "Even if we grant equality for women—political, economic, and social—why should that prevent me from spending one evening a month with friends of my own choosing who just happen to be male?"

Avalon said, "You know better than that, Manny. They don't just happen to be male. They are forbidden by the rules of the club to be anything but male."

"And anything but intelligent," said Rubin, "and anything but compatible. If any one of us takes a dislike to anyone proposed for membership, however trivial or even nonexistent the cause of that dislike might be, that potential member can be blackballed. Just one of us can do it, regardless of the wishes of the rest, and we don't have to explain either."

"Manny," said Avalon, "you're not usually so obtuse. A woman can't be blackballed, because she can't even be *proposed* for membership. Don't you see the difference? Whichever one of us is host for the evening can bring any guest he wishes, even one who would be instantly blackballed if he were proposed for membership. But the guest must be male. No women can be brought. Don't you see the difference?"

"Exactly," said Halsted. "If it were a black that we ruled out, or a Jew, or an Irishman, that would be bigotry and not one of us could live with it. But since it's only women, we don't seem to mind. What moral blindness!"

"Well, then," said Rubin, "are you two suggesting that we permit women to join the society?"

"No," said Avalon and Halsted in quick and emphatic simultaneity.

"Then what are we arguing about?"

Halsted said, "I'm just pointing out that we ought to recognize the immorality of it."

"You mean as long as we know something is immoral, we are free to be immoral."

"Of course I don't," said Halsted. "I happen to think that hypocrisy aggravates any sin. Nothing is so male chauvinist as to say, 'I'm not a male chauvinist, but . . .' as I've heard Manny say."

Mario Gonzalo joined them and said with clear self-satisfaction. "I don't say, 'I'm not a male chauvinist, but . . .' I *am* a male chauvinist. I expect a woman to take care of me."

"That's just an admission you can't take care of yourself," said Rubin, "which is something I've always suspected, Mario."

Gonzalo looked over his shoulder hurriedly in the direction of his guest and then said, in a low voice, "Listen, keep talking feminism during the dinner, off and on. It's a stroke of luck you've started on your own."

"Why?" said Avalon in a voice that had not been hushed since its invention. "What dire plot are you . . ."

"Shh," said Gonzalo. "I want to draw out my guest. He's got something eating him he won't talk about. That's why I brought him. It could be interesting."

"Do you know what it is?" asked Halsted.

"Only in a general way . . ." said Gonzalo.

Henry, whose elegant service at the banquets ennobled the occasion, interrupted in his soft way. "If you don't mind, Mr. Gonzalo, dinner is served."

Gonzalo placed his guest immediately to his right and said, "Has everyone met Mr. Washburn now?"

There was a general murmur of agreement. Lionel Washburn was an almost classically handsome individual with a head of thick, dark hair cut neatly, with black-rimmed glasses, white shirt, dark-blue suit, and shiny black shoes. He looked dressed up without being uncomfortable. He did not yet seem to have passed his thirtieth birthday.

He said to Gonzalo somberly, "Is there some argument about whether the organization is to be stag, Mario? I heard . . ."

"No argument," said Gonzalo quickly. "It *is* stag. I invited *you*. I didn't suggest you bring a girlfriend."

"I don't have one," said Washburn, biting off each word. Then, more normally, "How long have you been stag?"

"From the start, but it's Jim's story. Jim, my guest would like to hear how the society got its start—if you don't mind, that is."

James Drake smiled and held his cigarette to one side so that he could see the other's face clearly. "I don't mind, though I'm sure the others are pretty sick of it. Still—any objections?"

Thomas Trumbull, who was cutting into his rack of lamb, said, "Plenty of objections, but you go ahead and I'll attend to the inner man. Henry, if you can scare up an extra helping of mint sauce, I would be infinitely appreciative. And Jim, I would suggest you get our personal Book of Genesis printed up and handed out at the start of each banquet to the guest. The rest of us can then be spared. Thank you, Henry."

Drake said, "Now that we have Tom out of the way, I'll go on. About thirty years ago, I married, but then we all make mistakes, don't we? I believe I was fascinated at the time, though I don't remember why. My friends, however, were not fascinated."

Avalon drew in his breath in a long, rumbling sniff. "*We* remember why."

"I'm sure you do," agreed Drake good-humoredly. "As a result, I found myself outcast. My friends fell away and I couldn't endure *her* friends or, after a time, her. It occurred to Ralph Ottur, then—He lives in California now, I'm sorry to say—to start a club for the sole purpose of seeing me without my wife. Naturally, this would only work if the club were stag. So there you are. We called it the Black Widowers because black widow spiders are quite apt to devour their mates, and we were determined to survive."

Washburn said, "And does your wife know the nature of the origin of the club?"

"She's not my wife," said Drake. "Anymore, that is. I divorced her after seven years."

"And were you all members at the start?"

Drake shook his head. "Geoff, Tom, and I are charter members. The others joined later. Some members have died or now live too far away to attend."

"But the reason for the men-only character of the club is gone. Why do you . . ."

"Because we want to," said Gonzalo quickly. "Because I like women in their place and I know exactly where that place is and here isn't it."

"That's a disgusting statement," said Halsted, with a slight stutter that came when he grew emotional.

Gonzalo said coolly, "You've got to say that because you're married and you're afraid that if you don't keep in practice, you'll let something chauvinistic, so-called, slip in front of your wife and then you'll be in trouble. I'm not married so I'm a free man. My girlfriends know where I stand, and if they don't like it, they can leave."

Avalon said, "There's an uncomfortable Don Juanism about that statement. Don't you care if they leave?"

"Sometimes," admitted Gonzalo, "but I'd care a lot more if they stayed and argued with me. And there are always others."

"Disgusting," said Halsted again.

"The truth usually is," said Gonzalo. "Why don't all you highly moral feminists tell me why you don't want women at these meetings and see if you can make the reason non-chauvinist?"

There was an uncomfortable silence about the table, and Gonzalo said, "Henry, you're a Black Widower, too, and I'm not letting you escape. Would you like to see women at these meetings?"

Henry's face crinkled into a pleasant smile. "No, Mr. Gonzalo, I would not."

"Aha," said Gonzalo. "Now, you're an honest man, Henry, unlike these Black Hypocriticers you wait on. Tell me why not."

Henry said, "Like you, Mr. Gonzalo, I am not married, but I'm afraid I lack your variegated experience with young women."

"What's that got to do with it?"

Henry said, "I was merely explaining the situation in case my theory on the subject should prove to be childishly foolish to other, more experienced men. It seems to me that most men during their childhood have had their mothers as their chief authority figures. Even when the father is held up as a mysterious and ogreish dispenser of punishments, it is, in fact, the mother whose outcries, yanks, pushes, and slaps perpetually stand in the way of what we want to do. And we never recover."

Rubin said, in a voice of deep, masculine disdain, "Come, Henry, are you trying to say that men are afraid of women?"

Henry said, "I believe many are. Certainly, many feel a sense of relief and freedom when in the company of men only and feel particularly free when women are not allowed to intrude. This society originated as a haven from women under the guise of being one from a particular woman. The particular woman is gone but the haven is still needed and still persists."

Avalon said, "Well, that is at least not an example of outright chauvinism."

"And totally untrue," said Rubin, his eyes flashing behind the thick lenses that covered them. "How many here are afraid of women?"

It was Washburn who intervened at this point. With his handsome face contorted into a mask of fury, he brought his fist down with a smash that rattled the dishes and caused Henry to pause in his task of pouring the coffee.

Washburn said, "You don't expect anyone to admit it, do you? Your waiter is correct, but he doesn't go far enough. Of course, we're afraid of women. Why shouldn't we be? They're man-eaters, cannibals, harpies. They're bound by no rules, no canons of sportsmanship. They're the ruin of men and of all that is decent and human. I don't care if I never see another one in my life."

He paused, drew a deep breath, then passed a hand over his forehead, which had dampened with perspiration and said, "Pardon me, gentlemen, I did not mean to lose my temper."

Trumbull said, "But why . . ." and stopped at Gonzalo's raised hand.

Gonzalo was grinning in triumph. "Later, Tom. It's almost grilling time and I'll choose you as inquisitor and you can ask your question."

And, indeed, it was not long before Gonzalo began the ritualistic tapping of the water glass as the brandy was being distributed. He said, "It's up to you, Tom."

Trumbull frowned ferociously under his white and crisply waved hair and said, "I will assume, Mr. Washburn, that Mario has explained to you that the payment, for what we hope you will agree is a fine dinner and at least partly edifying conversation, is a grilling. To our questions, you will be expected to answer fully and truthfully, even when that may be embarrassing. I must assure you that nothing said here ever leaves these four walls.

"With that preamble, let me say this. I am not a judge of masculine pulchritude, Mr. Washburn, but it seems to me that women would judge you to be handsome."

Washburn flushed and said, "I would not try to account for women's tastes. Still it is true that I have found that I can, on occasion, attract women."

"That's a very modest way of putting it," said Trumbull. "Does the converse hold as well? Do women attract you?"

For a moment, Washburn looked puzzled. Then he frowned and said, "Are you asking me if I am gay?"

Trumbull shrugged and said in a level voice, "In these times, it is a permissible question, and it is even permissible to answer in an open affirmative, if that should happen to be the case. I ask out of no personal interest, I assure you, but merely out of curiosity over your earlier angry remarks about women as a group."

Washburn relaxed. "I see your point. No, I'm interested in women. Far too interested. And it was not the sex as a whole that I was really berating. I was striking out at one! One woman! And myself!"

Trumbull hesitated. "The logical thing," he said, "would be to question you, Mr. Washburn, concerning this woman who so distresses you. Yet I hesitate. On the one hand, it is a peculiarly private matter, which I do not wish to probe and, on the other, if you don't mind my saying so, the details are likely to be peculiarly uninteresting. I suppose every one of us in our time . . ."

Avalon interrupted. "If *you* don't mind, Tom, you are displaying an uncommon combination of delicacy and insensitivity. I am prepared, with your permission, to take over the grilling."

"If you think you can do so, Geoff, within the bounds of good taste," said Trumbull huffily.

Avalon lifted his dense eyebrows to maximum and said, "I think highly of you, Tom, and yet have never considered you an arbiter of good taste. Mr. Washburn, I have no wish to probe wounds unnecessarily, but let me guess. Your outburst came during a discussion of the pros and cons of feminism. May we take it, then, that your unhappy experience, whatever it was, involved feminism?"

Washburn nodded and said, "It sure as hell did."

"Good! Now it may be superfluous to ask this, but was whatever it was that happened something that has happened to many others? Putting aside the great pain it may have caused you and the unique unhappiness you may consider you have felt, would you in your calmer moments think that it might be the common lot of male humanity?"

Washburn seemed lost in thought, and Avalon went on as gently as he could. "After all, millions have been jilted, millions have been sold out, millions have been betrayed by their lovers and their friends."

"What happened to me," said Washburn, between remarkably white and even teeth, "has in a way happened to very many, as you suggest. I recognize that. To lose the woman one loves is not so rare. To be laughed at and humiliated," he swallowed, "may be the lot of many. But in one respect, I have been ill used particularly. In one respect."

Avalon nodded. "Very good. I won't ask you any leading questions. Just tell us about that one respect."

Washburn bent his glance down to his brandy snifter and spoke in a hurried tone of voice. "I fell in love. It wasn't the first time. She was—she was not the most beautiful woman I have ever known—nor the pleasantest. In fact, we did not get along. Her company was always a maddening bumpy ride in a springless cart down a rough road. But, oh God, I couldn't help myself. I still can't seem to. Don't ask me to analyze it. All I can say is that I was caught, tangled, trapped, and I wanted her. And I couldn't get her.

"She acted as though she hated me. She acted as though she wanted me to want her, just so she could show the world I couldn't have her.

"She was a feminist. Her nerve endings stuck out six inches beyond her skin on that subject. She was successful. She was a magazine illustrator at the top of her field and commanded high fees. It wasn't enough, though. To make it right for her, I had to fail.

"And there was no way I could argue effectively with her. She won every time. Of course, she was an intellectual and I'm not—though I like to think I'm intelligent. . . ."

Rubin said, "Intelligence is the diamond and intellectualism only the facets. I've known many a beautifully faceted rhinestone. What do you do for a living?"

Washburn said, "I'm a stockbroker."

"Do you do well? I mean, as well as your feminist?"

Washburn flushed. "Yes. And I've inherited a rather sizable trust fund. She seemed to resent that."

"Let me guess," said Rubin dryly. "You make more money with less brains because you're a man. You get farther with less deserving because you're a man. You probably even inherited the trust fund because you were a man. Your sister would have gotten less."

"That's about it," said Washburn. "She said the way I dressed, the way I held myself, everything about me was designed to show my masculine wealth and power. She said I might as well wear a neon sign saying, 'I can buy women.' "

Trumbull said, "Did you ever try to defend yourself?"

"Sure," said Washburn, "and that meant a fight. I asked her why, if she thought she should be considered as a human being and as an intellectual, without being penalized for her sex, she insisted on emphasizing her sex? Why didn't she remove her makeup and meet the world with an unpainted face as men did? Why didn't she wear less revealing clothes, and accentuate her breasts and hips less? I said she might as well wear a neon sign saying, 'I sell for a high price.' "

"She must have loved that," muttered Rubin.

"You bet she didn't," said Washburn grimly. "She said a masculine society forced that on her in self-defense, and she wouldn't give up the only weapon they granted her. I said she needed no weapon with me. I said I would marry her without enticement or allure, straight out of the shower with wet hair and a pimple on her shoulder if she had one. And she said, 'To do what? To cook your dinner and clean your house for you?' And I said, 'I have a housekeeper for that.' And she said, 'Of course; another woman.' "

Halsted said, "What good would it have done you to marry her? You would have fought like that every day. It would have been a purgatory. Why not just walk away from that?"

"Why not?" said Washburn. "Sure, why not? Why not just kick the heroin habit? Why not just stop breathing if the air gets polluted? How do I know why not? It's not the sort of thing you can reason out. Maybe—maybe—if I had the chance, I could win her over."

"You wouldn't have," said Rubin flatly. "She's a ballbuster, and she'd stay one."

Halsted said, "That's a stupid phrase, Manny. It's part of the routine bigotry of the chauvinist. A man is ambitious; a woman is unscrupulous. A man is firm; a woman is stubborn. A man is witty; a woman is bitchy. A man is competitive; a woman is abrasive. A man is a hard-driving leader; a woman is a ballbuster."

Rubin said, "Call it what you want. Say she's a lily of the valley if you want. I say her ambition and occupation would have been to make our friend here wish he had never been born, and she would have succeeded."

Turning to Washburn, he said, "I assume from your early outburst, your failure with her was complete. If so, I congratulate you, and if I knew of a way to help you succeed, I would refuse to give it to you."

Washburn shook his head. "No fear. She's married someone else—a dumb creep—and the last I've heard she *is* cooking and cleaning house."

"Did she give up her career?" said Avalon in astonishment.

"No," said Washburn, "but she does the other, too. What I'll never understand is why *him*."

Trumbull said, "There's no accounting for the nature of attraction. Maybe this other fellow makes her laugh. Maybe he dominates her without bothering to argue the point. Maybe she likes the way he smells. How can you tell? How do you account for the way she attracts you? Nothing you've said makes her attractive to me."

"If she liked him better," said Washburn, fuming, "why not say so, for whatever reason—or for no reason? Why make it look like a straightforward test? Why humiliate me?"

"Test?" said Rubin. "What test?"

"That's what I referred to when I said earlier that in one way I had been particularly ill used. She said she would see if I were the kind of man she could live with. She dared me to give her a one-syllable middle name to represent what every schoolchild knew—and yet didn't know. She implied that she was giving the other fellow the same test. I knew about him and I didn't worry about him. My God, he was a stupid advertising copy writer who shambled about in turtleneck sweaters and drank beer."

Avalon said, "Surely, you couldn't believe a woman would choose one man over another according to whether he could solve a puzzle. That happens in fairytales perhaps; otherwise, not."

Washburn said, "I see that *now*. She married him, though. She said he had the answer. That idiot passed, she said, and I failed. Not getting her was bad enough, but she arranged to make me lose in a battle of wits to someone I despised—or at least she *said* I had lost. It wasn't a *test*. It was nonsense. Suppose you chose a middle name with one syllable—John, Charles, Ray, George—any one of them. Who's to say the answer is right or wrong, except her?"

"If she were going to marry him anyway, she might have done that without going out of her way to make me look foolish in my own eyes."

Halsted said, "What if the question were a legitimate one? What if he had gotten the correct answer and you hadn't? Would that make you feel better?"

"I suppose so," said Washburn, "but the more I think of it, the more certain I am that it's a fake."

"Let's see now," said Halsted thoughtfully. "We need a one-syllable middle name that every schoolboy knows—and yet doesn't know."

"Schoolchild," growled Washburn. "Schoolboy is chauvinistic."

Gonzalo said, "Go ahead, Roger. You teach school. What does every schoolchild know—and yet not know?"

"In my class at the junior high school," said Halsted, gloomily, "every schoolchild knows he ought to know algebra, and what he doesn't know is algebra. If algebra were a one-syllable middle name that would be the answer."

Drake said, "Let's be systematic. Only people have middle names in the usual meaning of the word, so we can start with that. If we find a person whom every schoolchild knows—and yet doesn't know, then that person will have a middle name and that middle name will be the answer."

"And if you think that," said Washburn, "where does it get you? For one thing, how is it possible to know something or someone—and yet not know? And if it *were* possible, then it's quite impossible that this should be true of only one person.

How would you pick out the correct person? No, that witch was playing games."

"Actually," said Avalon, "middle names are, on the whole, uncommon. Nowadays, everyone gets one, but they were much against the rule in the past, it seems to me. Think of some famous people—George Washington, Abraham Lincoln, Napoleon Bonaparte, William Shakespeare—no middle names in the lot. The Greeks had only one name—Socrates, Plato, Demosthenes, Creon. It limits the field somewhat."

Halsted said, "There's Robert Louis Stevenson, Franklin Delano Roosevelt, Gustavus Adolphus Vasa."

"Who's Gustavus Adolphus Vasa?" asked Gonzalo.

"A King of Sweden in the early 1600s," said Halsted.

Gonzalo said, "I suppose every Swedish schoolchild would know him, but we should stick to the knowledge of American schoolchildren."

"I agree," said Avalon.

Rubin said thoughtfully, "The Romans had three names as a matter of course. Julius Caesar was really Gaius Julius Caesar. His assassin, Cassius, was Gaius Cassius Longinus. Every American schoolchild would know the names Julius Caesar and Cassius from Shakespeare's play *Julius Caesar*, which every American schoolchild is put through. Yet he wouldn't know the names Gaius Julius Caesar and Gaius Cassius Longinus. He would think Julius was a first name and Cassius was a last name, but each would be a middle name. That would be the sort of thing we're after."

Avalon said, "Many cultures use patronymics as routine middle names. Every Russian has one. Peter I of Russia, or Peter the Great, as he's usually known, was really Peter Alexeievich Romanov. Every schoolchild knows Peter the Great and yet doesn't know his middle name, or even that he has one."

Rubin said, "There are other possibilities. Some middle names are treated as first names even for Americans. President Grover Cleveland was really Stephen Grover Cleveland. He dropped his first name and used his middle name, so every schoolchild knows Grover Cleveland and doesn't know Stephen Grover Cleveland. The same is true for Thomas Woodrow Wilson and John Calvin Coolidge.

"Then again, some middle names are lost in pen names. Mark Twain was really Samuel Langhorne Clemens, and

Lewis Carroll was really Charles Lutwidge Dodgson. Every schoolchild knows Mark Twain and Lewis Carroll but probably doesn't know Langhorne and Lutwidge."

Washburn said impatiently, "Pardon me, gentlemen, but what good is all this? How does it help with the problem? You can rattle off a million middle names, but which one did that female *want?*"

Avalon said solemnly, "We are merely outlining the dimensions of the problem, Mr. Washburn."

"And doing it all wrong," said Gonzalo. "Look, every middle name I've heard from Julius to Lutwidge has more than one syllable. Why not think of a one-syllable middle name and work backward? If we want to consider American Presidents, we can start with the letter 's.' You can't be more one-syllable than a single letter. Well, it was Harry S Truman; and the S was just S and stood for nothing. Every schoolchild has heard of Harry S Truman, but how many of them know S doesn't stand for anything?"

Drake said, "For that matter, every schoolchild knows Jimmy Carter; but his name really is James Earl Carter, Jr. The schoolchildren don't know about Earl, and that's one-syllable."

Washburn said, "You still have a million answers, and you don't have *one.*"

Trumbull suddenly roared out angrily, "Damn it to hell, gentlemen, you're leaving out the third and crucial clue. I'm sitting here waiting for one of you to realize this fact, and you just run around in solemn pedantic circles."

"What third clue, Tom?" asked Avalon quietly.

"You need a one-syllable middle name; that's one. You need that rigmarole about schoolchildren; that's two. And you have the fact that the woman said that the puzzle was intended to indicate whether Washburn was a man she could live with. *That's* three. It means that the puzzle must somehow involve male chauvinism, since the woman is an ardent feminist. The implication is that a male chauvinist, such as she firmly believes Washburn to be, would not get the answer."

Rubin said, "Good Lord, Tom, you've made sense. What next? Don't tell me you've worked out the answer, too."

Trumbull shook his head. "Not exactly, but I suggest we confine ourselves to women's names. A feminist would argue that many women have played important roles in history but that male chauvinism tends to blot them out. Therefore every schoolchild *should* know them, but doesn't."

Halsted said, "No, Tom. That's not the clue. It's not something every schoolchild *should* know but doesn't. It's something every schoolchild *knows* and doesn't. That's different."

"Besides," said Rubin, "even if we confine ourselves to women, we have no clear route to the answer. If we stick to historic feminists, for instance, we have Susan Brownell Anthony, Carrie Chapman Catt, Helen Gurley Brown, Gloria Steinem. Betty Friedan—who's got a one-syllable middle name?"

Drake said, "It needn't be a feminist." His little eyes seemed to peer thoughtfully into the middle distance. "It might just be a woman who contributed to history—like the one who wrote *Uncle Tom's Cabin* and helped cause the Civil War, as Lincoln said."

"Harriet Beecher Stowe," said Rubin impatiently, "and Beecher has two syllables."

"Yes," said Drake, "but I merely mentioned it as an example. What about the woman who wrote 'The Battle Hymn of the Republic,' Julia Ward Howe? How many syllables in Ward?"

Avalon said, "How is that something every schoolchild knows and yet doesn't know?"

Drake said, "Every schoolchild knows, 'Mine eyes have seen the glory of the coming of the Lord' and yet doesn't know the author, because she's a woman. At least that's what a feminist might claim."

There was a confused outcry of objections, and Avalon's deep voice suddenly rose into an overtopping bellow, "How about *Little Women*, which was written by Louisa May Alcott? Which would the answer be: Ward or May?"

Washburn suddenly cut in sharply, "Neither one."

Drake said, "Why not? How do you know?"

Washburn said, "Because she sent me what she said was the answer when she wrote to say she was married. And it isn't either Ward or May."

Rubin said indignantly, "You've withheld information, sir."

"No, I haven't," said Washburn. "I didn't have that information when I tried to get the answer, and now that I have it, I still don't see *why*. I think she just chose an answer at random as a continuing part of her intention of making me feel like an idiot.

"Nor will I give you the solution *now,* since you'll be able to dream up a reason once you have the name, and that's not good. The point is to be able to get a solution and reason it out without knowing the answer in advance—though she *did* hand me a feminine name. I'll give Mr. Trumbull that much."

Gonzalo said, "If we can reason out the name she gave and tell you what it is and why, will you feel better?"

Washburn said gloomily, "I think so. At least I might imagine it was a fair test and that I might have had her if I were brighter, and she wasn't just laughing at me. But can anyone tell me what the middle name is?"

He looked about the table and met six thoughtful stares.

Gonzalo said, "Do *you* have any ideas on the subject, Henry?"

The waiter, who was removing the brandy glasses, said, quietly, "Unless the middle name in question is Ann, Mr. Gonzalo, I'm afraid I am helpless."

Washburn let out an incoherent cry, pushed back his chair with a loud scraping noise, and jumped up.

"But it *is* Ann," he cried out. "How did you come to decide on that? Was it a guess or do you have a reason?"

He had reached out almost as though he were going to seize Henry by his shoulders and shake the answers out of him, but controlled himself with obvious difficulty.

Henry said, "The gentlemen of the Black Widowers supplied the pieces, sir. I needed only to put them together. Mr. Rubin said that a middle name might be hidden by a pseudonym, as in the case of Mark Twain. Mr. Trumbull pointed out that feminism was involved. It seemed to me quite possible that at times in history someone who was a woman might hide under a male pseudonym, and I pondered over whether there were such a case in connection with something every schoolchild would know.

"Surely, one book that schoolchildren have notoriously been required to read for decade after decade has been *Silas Marner.* Every schoolchild knows it, and the further fact that it was written by George Eliot. It seemed to me, though, that that was a pseudonym. I checked it in the encyclopedia on the reference shelf, while the discussion raged, and I found that Eliot's real name is Mary Ann Evans."

Washburn said, eyes big with wonder. "Then it *was* a fair question. I'm glad of *that*. But do you mean that the jerk she married figured it out?"

Henry said, "He may well have. I think it would be best for you, sir, to believe that he did."

"Middle Name"—Afterword

This story was written on a train trip to Richmond, Virginia, where I was slated to keynote a conference, and during my stay in Richmond.

The Trap Door Spiders and, therefore, the Black Widowers too, are indeed stag organizations. Only men can be members; only men can be guests. What's more, the Trap Door Spiders actually had their beginnings in the way attributed, in this story, to the Black Widowers.

Stag organizations are, of course, outmoded things in these days. I cannot speak for the other Trap Door Spiders, but my conscience hurts me over the matter. Janet, fortunately, is a very tolerant woman and is rather foolishly besotted with me so that she is willing to allow me to stay with not only one, but four, stag organizations, since she feels I enjoy them.

Well, I *do* enjoy them and I quiet my conscience by agitating from within in favor of open membership for women as well as men—but so far vainly in every case.

12.

To the Barest

Emmanuel Rubin said in a scandalized whisper, "He offered to *pay* for the dinner." He glanced with owlish ferocity at the guest who was attending that month's Black Widowers' banquet.

"Yes, he did," said Mario Gonzalo casually.

"And I suppose you accepted," said Rubin.

"No, I didn't, though I don't see why he shouldn't if he wants to. If someone is anxious to pay for the privilege of dining with us, why not let him?"

"Because we would be selling our freedom of choice, you idiot, and that is without price to the rest of us. Do you think I'm willing to eat with anyone who'll pick up my check? I *choose* my companions. Damn it, Mario, if he offered to buy us that should in itself instantly disqualify him as a guest."

"Well, it doesn't, so why not calm down, Manny, and listen? I've told the others already and saved you for last because I knew you'd rant away. He got in touch with me. . . ."

"Do you know him?"

"No, but he introduced himself. He's Matthew Parris, and he's a lawyer. He knew of the Black Widowers. He knew I was to be the next host and he wanted to see us professionally, *all* of us. He asked to join us at our banquet and offered to pay if that would help. He seemed like an interesting guy, so why not?"

Rubin said discontentedly, "Why should professional matters intrude on the banquet? What does he want to do, serve us with summonses?"

"No," said Gonzalo with an affectation of eye-rolling impatience. "He represents Ralph Ottur. We still send Ralph invitations, and that's how this guy, Parris, knew I was the next host. He got in touch with me at Ralph's instructions. I suppose you remember Ralph."

Rubin's eyes flashed behind his thick-lensed glasses. "Of course I remember him. I'm surprised you do. I didn't know you had become a member before he left."

"Memory decays with age, Manny."

Rubin ignored that. "That was twelve, fifteen years ago when he left us, when the Black Widowers were just beginning. That was before we met at the Milano—before Henry's time." He looked in Henry's direction with a smile and said, "It doesn't seem possible we could have had meetings of the Black Widowers without Henry. But then, in those days we wouldn't have believed it possible to have dinners without Ralph. It was in '65 he went to California, wasn't it? We were kids then."

"I believe," said Geoffrey Avalon, who had drifted toward them, his neatly bearded face solemn, "that you and I, Manny, were fortyish even then. Scarcely kids."

"Oh well," Rubin said. "What does Ralph want with us, Mario?"

"I don't know," said Gonzalo. "Parris wouldn't say. Have you heard from him lately?"

"Not a word in years. He doesn't even send in a refusal card to the invitations. Have you heard from him, Geoff?"

"No," said Avalon. "Tom Trumbull says Ralph is teaching navigation at CIT but has had no personal communication."

"Well, then, Geoff, what do we do about this lawyer Mario has dragged in?"

"Treat him as any other guest. What else can we do?"

Henry approached, his smooth and unwrinkled face radiating the efficiency that was characteristic of this best of waiters. He said, "Mr. Gonzalo, we are ready to begin dinner if you will be so kind as to call the meeting to order."

* * *

The dinner was quieter than usual as Matthew Parris somehow absorbed the attention of the others. He seemed oblivious to that, however, his smooth-shaven face shining pinkly, his graying hair slicked smoothly back, his smile wide and unaffected, his speech precise and with a flat midwestern accent.

At no time did he refer to the business at hand, but confined himself to discussing the Middle Eastern situation. The trouble, he said, was that both sides were playing for time. The Arabs felt that as oil supplies dwindled, world hunger for energy would bring victory. Israel felt that as oil supplies dwindled, Arab influence would dwindle with it.

To which James Drake said somberly that as oil supplies dwindled, civilization might break down and the whole matter of victory (quote, unquote, he said) in the Middle East or anywhere else would be irrelevant.

"Ah," said Parris, "but your fiery ideolog doesn't care about trivial things such as survival. He would rather win in hell than lose in heaven."

Mario Gonzalo, who had put aside his rather blinding pea-green jacket and was eating veal cordon bleu in his striped shirt-sleeves, leaned toward Thomas Trumbull and whispered, "This whole thing may be a practical joke, Tom. I only met Ralph two or three times before he left. He was a peculiar fellow as I recall."

Trumbull's bronzed forehead furrowed under his white thatch of hair. "So are we all, I hope. Ralph Ottur founded this club. We used to eat at his house during the first two or three years. He was a widower, a gourmet cook, an astronomer, and a word buff."

"That's what I remember. The word-buff bit."

"Yes," said Trumbull. "He's written books on acrostics and on novelty verse of all kinds. Conundrums involving word play and puns were a specialty of his. He's the one who got Roger Halsted interested in limericks."

Gonzalo laughed. "How did you stand it, Tom?"

Trumbull shrugged. "It wasn't the sole topic of conversation, and I was younger then. However, Ralph remarried, as you probably remember, went to the West Coast, and we never heard from him again. Then Jim Drake and I found the

Milano, and the Black Widowers has been here ever since, better than ever."

Henry refilled the coffee cups, and Gonzalo played a melodious tattoo on his water glass with his spoon.

"Jim," he said, "as the oldest member and the one who best knew Ralph Ottur in the old days when even Manny claims to have been a kid, would you do the grilling honors?"

James Drake lit a fresh cigarette and said, "Mr. Parris, how do you justify your existence?"

"At the moment," said Parris, "by attempting to make you somewhat richer than you have been hitherto. Or if not you, Dr. Drake, then another one of you."

"Don't you know which?"

"I'm afraid not, gentlemen. In order to know, I must complete the reading of the will."

"Will? What will?" Drake took the cigarette from his mouth, placed it in an ashtray, and looked uneasy.

A heavy silence descended on the rest of the table. Henry, who had been serving brandy, desisted.

Parris said seriously, "I was instructed to say nothing concerning the matter till I was a guest at a Black Widowers' banquet and till I was being grilled. Not till this moment."

Drake said, "It *is* this moment. Go on."

Parris said, "I'm sorry to have to tell you that Mr. Ralph Ottur died last month. He had been pretty much of a recluse since his second wife died three years ago and, at his request, no announcement of his death was made. Though he had made a clean break with his life in New York after he left for California, he did not, apparently, forget his old friends of the Black Widowers. He asked that I hand out one of these to each of you, provided all six were present, and you all are."

Envelopes were passed out to each of the stunned Black Widowers. Each bore the name of a Black Widower in careful India ink lettering.

Drake muttered, "There's his monogram." Each envelope bore a stylized sketch of what was unmistakably an otter with a fish in its mouth.

Trumbull said, "Did we each get the same?"

Gonzalo said, "Read it and we'll see."

Trumbull hesitated, then read in a low monotone, " 'Well, don't sit there like idiots. There's no reason to get into a mood. Remember, "mood" spelled backward is "doom." I've been with you in spirit every month since I left, even if you haven't heard from me, and I'm with you again now, ready for our last game.' "

"That's what mine says," said Gonzalo.

There was a murmur of agreement from the rest.

"Well, then," said Parris briskly, "I'll now read the will—not the entire will, you understand, but only that portion that applies to the club. If you're ready . . ."

There was silence and Parris read, "It is my further wish and desire to make a bequest to the Black Widowers, a club I helped found and for the members of which I have always had a profound affection. Therefore, I wish to leave a sum of money, which, after taxes are paid, is to come to ten thousand dollars. This sum is to go to one of the following gentlemen, all of whom were members of the club at the last meeting I attended and all of whom, I believe, are still alive. They are: Thomas Trumbull, James Drake, Emmanuel Rubin, Geoffrey Avalon, Roger Halsted, and Mario Gonzalo."

Parris looked up and said, "For the record, there are six of you at the table and I believe you are the six whose names I have read off. Are there any discrepancies?"

Gonzalo said, "There is a seventh member. Henry, our waiter, is the best Black Widower of them all."

Halsted said, "He wasn't a member in Ralph's day. Hell, I can't believe he's dead. Do you remember that time he asked us to find a common English word that contained the letters "ufa" in that order? It kept us quiet all that evening."

"Yes," said Drake, "and it was you who got it. That's why you remember."

Rubin said, *"Quiet!"* His straggly beard bristled. "I demand silence. The will hasn't been read yet. What does Ralph mean that *one* of us will get the money? Why only one and which one?"

Parris cleared his throat. "I don't know. It is at this point I have been instructed to open a small envelope labeled, 'One.' Here it is."

"Well, don't open it just yet," said Rubin violently. "Mario, you're the host, but listen to me. If any bequest were left to the club or to the six of us in equal division, that would be all right. To leave it to only one of us would, however, create hard feelings. Let's agree, then, that whoever gets the money sets up a fund for the use of the Black Widowers as an entity."

Gonzalo said, "I'm willing. Any arguments?"

There was none, and Gonzalo said, "Open the envelope, Mr. Parris."

Parris opened it, withdrew a three-by-five card, glanced at it, looked surprised, and said, "It says, 'To the barest.'"

"What?" said Trumbull indignantly.

Parris looked on the other side, shook his head, and said, "That's all it says. See for yourselves." The card was passed around.

Avalon chuckled and said, "Don't you get it? He said in his note there would be a last game and this is it."

"What kind of game?" said Gonzalo.

Rubin snorted and said, "Not one of his good ones. Go ahead and explain, Geoff."

Avalon looked solemn and said, "In the Greek myths, the sea nymph Thetis married the mortal Peleus, and to the wedding all the gods and goddesses were invited. The goddess of discord, Eris, was overlooked. Furious, she appeared unbidden and, into the happy throng, tossed a golden apple, then left. Hermes picked it up and noticed a small message attached. What it said was, 'To the fairest.' Three goddesses at once reached for it—Hera, the queen of heaven; Athena, the goddess of wisdom; and Aphrodite, the goddess of love and beauty. The quarrel that resulted ended in the Trojan War."

"Exactly," said Rubin, "and I suggest we not play Ralph's game. I don't know what the hell he means by the barest, but if we start arguing about which one of us qualifies for ten thousand dollars we will end with everyone of us aggrieved, winner and losers alike, even if we put the money into a fund. Earlier, Mr. Parris said that ideologs valued victory above survival, but I don't. I don't want to see the Black Widowers come to an end over the question of who wins ten thousand dollars."

"Hear, hear," said Gonzalo. "Even you say something sensible now and then, Manny. Let's agree that each one of us is in a six-way tie for barest, take the money, and put it into the fund."

"Excellent," said Avalon. "I don't see that there would be any objection to that."

Again, there was a silence, but Parris said, "I'm afraid my

instructions were to allow discussion and then to open another small envelope marked 'Two.' "

Gonzalo looked surprised and said, "Well, open it."

Parris opened the second envelope, removed a folded piece of paper, and unfolded it to find a single-spaced typewritten message. He glanced over it and chuckled.

He said, "Here is what it says: 'I have no doubt that Geoff Avalon, in his endearingly pedantic way, will have by now explained the connection of the message with the apple of discord at the wedding of Thetis and Peleus. . . .' "

Avalon, having flushed to his hairline, said stiffly, "I have never denied that I have a touch of pedantry about me. I trust that I have never been offensively so, or if I have, that I may count on my outspoken comrades of the Black Widowers to tell me so."

"Don't get defensive, Geoff," said Trumbull. "We're all pedants. Go on, Mr. Parris."

Parris nodded and said, " '. . . of Thetis and Peleus. It may also be that someone, possibly Manny Rubin, will suggest that the game be refused and that the money be shared. Not so! Sorry to insist, but only one person gets the money, and that person will be he who can demonstrate himself to be the barest to the satisfaction of the executor of the will. Failing that, no one of them will get the money. I dare say Geoff can explain the appropriateness of this, if he has not already done so."

Avalon cleared his throat and looked harassed. "I don't think it's necessary I do so."

Rubin said, "It's all right, Geoff. I'll take over. Everyone knows *I'm* no pedant."

"Not bright enough," muttered Gonzalo.

Rubin, glaring briefly at Gonzalo, said, "As Geoff said, three goddesses claimed that apple. Hermes, who had picked it up, could see at once that this was no place for an innocent god, and he absolutely declined to make a decision. One by one, the other gods also declined. After considerable discussion, someone suggested that some poor mortal be stuck with the task. The one selected was a shepherd boy on the slopes of Mount Ida near Troy.

"The three goddesses appeared to him in all their magnificence, and each, fearing she might not win in a fair contest, attempted to bribe the judge. Hera offered him world conquest; Athena offered him the crown of wisdom; and Aphrodite offered him the most beautiful girl in the world as his wife.

"The shepherd boy was young enough to find the third bribe the most attractive, and chose Aphrodite. Undoubtedly, she would have won in a fair contest of fairness, but it was a disastrous choice just the same. The most beautiful girl in the world was Helen, queen of Sparta, and the shepherd boy some years later carried her off with Aphrodite's help, and that started the Trojan War.

"The shepherd boy's name was Paris, and he was one of the fifty sons of Priam, king of Troy. The decision among the goddesses is a favorite scene among artists and is commonly referred to as 'The Judgment of Paris.' Clearly, Ralph couldn't resist playing on words and setting up 'The Judgment of Parris'—two r's."

Parris smiled and said, "I seem to have the worst of it. Instead of choosing among three glorious goddesses, I am faced with deciding among six not particularly attractive men."

Rubin said, "You're not faced with any decision at all, actually. Ralph can't make us play the game. If the only way we can get the ten thousand dollars is to compete for it, then I suggest we let the whole thing go. Ten thousand dollars is something we can live without—we have lived without it all these years. What we can't live without is our mutual friendship."

Halsted looked regretful. "Well, now, we can use the money. It could defray part of the costs of the banquets. What with inflation, I, for one, am finding it difficult to cover the expenses. Since I'm the most nearly bald member of the group, can't we say I'm obviously the barest and let it go at that?"

Gonzalo said, "We could decide that 'barest' means 'the most nearly nude.' Then I can strip to my underwear, collect, and we'll set up the fund."

"Oh God," said Rubin. "Look, I'd pay you ten thousand dollars, if I had it to spare, *not* to strip."

Drake said dreamily, "If we were ecdysiasts, it would all be simple. A nice six-way tie."

Parris said, "Now, gentlemen, wait. This is serious. I disapprove of wills such as this one, but I am the executor and I must treat it seriously. I don't know what Mr. Ottur means by the 'barest,' but it is undoubtedly something that is first, not obvious, and second, compelling. If one of you can demonstrate what is meant by 'barest' and then show compellingly that one or another of you is 'barest,' I will release the money. Otherwise I can't. Baldness and, for that matter, nudity, do not strike me as clever explanations of the meaning of the phrase. Try again."

"No, we won't," said Rubin. "You ought to be ashamed of yourself, Roger, for that baldness suggestion. If you need money that badly, I'll contribute to the payment when it's your turn to host."

Halsted turned red and he pointed an angry finger at Rubin, "I don't need money that badly; and I wouldn't come to you for help if I were starving."

Avalon said, "Well, the apple of discord is beginning to do its work, obviously. Manny is right. Let's let it go, while we're still on speaking terms."

Halsted frowned as he passed the palm of his hand over his high forehead, but he kept quiet.

Rubin muttered, "Sorry, Rog. I meant no offense."

Halsted waved a briefly forgiving hand.

Parris said, with considerably more than a trace of apology, "My instructions are that after you have had time for discussion, I am to open the small envelope marked, 'Three.' "

Drake said softly, "How many envelopes do you have, Mr. Parris? This can go on all night."

"This is the last envelope," said Parris.

"Don't open it," roared Rubin. "There's nothing he can say that will change our minds."

Parris said, "I am compelled to open and read this third message by the ethics of my profession. I can't compel you to listen, of course, so if any of you wish to leave the room, you may."

No one did, however; not even Rubin.

Parris opened the third envelope and this time he looked grim as he scanned the message.

"I think you had better listen," he said. "The message reads, 'I think it possible that the group may decide to turn down the bequest rather than play the game. If they do so, or if they play but do not solve the riddle, I do will and bequeath the money, unconditionally, to the American Nazi Party.'"

There was a unanimous wordless rumble from the Black Widowers.

Parris nodded. "That's what it says. See for yourselves."

"You can't do that," said Halsted.

"I am legally compelled to do so," said Parris, "if you refuse to play the game. I am just a sluice through which the money passes. I cannot take independent action. Of course, any or all of you may contest the will, but I don't see what grounds you can possibly have—what legal grounds, that is. A man can do as he wishes with his property within certain clearly defined legal limits, and those limits don't seem to be transgressed here."

"Then let's play the game," said Halsted. "I say I'm the barest because I'm the baldest. I don't say that to win the money, Manny; I say it to keep it out of the hands of the Nazis. Now if you'll agree to that, Mr. Parris, you can hand over the money, and we'll put it into the fund, and that's that."

Parris hesitated. "I'd like to. I would really like to. The trouble is I can't."

"Why not? Do you want the money to go to the Nazis?"

"Of course not," said Parris, with some indignation, "but my only duty here is to respect the will of my client, and he wants one of you to demonstrate that he is the barest in so clever and unmistakable a way that I will be compelled to accept it and to select one of the six of you as the winner. After that, the money is the property of the winner and he is free to do with it as he wishes—keep it, divide it equally among the six of you, set up a trust fund for whatever legal purpose, or anything else."

"Are you sure?" said Trumbull. "No more clever little notes?"

"No more," said Parris. "The reading is complete. I must remind you now that it's a case of 'The Judgment of Parris.' You have to convince me of the validity of the solution or I have to give the money to—to— I have no choice."

Gonzalo said, "According to Manny, Paris—the original Paris—was bribed into giving his judgment. Does that mean . . ."

Parris said seriously, "Please don't finish that remark, Mr. Gonzalo. It will not be funny."

Rubin said, "Then we have no choice. We have to play the game. Who's the barest?"

Halsted says, "We can't answer that until we find out what the old b— Well, *nil nisi bonum* and all that. What does Ralph mean by 'barest,' if he doesn't mean baldest?"

"He may mean 'poorest,' the person who is barest of money," said Gonzalo. "I think I'm in the running for that."

"Or shortest," said Avalon, "the one who most nearly barely exists, so to speak. That's you, Manny."

"You may have eight inches on me, Geoff," said Rubin, "but that could be eight inches of solid bone. How about the one with the smallest wardrobe, which eliminates Mario, or else the lowest IQ, which puts him right back in the running again?"

"Gentlemen, gentlemen," interposed Parris, "none of this sounds in the least convincing. Please be serious."

"You're right," said Rubin, "this is too serious a matter for fooling, but I hate this thing too much to be able to think clearly about it. I say we get Henry into the thing right now."

Henry, who had been standing at the sideboard, listening attentively, now shook his head. "I'm sorry, gentlemen, but that would not be fitting. The deceased did not know of me, did not consider me a member of the club, and I do not qualify to play the game."

"You're a member now," said Trumbull gruffly. "You may not qualify to inherit the money, but you qualify to advise us as to who may. Go on and tell us, Henry."

Henry said, "I don't think I can, Mr. Trumbull. If I am a member of the Black Widowers, I am the only member who has never met Mr. Ottur. I do not know the cast of his thought."

Trumbull said, "There's no mystery there. You've heard us discussing him. He was a word nut. Come on, Henry, if you didn't know Ralph, neither did he know you. He didn't know your faculty for seeing the simple things."

Henry sighed. "I will do my best, sir. May I ask some questions? For instance, am I correct in taking it for granted that the deceased was not a Nazi sympathizer?"

"Hell, no," said Rubin with a snort. "Quite the reverse. During the 1950s he was in trouble because some people thought his views were too leftist."

"Then he doesn't want the money to be left to the Nazis?"

"Of course not."

"So he expects you to win."

Avalon said, "He expects us to do so, but he may overestimate our abilities."

Henry said, "Do you suppose his eagerness to have you win would extend to his giving you a hint?"

Gonzalo said, "What kind of a hint?"

"I'm not sure, Mr. Gonzalo, but let us see. Is Mr. Ottur's name spelled in the usual way?"

"You mean like the animal?" said Trumbull. "O-t-t-e-r? No. It's spelled O-t-t-u-r. With a 'u.' "

Henry said, "I believe that when the preliminary envelopes were handed out, Dr. Drake said something about Mr. Ottur's monogram."

Drake said, "I meant this sketch on the envelope."

"Yes. I had thought that might possibly be so. Has he always used that monogram, Dr. Drake?"

"As long as I've known him, and that goes back a long time."

Henry said, "I can understand the otter, which is a clear reference to Mr. Ottur's name, in a punning sort of way. May I ask if it is known whether the fish in the otter's mouth is a trout?"

There was no reply at first, but finally Avalon said, "I don't know that I gave that any thought. It could be a trout, I suppose. Why do you ask?"

"Only because trout, t-r-o-u-t, is an anagram of Ottur, o-t-t-u-r. The two words consist of the same letters in different arrangements. An otter holding a trout is double reference to his last name by way of a pun and an anagram. Does that fit his character?"

"Absolutely," said Rubin. "The otter was obvious to all of us but I never thought of the trout. He never explained that, as far as I can recall, but then he never explained anything. He wanted everything worked out. But what does all this have to do with the problem facing us, Henry?"

"It seemed to me, gentlemen, that the preliminary message was not really a neccessary prelude to the will and might well have been omitted. Furthermore, I saw no point in giving each one of you an identical message. A single message read out would have done as well, as in the case of the three messages in the three envelopes that were part of the will.

"Looking at it in that fashion," Henry went on, "it occurs to me that he was really handing out his monogram and making sure that each one of you got a good look at it, and will therefore perhaps think of using it as a clue to the nature of the game. The monogram is a pun and anagram on Mr. Ottur's last name. The solution to the problem facing us may rest in just that—puns and anagrams on last names."

The six Black Widowers looked thoughtful at that, each in his own way, and finally Drake stirred.

He said, "You know, that sounds like Ralph, and if so, let me point out that d-r-a-k-e can be rearranged into r-a-k-e-d, and a piece of ground that has been raked is bare, so say nothing of the fact that it is only one letter removed from n-a-k-e-d, which is certainly barest."

Parris said, " 'Raked' doesn't sound compelling to me, and 'naked' is completely impermissible. I don't think we would be allowed to substitute letters."

Rubin said, "Let me offer a pun, then. We don't have to rearrange the letters r-u-b-i-n. Just change it into two words, r-u-b i-n, 'rub in.' Cold cream, which is rubbed into the skin, appears to vanish and leave the skin bare. How about that?"

"Even more farfetched than 'raked,' " said Parris.

Gonzalo said, "g-o-n-z-a-l-o can be rearranged to a-z-o-l-o-n-g, which is 'a so long' in a German accent. A good-bye, in other words, and when everyone says good-bye, you're left bare of company."

"Good God!" said Rubin.

"I can't think of anything else," said Gonzalo defensively.

"If we're going to misspell," said Halsted, "my name can be rearranged into s-t-e-a-l-d-h, which is a misspelling of 'stealth,' and if people steal away, the place is left bare."

"Worse and worse," said Rubin.

"I'm worst of all," said Trumbull, scowling. "The only vowels in my name are two u's, and I can't do anything with that."

Parris said impatiently, "You are still not serious, gentlemen. None of this is worth anything at all. Please! If you want to keep the money from falling into vile hands, you *must* do better."

Avalon, who had had a tight smile on his face for the preceding few minutes, now hunched his magnificent eyebrows down over his eyes and let out a satanic cackle. "But I have it, gentlemen, and I'm delighted to be able to say that Henry, our unexcelled waiter, has overlooked the key clue. No matter, Henry. Even Homer nods."

"Far less often than I do, Mr. Avalon. What clue did I overlook, sir?"

"Why, in the preliminary message, there is not only the monogram, as you correctly pointed out, Henry, but also a reference to the fact that m-o-o-d, spelled backward, is d-o-o-m. That statement is rather a *non sequitur,* and we have a right to wonder why it's brought in at all."

"Because that's the way Ralph thinks—or thought," said Drake.

"Undoubtedly, but if you will take the trouble to spell Avalon backward, you have n-o l-a-v-a. No puns, no rear-rangements, just do as Ralph did in the message."

Parris clenched both hands in excitement. "Now, that's the most interesting thing I've heard yet. But why 'no lava'?"

Avalon said, "A piece of ground over which lava has not flowed is bare."

Parris considered this and shook his head. "We might just as easily consider that ground over which lava has not flowed is rich in vegetation and is *not* bare. In that sense, it would be land which lava *has* flowed that would be bare."

Avalon said, "Very well, then, we can rearrange the let-ters slightly and we have o-n l-a-v-a. By Councilor Parris's argument there would be no vegetation on lava, and that anagram represents bareness."

"What about the reversed lettering?" said Gonzalo. "Mood to doom and all that."

"Well," said Avalon, "we'll have to eliminate that."

Parris said, "I liked 'no lava,' but it was not convincing. The reason I liked it, though, was that the backward spelling did seem to be a reasonable solution. 'On lava' without the backward spelling has nothing to recommend it."

There was a moment of silence and Rubin said, "You know, this is getting less funny all the time. Are we going to end up giving the money to the Nazis, even with Henry's help?"

Gonzalo said, "Well, let's ask him. What are we doing wrong, Henry?"

Henry said, "I'm not sure, Mr. Gonzalo. It does occur to me, though, that so far we have been punning and anagramming our last names—that is, the potential answers. Ought we to be working the question as well?"

"I don't see what you mean, Henry," said Avalon.

"It strikes me, Mr. Avalon, that the phrase 'to the barest' might just possibly be punned into 'to the bearest'; that is, b-e-a-r-e-s-t, the Black Widower most like a bear."

Trumbull said, "Terrible! It's a terrible pun and it's a terrible suggestion. I don't see how we can get any one of us to be clearly most like a bear anymore than we can get any one of us most bare."

Gonzalo said, "I don't know, Tom. You've got a terrible temper. You're the most bearish."

"Not while Manny is alive," said Trumbull hotly.

"I've never lost my temper in my life, damn it," shouted Rubin, just as hotly.

"Yes, like now," said Halsted.

Parris said, "Gentlemen, this is getting us nowhere either. Unless someone can think of something, we'll have to give up."

Henry said, "But we now have our solution, to my way of thinking, Mr. Parris. If we take the challenge to be that of finding the Black Widower most like a bear, may I point out that if we change the position of but one letter in r-u-b-i-n, we get b-r-u-i-n, the common name for the bear in the medieval animal epics, and still used today. I believe there is a hockey team known as the 'Bruins.' "

Parris said energetically, "I'll buy that. It is a clear solution that fits and is unique."

The Black Widowers broke into applause, and Henry turned pink.

Rubin said, "Since the money is mine, then, I will set up the trust fund with directions that the earned interest be turned over to Henry as an honorarium for his services to the club."

There was applause again.

Henry said, "Gentlemen, please don't. I will be overpaid."

"Come, come, Henry," said Rubin, "Are you refusing?"

Henry considered, sighed, and said, "I accept, sir, with thanks."

"To the Barest"—Afterword

I don't want the Black Widowers to be part of the real world. In the case of the Trap Door Spiders, deaths have occurred, and new members have been elected, but I don't intend to let that happen to the Black Widowers. No one is going to die and no new member is going to be elected.

Nor is anyone going to age. Henry was "sixtyish" in the first story, and though nearly a decade has passed he is still "sixtyish," and he is going to stay that no matter how long I live and the stories continue. Avalon will continue to stare down from his seventy-four inches of height, and Rubin's beard will continue to be straggly.

And yet, the exigencies of the plot and the tug of nostalgia lured me on to introduce Ralph Ottur as the founder of the Black Widowers and to depict him as having died. Of course, the Trap Door Spiders were founded by science-fiction writer and naval historian Fletcher Pratt, who died over twenty years ago, and is fondly remembered by all who knew him.

"To the Barest" appeared in the August 1979 *EQMM*.

With that, then, I will say farewell to my Gentle Readers—with my usual promise to keep on recording the proceedings of the Black Widowers while life and breath do last.

Isaac Asimov, master of science, science fiction, and practically everything else, is indeed a strange and wonderful phenomenon. To date he has published 210 books, among them the story of the early years of his own life—*In Memory Yet Green*. The other 209 have ranged from Byron to physics, from black holes to biology, from Greek history to tales of the Galactic Empire. And in addition to the present volume, he has authored the equally enchanting *Tales of the Black Widowers* and *More Tales of the Black Widowers*.

THRILLS * CHILLS * MYSTERY
from FAWCETT BOOKS